David Cliff is a successful author as this is his third book. However, this is the first thriller he has written. He is not new to publishing given he was employed in journalism for six years at Woman's Own magazine before changing to an academic career. He studied at London and other universities gaining his bachelor, master and PhD qualifications.

During the past ten years, he was an academic advisor and teacher in China, where he was deemed a 'National Distinguished Expert' having gained a prestigious Chinese award. His experiences in China inform the basis of the culture and places in this book. Currently living in Surrey, he loves the countryside, travel, jazz and art. Creativity is his passion and any outlet for this gives him inspiration.

To all my family and friends, present and past.

2022
Best Wishes

Eagle's IMPACT

DAVID CLIFF

EAGLE'S IMPACT
David Cliff

FICTION / Thrillers / Suspense

PB £9.99 9781528997539

EB £3.50 9781398427914

Harry Long is sent to China in order to unravel the secrets of a Chinese military experiment that may have gone wrong. He goes undercover in a Chinese university in order to solve the mystery about the deaths of two Chinese students involved in the experiment. Harry cleverly uncovers different sinister plans and motives. But we also witness his dealings with different individuals. The association with Lily Wang, academic colleagues and British Intelligence all have an impact on him. This is especially the case with his relationship with Lily Wang and their discussions. We can experience the impacts and changes in Harry as he learns that Chinese culture offers him a different way of thinking. Things finally get complicated when he has to take some difficult loyalty decisions. The impact of his experiences in China and questions about moral principles leads him to take self-determining decisions.

"This captivating thriller offers a masterclass in understanding how an individual can be so mesmerised by a culture that they revise their worldview."

"Eagle's Impact provides an action-packed book which takes place in China. The author shows a depth of knowledge of Chinese culture that will fascinate the reader."

- ✂ - -

Please send me ...... copy/ies of
Eagle's Impact
David Cliff

Please add the following postage per book:
United Kingdom £3.00 / Europe £7.50 /
Rest of World £12.00

Delivery and Payment Details

Format	Price	Qty	Total
Paperback ☐			
Subtotal			
Postage			
Total			

Full name: ....

Street Address ....

City:.. County:...

Postcode: .... Country: ....

Phone number (inc. area code): .... Email: ....

I enclose a cheque for £.................. payable to Austin Macauley Publishers LTD.

Please send to: Austin Macauley, CGC-33-01, 25 Canada Square, Canary Wharf, London, E14 5LQ

Tel: +44 (0) 207 038 8212
Fax: +44 (0) 207 038 8100
orders@austinmacauley.com
www.austinmacauley.com

AUSTIN MACAULEY PUBLISHERS™
LONDON · CAMBRIDGE · NEW YORK · SHARJAH

David Cliff

EAGLE'S IMPACT

AUSTIN MACAULEY PUBLISHERS™

LONDON * CAMBRIDGE * NEW YORK * SHARJAH

A CIP catalogue record for this title is available from the British Library.

ISBN 9781528997539 (Paperback)
ISBN 9781398427914 (ePub e-book)

www.austinmacauley.com

First Published (2021)
Austin Macauley Publishers Ltd
25 Canada Square
Canary Wharf
London
E14 5LQ

Thank you to all those people in China and elsewhere whose impact helped me unravel life a little more.

Table of Contents

Chapter 1
Dalian Taxi Ride

I flipped shut the computer and focused my thoughts. It was time to leave for the institute where the experiments were taking place. I grabbed my keys, punched in a text on my phone saying I was leaving, double-checked the number and hit the green button. I slipped the phone back in my pocket, feeling an urge to get things moving. Then left the room in high spirits given this was the start of my new assignment.

My high spirits were similar to those felt when on holiday. However, the experience would be the antithesis of a normal vacation, as nothing about my mission would be relaxing. I was in Asia for the first time. While everything seemed intriguing, I couldn't do what I fancied; there was no free will over choice. My time spent in China would be work: undercover, secret agent work. To be exact, my journey to the Chinese Institute of Technology was to carry out covert surveillance. This was a scoping exercise to find out what secrets the Chinese had in developing DNA warfare. Therefore, nothing was being left to chance and I was in China to figure things out.

I needed to identify my taxi. The taxi was due to arrive at the main entrance of the university to take me to the Institute of Technology. This was no ordinary taxi though, as this one was linked to the secret intelligence unit in Dalian. This ground unit carried out secret intercepts to target and monitor Chinese communications. Nothing was unusual about this covert MI6 base. The base in Dalian was just one of the many regional arms of the UK's global spying network.

At two o'clock, as arranged, I arrived at the front of the Donghai University building and stood on the wide pavement. Rectangular shadows crossed the pavement and the sun's heat shimmered off passing traffic. Squinting in the bright light, I tried to identify my pick up. It wasn't easy as the road was congested and cars merged into each other. I pulled out my sunglasses and put them on to reduce the glare. A taxi cruised into sight with its red for hire light switched off. It was a standard Volkswagen with a livery like other taxis in the area. No difference, and no standing out from the others. It was just another boxy, stock-standard local taxi. However, this one had the feature of painted green wheel hubs to signal it was my arranged pick up. It rolled along hugging the kerb.

The driver was leaning forward, observing people along the street. His gaze fixed on me once I'd been spotted. I wasn't difficult to spot, because as a Westerner in China, I stood out from the crowd. The taxi pulled up with a slight screech of brakes. I opened the door and slid into the front seat. The first impression was unpleasant as my nostrils reacted to an unfamiliar odour. I took shallow breaths. Plastic and soya sauce smells intermingled in the heat of the day. A fan was working its hardest, but was simply recirculating nauseating smells. I rolled down the window and fastened my seat belt. I turned and smiled, but there was no response. The Chinese driver sat expressionless, watching me while I settled in.

"Where's the best English place in town?" it was the prearranged question.

The composed look and a nod from the driver indicated I'd chosen the right taxi. However, it was later I realised this could have been misleading as my driver often assumed a serene, hooded eye expression when confused. The driver spoke, but his English wasn't clear. "Hi ahh, Harry." He nodded again. "You're fitting his description." He engaged a gear and we accelerated off into the rush of cars jostling for position.

"Good meeting yer." He glanced sideways, "I'm, Leo." Leo pulled back his mouth when talking, which exposed his teeth. "Will need update you, ah."

He talked with his mouth hardly moving and his lips pulled back. This hampered his tones and communication, but provided for a continuous, pleasant smile. The smile showed his teeth were a little stained but quite regular. His face was moon-shaped and his eyes full of fun. Like many Northern Chinese men, he was relatively tall. Perhaps, he was around 1.85 metres, and a few centimetres shorter than me. He wore a short-sleeved shirt and his smooth arms lacked hair. He seemed stress-free as he drove. Fixed to the dashboard was a taxi driver permit alongside a small Buddha statue. A new briefcase was on the floor.

Leo's expression seemed relaxed and compliant. It was noticeable that he didn't seem to fit in as an intelligence or military type. There was softness to his character and slackness in his posture. The first impression was he must be a low-level operative. I couldn't help thinking he looked something of an anomaly. Perhaps he'd been recruited due to a personal grudge against the political regime rather than his expertise.

"Hello, Leo. Thanks for being on time."

"Oh, okay. Good we met."

"Can you update me on what's been happening?"

"Yes, things happening," Leo spoke in clipped tones. "Our electric …'vestigation knows big thing with, Jinying med…ical test. The Jinying test happens with two deaths."

I cut in, "We say electronic surveillance."

"Oh. My English no good. Sorry." He gazed sideways at me. "I understand more than speak."

"What does Jinying mean?" I asked.

"Oh. In Chinese, it's mean eagle. Jinying is the code secret test uses." He looked to see if I understood. "You know what's eagle bird, ah?"

"Yes." I visualised one swooping down on its prey.

My focus became fixed on the road. The taxi was navigated precariously through the veering angles of other vehicles. I stamped my foot on the floor when a car cut in front of us. Leo glanced at me and smiled in his broad mouthed way. He didn't change his driving. I felt impatience and was at the point of needing to say something.

"How safe is this taxi – with all these dangerous drivers on the roads?"

Leo didn't understand my meaning and simply explained the taxi's modifications. "Emm, some bullet proof bits, and windows no break it."

"Yes – BUT am I safe from an accident? Like a crash with other cars! The drivers here take lots of chances."

"What you mean? I'm not good." He was bemused, so I decided the subject was not worth pursuing.

"I'm sure we'll be able to work well together…but you'll see that I like to do things properly. That may make me seem awkward," I explained.

"No problem."

"Okay. So, get us there without an accident. We need to remain secret."

We drove on through the grid pattern streets. I watched the other cars change direction or swerve, listened to inconsequential horn noises and waited for an accident. The scene was like a weird computer game played out in real time. Leo shouted something in Chinese when a car emerged from a side turning without warning.

"Shit. We don't need to hurry?" I decided the double white lines of the lane markings were a waste of paint. "There's no lane discipline," I commented, but was relieved to see Leo checked his mirrors before changing lane.

"In briefcase, there's plan. It's Jinying building we're going to see." He pointed at a briefcase behind his seat. "We see building soon and we can look at outside."

"It's the Institute of Technology. That's its name."

"Yer. Jinying in that building."

I felt perplexed at being with Leo. I thought driving on the roads in Dalian wasn't safe at times, and he could have been more forthcoming about our mission. I realised I would have to follow up in other ways to get more details of the experiments. He was compliant but probably not as focussed as me. So, I wanted him to understand how serious I was about the mission. "This Jinying eagle secret is important to understand. We need to do a good job, Leo. This is a military secret that we must uncover. I'm relying on your back up."

"Yer. I understand, Harry – oh, but be careful today. It's fourth month, fourth day. Our four no good as Chinese number."

I turned to look out the window. 'Four not good'. I'd no idea what Leo was talking about. Possibly it was an unlucky number. It was better to ignore superstition and to focus on what lay ahead. As we drove on, the traffic became lighter and the roads quieter.

Chapter 2
Institute of Technology
Drive-By

My mobile beeped. "Donghai one." I gave my code.

"Hello, we've tracked your mobile to the taxi," the voice was of a female operative with an educated English accent. "Just checking with you."

"It's clear to talk," I responded. I'd been briefed in Beijing about the amount of bugging in China, especially in buildings with accommodation for international people. I waited but the female voice offered no reaction, so I informed her, "I'm on my way to see the target building."

"Is everything going well?"

"It's going well, as we're almost at the institute. Only thing here is the standard of everyone's driving. I think it lacks discipline."

"The driving takes some getting used to in Dalian. Also, Leo's English is poor as we always speak to him in Chinese."

"You're right, but I'm sure we'll work well together. It's not a big problem."

"I'm glad about that. All the final arrangements for you to act covertly as an English teacher in Donghai University have been made. That will allow you to speak to the English teachers in the department where the two dead students studied. You need to meet with the head of school, James Davis."

"Thanks. I've already been briefed by the British Council that it was all arranged. I'll start by seeing the English teaching staff tomorrow afternoon."

"All seems well then. Ring us if you need to. Bye." The phone went dead. I knew the rule. The call was not meant to last more than a minute to ensure it was untraceable. Nothing was left to chance as there was also a belt and braces approach with scrambling devices for communications.

"Ai ya!" exclaimed Leo. He braked; a car sped in front of us and almost clipped the front wing of the taxi. I braced myself against the dashboard. Leo simply switched direction into the bus lane. This gave him a clear lane to drive along, but one that was not legal.

We motored on past new buildings interspersed by forests of cranes perched around new building developments. It was Dalian's development zone. All was calm as traffic in this area was lighter than elsewhere. Leo focussed my thoughts.

"We at In…stitute building," said Leo.

We turned the corner. Looming before our taxi was the target building the surveillance data had identified. It was an ultra-modern office block finished with white cladding and glass. It formed a large three-story building, international in design, with a bowl-shaped curve at one end. The curve helped to soften the stark rectangular form of the building. Although it could have won an award, I felt its architecture was simply a foil for the experiments and secrets hidden in its inner space.

Leo slowed the taxi and we glided past. "How you get secret out?" He looked up at the building. "Not good, you Western. You're 'dabizi'." Wrinkles formed across his brow.

"*Dabizi?*"

Leo looked at me from the corner of his eye. "Oh, that's mean big nose, all Westerners called *dabizi*."

I was confident I wouldn't fail given everything was carefully planned. My mission was to identify if there was a dangerous military purpose to what was going on. Today's reconnoitre of the building was a first phase survey of the building's layout. It would reduce the possibility of things going wrong.

The taxi passed by the front of the building. A set of broad marble steps curved their way up to the entrance. The curve was enhanced by a modern stainless-steel handrail. There was a gleaming newness to the steelwork and whiteness of the building. It glinted in the sun. My eye was drawn to some people on the steps. Holding the handrail, at the top of the stairs, was a Western person exiting the building. A couple of Asian people and the westerner were in conversation. I focussed on them. The Western person was saying goodbye to two official Chinese people, dressed in dark suits. It seemed a formal farewell. I looked and noticed the Western man, wearing a grey sports jacket, was walking down the steps of the institute. A man-bag was across his shoulder. I wondered if a man-bag, rather than briefcase, revealed anything about him. Whoever it was, his visit was evidence that foreigners were arriving at the institute without any problems. That meant my Western face would be acceptable.

"Any idea about who those two well-dressed Chinese guys could be?" I enquired.

"Look like important officials. Yes, two big potatoes say goodbye."

We took a slow drive around the block. We were circling for a second viewing when Leo let out a sigh. "How you getting in, ah?"

"You'll be pleased to know I've got a good plan."

The goods' area was chosen as the most suitable entrance to obtain direct access during the daytime. Information had already been collected on the pattern of the different types of deliveries to the institute. A regular delivery seldom attracted security attention, apart from a cursory check on the driver's paperwork. There was one specific van identified as the best solution to get access because of its pattern of delivery. The van was chosen as it delivered at the same time each day, with a single driver. A rough plan had been worked out, which needed a final check on the goods' delivery area. I wanted to check whether their security could be got past with acceptable risk.

Leo drove around the corner and parked, so I could view the building from the back. At the rear of the building, a gate led to the selected goods' delivery area. I assessed the area carefully noting the guard on the gate, and the short entrance road to the loading bay area. From what I could see, the plan would work.

I moved my head sideways to motion Leo to continue on round the next corner. We rounded the corner and slowed to another stop. I assessed the types of windows on the building. Our pre-checks were going well. Unfortunately, things were about to change. My gaze was upward, so I failed to see a large car turn into the road we had just parked on. Leo tapped my leg and pointed backwards.

"A car follows us," said Leo. I looked and realised a large black car had rolled up behind us. Leo was watching it in his rear-view mirror.

"That car's stopped and its engine is still running. That seems strange," I commented, on hearing the soft humming against the quiet of the road. "Perhaps driving by the building wasn't a good idea. We have attracted unwanted attention."

"No police, no government, perhaps important car," he responded, while watching in his mirror.

The car was parked about twenty metres behind us on our side of the road. If it wasn't the government or police, then who was it? Who else could be interested in us or what was happening at the institute? I needed to find out.

Chapter 3
Unexpected Encounter

I half turned in my seat and used the wing mirror to check the car behind us. It was a large black, S-class Mercedes that had pulled into the kerb.

"Can we check them out?"

"It not government. Because it isn't big Audi." He looked at me "Why it follow us?"

Leo flipped a button on the side of his door that looked like the door-locking device. This provided direct radio contact to the emergency centre at the Dalian base. There was a beep as it activated. He looked my way, "Need know car plate, ah?" I half turned and read it to him. Leo used a request in Chinese to the Dalian field base. He spoke loudly and quickly. I could detect his concern.

I tried to assess our situation. Unlike our taxi, the large Mercedes car wasn't chosen to blend in with other traffic. Perhaps it was an official car given its expense and status. However, I knew that Leo was suspicious, which meant it could be the start of an unwanted confrontation. It wasn't clear what was happening, and my body responded with a trickle of adrenaline into my system. This was heightened by feeling we were in some sort of standoff, where the waiting stretched and warped time. I assumed the Mercedes' occupants were checking our number plates to find out who we were. What other reason could there be? Why else would a large Mercedes car be parked behind us in a quiet side road?

As time ticked by, one thing was clear to me: we were under surveillance.

The large black car started to close the short distance between us. It was like a big black animal closing in on its prey. At the push of a button under the dashboard, Leo made a gun drop down offering its butt end. Its frame and finish, with its black plastic grip, indicated it was an older German made

Walther PPK. The small size allowed it to be easily concealed in the taxi, but its calibre didn't offer much stopping power.

The voice activated mobile device crackled. A message was repeated twice in English, "The car trace suggests an international FSB source." There was no need for the second communication. 'A*lways strike first*' was the phrase driven into me in training. The FSB occupants were not going to offer a welcome to us. This required our taking control of the situation, given we were confronting trained professional agents. I could only assume that serious shit was about to happen.

The Mercedes stopped a car length from us. I judged it better to take the initiative before they did. I took off my sunglasses and placed them on the top of the dashboard. Leo shoved the gun into the side of his trousers and looked at me. His hooded eye expression returned and he seemed lost, not knowing what we should do.

"Should we go?" Leo gripped the steering wheel. "We should leave fast now, Harry," said Leo, in readiness to accelerate away.

"No. No don't. We need to find out what's going on," I took control.

"They can hurt us, yes?"

"Let's see," I said. "If they want to fight, it'll be good practice."

"Emm. Take care. You're a little mad, ah." Leo considered my facial expression. It was set with a strong jaw line.

"Let's not sit here as easy targets. Get out," I insisted. "Let's confront these people whoever they are." There was a stirring of my system. I was ready for fight, not flight.

As we left the taxi, four large men emerged from the Mercedes. They weren't Chinese. The characteristic look of Eastern Europeans was the first impression. Their baggy, cheap looking suits reinforced the image. I'd seen these tough types before.

"Why did you two get out the car?" the tone of the biggest of the group was abrupt. I was sure things were about to get awkward.

Four faces stared at us etched with menace. I glanced into their car and saw no one was left inside. Then, I checked their hands and realised they weren't carrying weapons. I squared my shoulders. The situation was going to escalate, so it was time to adopt tactical breathing. I started by quietly inhaling through my nose, controlling my diaphragm and exhaling through my mouth. My heart rate calmed and I became readied throughout my whole being. I was in the zone. I faced the group and tried to offer a neutral stance.

"This stupid taxi driver is lost," I offered as my opener. "Do any of you speak Chinese? It would help me. I need to tell him where I want to go."

"I don't think you're lost!" the obvious, more senior one in the middle of the group retorted. He had an abrupt East European accent. "It must be us you think stupid, as you're here for a reason." He looked us up and down. "Tell us something. Who are you two?"

"We're of no interest to you. Please leave." My eyes became steely.

"I'm asking who you are? You will answer me – right!" He sneered at me. His broad neck and flattened nose resembled a one-time pugilist.

"Tell me why I should," I responded.

"We've watched you circling the institute. You need tell us what you're planning here. If not, we beat the truth from you!" The one next to him nodded, which accentuated his shaved head. He seemed the number two of the group.

"Beat the truth from us – No way."

He gazed in disbelief at my words and responded, "It'll be easy. You'll see!"

"Look. Please leave us alone, while you can."

"Nyet. Go fuck you!" he went from anger to disbelief. "Oh. You joking, right?" A deep-throated chuckle emerged.

"Why don't you ignore us? I don't want to hurt you," I warned in a calm, rather than threatening tone. But it was obvious what was going to happen.

My words were received with empty looks. The senior looking one in the middle raised his eyes in disbelief and let off a second chuckle. He stepped forward, gripping and releasing his fists. I could feel the seriousness of the situation. They were intent on a confrontation.

Leo stood beside me. He didn't look the fighting type, so I emphasised my intent to handle the situation alone. "I need you to step back. I'm okay – So stay out of this." His mouth closed and tightened. Leo stepped back a couple of paces.

All four Russians focussed on me. They were getting ready to launch their attack. There was a need to choose my ground. I assumed a couple of them would attempt to outflank me. In anticipation, I backed up to the wall of the Institute.

These four were about to make their first mistake. The middle two relaxed their stances and showed more confidence. They seemed to have assessed their odds of winning. Therefore, my mind was fixed on taking on the middlemen first. I lowered my stance by placing one leg ahead of the other. This allowed me to react in any direction. An adrenaline surge raised the hairs on the back of my neck, and my mind became razor sharp. I was in the zone.

They all moved toward me, and as I expected those in the centre led the attack. Their arms rose to a boxing stance. Both came at me. I waited until the senior one was positioned at the right distance and square to me. Before he was able to strike me, my right leg snapped out and landed a gonad crushing strike. His shoulders lost their muscle tone and he sank to his knees, gasping with pain. My snap kick allowed me to regain my stance. The shaved-head Russian looked to his right at his gasping colleague. I aimed at his chin. There was a crunching sound as my knuckles struck. The shock to his nervous system was like an electricity failure. All his lights went out. His body hit the ground with an audible thump. The outside ones were closing in. I knew instinctively how to choose a perfect position to strike. I'd rehearsed my moves thousands of times. I twisted into one of the others and rammed my elbow into his face. As I turned, the man grabbed at my shirt to pull me down. Luckily, he never got a proper grip. I made direct contact with the bridge of his nose. The cartilage crunched as it burst open. Blood erupted out of his nostrils, streamed down over his mouth and dripped from his chin. He stumbled back, holding his nose.

My position wasn't good. I was spiralling backwards due to my last attack. I was out of position and open to the final attacker; he aimed a fist at my head. I reacted instantly. Ducking sideways, the punch brushed my face without much force. His arm continued and he was sideways to me. The momentum had twisted him round. That meant I was able to deliver a forceful chop with the side of my hand. The trauma of the blow against his neck worked. He fell down onto the back of his head, which left him in a prone, twisted heap. The odds were in my favour with two unconscious and two badly hurt.

Now the guy with the bleeding nose came for a second attack. He made a mistake by trying to football kick me. He lashed out with his foot aimed at my groin. This meant his leg became extended. It was a bad move. I caught his ankle and raised it to unbalance him. He tilted sideways. I delivered a telling sidekick to his head. It was a copybook kick, and one to relish. He lost motor control, and the ground rose up to meet him.

Things were moving fast and I realised the new odds were not in my favour. There was now a problem. The big Russian leader was about to raise the stakes of the fight. The pain from the groin kick must have been subsiding as his arm was reaching into his jacket. Given where he was reaching, the next move was clear. I needed to react, but the distance between us was too far to smother his action. I looked for where I could dive and roll away.

Leo stepped forward. "No – stop. Okay ah, ah!" he shouted, while aiming his gun at the big Russian leader's chest. "I not like you dead. Up with arms."

The leader froze, and along with his partner with the bleeding nose, raised his arms. While Leo moved to the side to cover the group, he signalled with his gun for them to keep their arms up. I reached into their jackets to remove their guns, but only the big Russian who led the fight had a gun. I gave Leo a nod in gratitude for his action. I was impressed with the way he covered the group. No need to tell him how to move. He was upright, had chosen a good firing line and used both hands to steady his gun. I noticed he knew how to widen his stance, angle his shoulders and put one leg further back. There was good balance from his stance. That meant his gun hand wasn't exposed to being grabbed. It was clear he knew the drill. I had underestimated Leo and was changing my mind about his abilities.

I joined Leo and covered the men in case they tried anything else. The Russian's gun felt heavy. The gun was an older Russian Yarygin PYa handgun, which is capable of using armour-piercing ammunition. Its weight indicated it had an oversize magazine.

I caught Leo's eye. "You did well." His broad smile returned.

We retreated to our taxi, never taking our eyes off the bemused Russians. A loathing look from the leader signalled his hatred of us. His colleagues were showing signs of movement and uttering low curses. Leo got in first, and as the taxi started to move forward, I jumped into the front seat. Turning in the seat, I looked out the back window. The scene wasn't one of pursuit but of recovery. I picked up my sunglasses from the dashboard by the bridge of the frame and put them on in one movement. As we drove away, the adrenaline rush and feeling of power subsided.

We turned a few corners and merged back into the fast-moving traffic. Leo shook his head as if to clear it. He then reported the fight with the four FSB to our base, using his voice-activated device. The base people were not surprised. They reported a Russian communique, with the code Jinying, had been picked up. They indicated it was clear the Russians were also involved in trying to find out more about the Institute of Technology experiments. Their response to our encounter indicated it had been a chance encounter. We were also informed by our female contact that after we had identified the Russian's car, the base had asked for satellite images. These satellite images indicated the S-class Mercedes had been circling different parts of the building. There was a relief in knowing we had stumbled on each other, rather than being followed. Therefore, this meant the Russians were competing to solve the question we had, of what was Jinying?

Leo constantly checked the rear and side mirrors. "Where'd you learn to fight, ah?"

"A Japanese karate master named Suzuki taught me. He used slaps and kicks to make me do what he wanted. Those kicks meant I learnt quickly."

"Him good kicking laoshi – ah?"

"He was the highest ranked black belt in the UK."

"Black belt. Why black?" Leo frowned. I was getting used to his expression when he didn't understand.

"Black is the highest-level belt colour. He was a good teacher but spoke poor English." I sat back in my seat waiting for Leo's response.

"Worse English than me, hey?" I grinned. Leo went on, "So, Harry, bad friends made with Russians today."

"The FSB agents are never friends. Just big, big problems."

Leo drove on through an older, poorer part of the city.

"This is different," I noted.

He saw me looking at the old villa-like buildings. "These old Japanese livings."

They looked like they'd been pretty villas many years ago. Their demolition reflected the city's recycling and refurbishment of old areas to build apartment complexes. It seemed a shame that old villas were being knocked down, but urban redevelopment had to keep pace with the population. The old China was disappearing, and this was its new face of modernism.

The journey back was uneventful apart from some vehicle drivers assuming everyone else should give way to them. We had passed through different districts of the city from the cleanliness of the development zone to dilapidated areas with old buildings, and then with an abrupt change, there was the modern architecture of the business centre. We motored on and came to a stop outside Donghai University.

"I'll check the information you gave me. When I'm happy, I'll finalise the plan and be in contact." I picked up the briefcase and exited without delay.

"Hope you happy soon. Bye," were his parting words.

A throng of chattering Chinese students, emerging through the university gate, slowed my progress. They streamed forward in a bustling mass of young faces without giving me a second glance. There were several red spots of blood on my clothes. I glanced down and decided on a shower and change of clothes. Nothing too serious had happened as there were no marks on my body. That meant I didn't need to worry about developing alternative reasons or excuses when I met the teachers.

I returned to the confines of my own room. Everything was as bland as expected. I entered and held my breath for a second. There was a need to adjust to the blend of linoleum, dampness and grimy furniture odour. A memory was triggered. The smell reminded me of boyhood visits to my grandparents' house. Their old Victorian house was associated with many happy boyhood memories, but I never enjoyed its musty smell.

After undressing, I folded my clothes and laid them on the bed. I felt the need to take a long shower. Turning on the taps brought the pleasant sound of falling water, like rain on a glass roof. It felt good to step within the heavy stream of the shower and relax. I looked up into the flow of water and let it wash over me. It washed away the tension from muscles, bones and joints. I was finally rejuvenated. Thoughts came more easily as my mind cleared and a song trickled out.

"Away from home, away from home,

away from home, away from home,

Lord, I'm five hundred miles away from home.

Not a shirt on my back…"

The sensation was good. My shower had engendered feelings of well-being. The feeling wasn't contained as I broke out in loud singing while I cleaned the walls and shower tray. The final task was to wash out my shirt in cold water and put it on the chair back to dry.

Once I'd dressed in fresh, clean clothes, I felt better and ready to start work. I looked around for a place to sit to update myself. It was an easy decision as sitting on my bed seemed the most comfortable place available. I propped myself up on the bed and my thoughts turned to our lack of information on Jinying. The briefing I'd been given had indicated the sparseness of anything for us to work on. I flipped open my computer and it pinged to life. I read through the information but there was little new intelligence to consider, apart from our recent involvement of the FSB and their competitive interest in Jinying. The hope for me was that our paths wouldn't cross and complicate my plans to break into the institute.

The computer wasn't fast in its processing capabilities due to its advanced protection features. There was a reason. Its design allowed information to be embedded electronically in a safe section of the computer's system. Protecting secrets is important, so the development of systems to protect data is relentlessly pursued. Sophisticated tracking is commonplace. This led to intelligence agencies ensuring data is more protected than ever before. In fact, the government-based communication codes in China had not been broken by our GCHQ experts. Only the pattern of electronic chatter and the frequencies of communications being sent could be monitored. That monitoring turned up a massive fingerprint of the use of the codename, Jinying. Our people gathered the number of communications, but unfortunately no detail of the content. At least links were identified. When the network fingerprint of communication was examined, links from different government bureaus were highlighted. The Institute of Technology's secret experimental role was clear. This underpinned the plan for me to enter the institute to obtain information about its research. It was hoped this could throw light on the Jinying secrets and help the UK decide if they needed to react to a threat.

I went to the shower room for a pee. I aimed my pee at the slow rivulet of water running down the toilet bowl. It was a relief the toilet was Western in design, but the cistern allowed water to constantly run down into the bowl. A green lime scale stain indicated the line of the flow. Washing my hands afterwards wasn't pleasant either, as the sink tap was loose and green mould covered its edges. Entering back to the room, my gaze was held by a mirror and my reflection. A smile formed as I nodded to the mirror. The nod was confirmation of my feeling of confidence. I was reassured to see a vision of strength, of character, of determination. My image was of someone who may appear friendly, but not someone to take advantage of. Not an ideal face for a fashion magazine perhaps, but the ideal face for an army recruitment campaign.

Once all my tasks were complete, I became aware that my stomach felt empty. This triggered my body clock as I realised it was time to eat. I wanted to select somewhere easy so I considered local places. I decided the clean dumpling place I'd seen on campus was a good choice. It was only a short walk away, so within minutes, I was satisfying my hunger and enjoying a cold beer. The combination of pork dumpling juices and beer were good. I ordered another beer, feeling it a reward for my day's work.

The day had gone well. I was happy that along with Leo, we had dealt with the Russians. However, knowing Russians were also interested in Jinying had come as a shock. I drew on my second beer and mulled over the need to find out more about the student deaths. I'd the advantage of having seen the institute building, and felt it was possible to enter without a problem. That was under control. The background to the student deaths was more difficult to deal with. I needed a timetable. My first task would be to make contact with anyone who was known to them. I could then identify their contacts to build a picture of what happened. With a list of key people, I could find out more about the circumstance surrounding the deaths. I knew the dead students were both friends and final year undergraduates. If their social network could be identified, an assessment of who should be targeted for more details would become clearer.

I thought about my following afternoon's meeting with the English language tutors. This would allow me to blend in with the staff to gain their confidence and to learn more about what had happened. Given my cover as an English teacher, I would have the chance to obtain first-hand information about the student's involvement in the experiments. I felt sure the academic staff would be able to provide background clues, given gossip and communication was bound to have circulated. So, I decided uncovering the background facts could be achieved.

My task was clearer. I returned to my room, placed the gun under my pillow and drifted off.

Chapter 4
Strange Morning

The day started with a strange early morning sound. I was roused by, 'oa...ah!' Then moments later another, 'oa...ah!' I emerged from sleep in a disoriented and confused state. I had little idea what it was, but the sounds kept repeating.

My head felt muddled as I struggled to understand the reason for the sounds. To improve things, I rubbed a hand across my stubble to regain my senses. I sat up and looked round. Nothing was clear. It was confusing as the sound didn't seem to come from any one direction.

Perhaps it was from the room above. I looked at the high ceiling as the sound could be from that direction. Yet another, 'oa...ah', delivered with high intensity. My gaze ran down to the dark-brown furniture and across to the window with its heavy, faded curtains. Another, 'oa...ah'. Adrenaline kicked in and the fuzziness subsided. It became clear the strange noises were coming from the direction of the window. In one movement, I threw back the cover, stepped from the bed and made my way to the window.

Looking out, things became clear as the puzzle was solved. In a sport's hall, opposite my room, an early morning Kung Fu class was taking place. A martial art group was visible through the many windows of a large hall. Now, the peculiar sounds could be linked to the activity. This answered the mystery of the source of the rhythmic sounds. I smiled a wry smile and folded my arms.

Feeling relaxed, I continued looking across at the Kung Fu class. Electric lights highlighted the sport's hall scene. The windows of the hall revealed a wave of movements, more like a stage performance than a martial art exercise. The regimented movement, of about 30 young Chinese people, coincided with kicks, thrusts and loud guttural moans. I realised the size of the group had provided the unusual, high intensity sounds. It was similar to the cadence of army marching exercises, where sound from a large group is delivered at full blast.

I lent my arms on the hard surface of the windowsill and watched the group's ebb and flow. It was an early time to hold the class. A glance at my watch showed it was just past six in the morning. I continued watching but my attention was only focussed on one person. The guttural sounds continued to pulse from the sport's hall but became background noise to what caught my eye. Surveying the group, moving to and fro, my attention was taken by a Chinese female. A Chinese female, in black leggings, was leading the group.

She stood at the head of the class giving instructions. It was impossible to ignore her. Her moves had a resolve and decisiveness about them. The scene resembled a theatre dance production. When she moved, a sea of white uniforms flashed into action. It was coordinated drill practice. An additional crack from the clothing arose as each leg or arm snapped in a strike movement. Step – punch – oa…ah; crack. Step – kick – oa…ah; crack. The class moved backwards and forwards in synchronised movements. It was difficult to separate any two of the class from each other. Step – punch; step – kick. It was captivating to watch the fluidity of movement.

All eyes focussed toward the leader. Her red blouse looked all the redder, due to the contrast against her jet-black hair and the white class uniforms. She was tall and boyish, being slim with small breasts and buttocks. Her hair was neatly tied back in a ponytail, which swung and bounced against the back of her neck with each kick or punch. The movements were fluid and exacting. At each thrust of the leader's arm, or leg, the guttural cry rang out as the class moved in physical unison. It was obvious she demonstrated the leadership to inspire her class to emulate her demanding exercises.

On command from the leader the, regimented group stopped their exercise and entered into deep breathing. I thought the class would break up but they then started to do Tai Chi exercises. These slower, more balletic exercises brought calmness to the scene. It was a more relaxed set of exercises, developing improved balance and allowing individual meditation.

The sight of the class reminded me of films I'd seen. With martial art films, it's the men, like Jackie Chan, who are mentioned as they dominate the ratings. Women have starred in films, but are less known. None of this makes sense. The female expert, like the one I was watching, was just as well trained and effective as the men.

29

My own memories became stimulated through watching the Kung Fu class. The mental images and the feeling created motivated me to do my own martial art exercise. I never underestimate the importance of regular practise for my karate. It helps to tone my body and gives me a better level of performance. As with all martial art training participants can be fitter, have better balance, increased strength, improved flexibility and be capable of dealing with any aggressor. These are benefits I admire as they favour my ability to win in a confrontation. I became motivated to do my own karate exercises to gain these benefits. I cleared away the small table to the side of the room. I now had space to go through a kata of movements.

Chapter 5
Entering the Zone

I'd learnt my karate from kata techniques. I enjoyed its practical nature. Karate was passed down in the form of kata exercises as it wasn't written down by the ancient masters. This convinced me of the benefit of learning by doing. Its actions develop the core strength of the body, and especially, force based upon using legs and hips to add power to strikes.

My kata combines flexing and tensing of arm and leg muscles – moving backwards and forwards in a series of set defensive or offensive strikes. A hiss of air is expelled after each move or strike. The karate hiss is different to the 'oa...ah' sound of the Kung Fu class. A proper breathing technique, where breath comes from low in the diaphragm, and not from the thorax, is essential.

The kata can transport me into my extreme performance zone. There's a benefit in entering a zone that's about achieving mental focus. The long-distance runner, the Olympic rower, the iron man competitor can find this zone. They can then face exhaustion, pain or fear without second thoughts. Special forces in the army are full of scrawny men, skinny men, who find they can achieve anything if they find the zone. I like and know the zone, because it's where I achieve super-human performance to be fitter, stronger, harder and better.

After ten minutes of the kata, it was time for deep breathing exercises. I felt good as the early morning exercise had heightened my concentration, focus and brain functioning. Taking a bottle of water, I stood looking round my boring excuse of a room. The room was four square and basic with no degree of comfort. Nothing about the room was relaxing. A cold floor was covered with linoleum and no mat. Energy saving bulbs hung on thin flex, and the ceiling was a dirty cream colour. Everything was dismal and depressing. Anything wooden was stained dark brown, making the room as shitty as its colour.

I went to the window to breath in the morning air. The cool breeze coming through the gap from the partly open window was refreshing. All outside was bathed in a watery light, and the breaking dawn offered the promise of a fine day to come.

By seven, I was showered and dressed. I left the room and walked down a broad staircase to a vast marble clad entrance hall. The area was impressive and seemed a surprising contrast to my dismal room. Pale light filtered into the hall through two heavy doors, which led out to a short flight of steps.

It was the start of a good day. Thin clouds were being burnt off by the rising sun. There were many morning aromas, including a trace of my own body lotions. I stood on the front steps and breathed in. The morning air heightened the fresh smell of my shower-gel. On a special task to take out a target, I wouldn't wash with soap as the scent would be too strong. My clothes would be washed in clear water and air-dried. It's the way of a hunter. I follow the ways of hunters as they're the best role models to emulate. The hunter wants to creep up on a target unannounced. They want a clean kill so as to have no misgivings. There's a connection, an overlap, between hunter and secret agent, with little difference between them. Both require similar skills of tracking, pursuing, trapping and eradicating.

My thoughts turned to dealing with the best way to start my day. I needed to find somewhere for coffee to kick-start things. Not just any place, as a place with good coffee was my main concern. A regular morning coffee fix was my set routine. However, these thoughts of where to go disappeared. After only a few steps, I spotted her leaving the hall. Walking in my direction was the Kung Fu instructor. Apart from the first impression of her shapely, attractive appearance, it was noticeable how tall she was for a Chinese person. Her tallness was matched to a slim, litheness of frame. A frame that looked deceptive. There are those people who think a slim person can't be powerful. Slenderness shouldn't be confused with the belief that an individual is lacking in strength. Bruce Lee or Jet Li had a slightness, which masked an inner strength that could explode into deadly action. They could find their inner performance zones when needed.

The Kung Fu leader was the sort of woman I could warm to. However, on a mission it was my rule not to get involved with anyone else. There are field agents who don't mind casual relationships when on assignments, but this could become their Achilles' heel. I keep the odds positive by never needing to worry about being figured out by a clever woman, having to answer questions or give explanations. I'm careful to make sure I don't compromise my mission.

The leader continued walking in my direction. She was wearing sunglasses, but I felt she'd looked toward me. We were on the same bearing, so the chances were we would cross paths. Her head lifted and she seemed to look my way. Then we were looking steadily at one another, while closing the few steps between us. It was going to be a chance meeting at any moment. My mouth formed into a soft smile.

"*Zao*," she wished me good morning.

Chapter 6
First Meeting

"*Zao an*," I responded. "Aren't you the lady who leads the Kung Fu class?"

"I am," she returned with a gentle smile.

"I noticed you run a very good martial art class." On my passing the comment about her class, her head lifted to consider me. She faced me and her soft smile didn't falter.

She responded with clear English, "Thank you. I enjoy running that class." She took off the sunglasses. "Have we met before?" I caught a hint of perfume in the air that seemed familiar.

I responded, "No. I'm new here. My name is Harry Long. I'm a new tutor, teaching English in the management school."

"Welcome, Harry. Perhaps we'll see more of each other. I'm also working in the management school." Her facial expression changed and became friendlier after knowing we would work together.

"I'm glad we've met before I start working at the school. Can I know your name?"

"I am Lily." Lily's smile broadened. "I'm Lily Wang. I'm sure we'll meet at some time."

"I'm going to the management school later. Perhaps you'll see me there."

"We could do. I'll probably be in the school this afternoon."

"I'll look out for you," I said, thinking she seemed a good first contact.

I started to respond positively about starting work at the university, but was cut off in mid-sentence as Lily took a call on her mobile. She frowned, raised her free hand and put her palm toward me to indicate our conversation was over. A fast stream of conversation took place between her and someone. She walked away talking into her phone, while putting her sunglasses back on. I didn't have the chance to say goodbye and so walked on.

After a few steps, I heard a motorbike. To my left came a powerful stutter and rumble. There was a click as the bike went into gear. Finally, the noises of pistons and tailpipes signalled the bike's departure. I was drawn to the powerful thudding, which signalled the noise of a super bike. To my surprise, Lily emerged from a side turning astride the bike. It looked like she owned a Honda 750cc Shadow without the full mudguards. The lines of the bike are appealing and easily recognisable. The image fascinated me, and my eyes narrowed in an attempt to look at the detail. The peanut shape fuel tank and the sweep of the twin tail pipes created a buzz of feelings.

Lily looked at me as she came along the road, but without any clear expression of recognition. She passed by and on her back was a tank bag. It looked like she had few possessions in it. The throaty noise of the Shadow disappeared and I considered the female biker. I like them as they're often more independent than other girls. Thinking of biking sent my mind back to earlier times. My elder brother introduced me to serious biking when I was young. We either played with his 'angry ninja girl rider' game or went out at weekends on his CB500 Honda. Girls were seldom bike owners in his group.

I strolled across the campus along the uneven paths, still recalling memories of riding on motorbikes. Students were everywhere. A surprising number of students were outside in the well-tended garden areas reciting English texts aloud or looking at textbooks.

My mind returned to the task of getting a coffee before meeting the teaching staff. I would be in the thick of it soon, trying to figure out as much as possible. On the previous day, I'd seen a Starbucks on a nearby corner. I decided it may be the only local outlet to offer a decent coffee. I quickened my pace.

Compared to other parts of China, Dalian was a good place to be sent to. It is a clean well-developed coastal city without a high level of pollution. That makes it a well-known summer resort offering a port, beaches, scenic places and a highly developed infrastructure. The UK had operated a secret base in Dalian for five years. It was the ideal geographical listening post to intercept information travelling between the different Asian countries of North and South Korea, Japan, and China. Dalian monitored and identified important communications within China and between these areas. A recent identification of genetic experiments, linked to the military, had triggered great concern in

London. The concern was we had no clear details as to the use, or importance, of what was happening at the Institute of Technology.

This was my first day to meet the teachers at the university to start gathering information. A day that was about to provide me with many different things to deal with.

My thoughts were interrupted by the ringing of my mobile.

Chapter 7
Morning Fix

I answered, "Hi, Donghai one."

"Hi, Harry. Glad you did well with the Russians."

"They've certainly complicated things."

"Was it difficult? Did they give you much trouble?"

"Not really. I handled it."

"We've got to be careful now we know they're sniffing around. They'll make everything more difficult for you."

"They're not amateurs. They'll follow up on things for sure."

"We're sure of it as well. But we don't think you've blown your cover."

"Good."

"We'll do what we can to protect you. But you need to watch out."

"Right. I always stay alert."

"Before you go, something else has been identified. It's very important. We traced a communique from the Chinese Ministry of National Defence production unit to the Wuhan Virology Institute. It was asking about the progress on virus development to be used in combination with the Jinying project. Unfortunately, we couldn't intercept any response to this."

"That means they're moving in parallel on the Jinying project."

"That's what we think."

"Makes my work here even more urgent."

"Well, soon you'll be carrying out your mission to get into the Institute of Technology. So we'll be better informed then."

"I'm looking forward to it."

"Good. That's all for now. Bye," she cut me off without further discussion.

The familiar Starbucks' brand name was reassuring when I spotted it. The round green logo with the crowned mermaid was welcoming. I went in and experienced the expected sweet smell of fresh Starbucks' coffee. The place had the normal mix of small tables, a few comfortable armchairs and a bar area. There were various cakes for sale in a chilled display cabinet. I looked up. On the wall behind the counter was a list of drinks, with their prices in Yuan. I stood in the queue, thinking about how non-Chinese speaking people could get what they wanted. Perhaps, it would be enough to point to café latte, which was listed on the wall? I arrived at the counter to give my order.

I looked up at the wall and pointed at café latte on the list of drinks. I then said, with an upward inflection, "Okay? Café latte."

"Lattier. You want large one?" asked a pleasant young girl, wearing a white blouse and green apron emblazoned with the Starbucks' logo. She displayed the amicable Starbucks' smile. Her hair was pulled back on one side, which accentuated her slender, giraffe-like neck. She was refreshingly direct and self-confident.

"Please," I requested.

The girl said, "Large, okay?"

I responded in Chinese, "*Shi*." I pronounced the 'yes' in Chinese as clearly as I could, because I was unsure about what tone to use. I had no idea what tone was right, or what was wrong. The Starbucks' person said something in Chinese, which was probably the amount to pay. She made a shape with her fingers, which I assumed was the amount. I'd no idea how much to pay so held out my Chinese money. She took what was required before responding, "*Xie, xie*, that's enough." The staff spoke reasonable English. I found the whole process was easier and more pleasant than expected.

My morning started by getting my caffeine fix from a few lattes before searching through the files on my laptop. The caffeine helped to clear my mind, which worked well to provide a good start to the day. I drank the coffee in a leisurely, relaxed way, enjoying the aroma and flavour. I found the ambience of the place comforting, so settled into my chair. Looking round, it struck me that although I was in China, this could be anywhere in the world. The branded merchandise surrounded me. Although Starbucks is international, I wrongly expected there would be more difference in Asia. I listened to the standard Starbucks' music being played from a good quality sound system. It was the same jazz music playing that I'd heard in European countries. This didn't feel like China, but I wasn't disappointed as its similarity to what I knew was comforting. I thought about it. Nothing I'd seen in China was as expected. The

China of travel brochures, of the Great Wall and Forbidden City, wasn't the China I was experiencing. I had entered a new China with a highly developed economy, populated with groups capable of purchasing exclusive brands, expensive cars – and Starbucks' coffee.

My nostrils reacted to cigarette smoke. Looking around, I noticed a few Chinese customers were smoking. I tried to ignore the unpleasant smell as I wanted to blend into the background. It was time to do some work. I flipped open my laptop. It bleeped its welcome and I was drawn to it. There was a need to study a map of the area, the plan of the institute and my correspondence. I'd always believed that detailed preparation can make the difference between being a winner or loser. Sun Tzu's book, *The Art of War*, stresses the need for prior calculations of everything in order for success. Good preparation is, therefore, a key to success. That means it's no good having the concentration span of a goldfish when planning a mission.

I thought about the recent deaths of the two university students. Young people die all the time in China, but not in circumstances when official Chinese departments send out copious communications. The signals were assessed from the masses of intelligence identified by the Dalian and GCHQ people. GCHQ was the key to this. They had the capacity to carry out data mining as part of the silent intelligence gathering defence of the UK. In this case, the student deaths were linked to unusual spikes in electronic chatter. Initially, the project didn't warrant my assignment. This changed when the nature of the deaths and blanket suppression of the information was identified.

I looked back at the screen to become acquainted with background details of the mission. I read about the progress made by the British MI6 field base in Dalian. Sophisticated software was able to break into different databases. They managed to tap into the hospital system to uncover the medical records of the dead students. The symptoms before the deaths were found to be complex. It was interesting that the hospital records showed both students had a similar condition. On admittance, both suffered from a lack of muscle function. This worsened to a high brain temperature and an inability to breathe normally. A rapid deterioration and organ failure occurred. It was reported both were placed on life support systems and ventilators, but their nervous systems shut down. Nothing more could be done for them.

One breakthrough was made in obtaining an important communication. There was one key communication that had not been properly coded by the

Chinese authorities. As part of the harvesting of important government emails, one was found that wasn't encrypted. The British intelligence group in Dalian found that the Institute of Technology had sent to the Ministry of State Security:

CONFIDENTIAL- Highest level. Treat as classified all Jinying information. All communication must be treated as Top Security. Urgent Autopsy Arrangement will be required. We need to check the DNA make-up of the Bao and Cheng case to see if the deaths are because we have failed with our Jinying military experiment to produce revised DNA. Tests are needed to see if we have changed their DNAs more quickly than required. Recovery of the bodies for urgent autopsy required, and details are to be coded and sent to the Military of Defence. This is a priority.

Our people believed the students were being treated to suppress or enhance their DNA to develop some military advantage. The intercepted communication showed the experiment to reprocess DNA had probably gone wrong. Scientists at Porton Down were asked about this. The Porton Down people, in the UK, indicated they knew nothing of this type of development. Their report indicated generating new virus strains for bio warfare would pale to insignificance if the current DNA experiments were successful. However, they stated nothing is new in the history of biological warfare. Russia was identified to be developing and using chemicals or radiological attacks involving advanced bio warfare. They pointed out Russia hadn't showed constraint in administering dioxin, novichok or radioisotopes, so were not to be trusted. The report indicated that developments are ongoing as generating or modifying viruses is far easier now. In recent years, new ways of utilising computer-generated change to viruses was reported to be common practice. They indicated they are worried that China does not comply with world standards, so are watched closely. China was identified as the most dangerous threat. They suspected Wuhan is a risk given it has the largest institute of virology in China, and is suspected of developing new viruses. Porton Down reported that DNA reprocessing could signal a step change in possible military advantage. Their main worry was while biological warfare had been banned by different treaties, nothing was banned for DNA reprocessing. One extra point they made was the possibility that China was planning to reduce the number of older people in the population. It was stated they could protect their leaders, while culling the older population with a coronavirus. So the purpose could be biological warfare targeting individuals or whole populations. Therefore, it could be used in standard or covert operations. All of this provided the reason for my mission to shed light on a threat, which we didn't know much about.

I flipped shut my computer. It was time to leave. I went to the toilet, combed my hair and checked myself in the mirror before strolling back. I felt eager to meet my new colleagues, as it could give me the opportunity to provide more insight to the mystery. My eagerness reflected the feeling we have when setting out to get new business or to play an important sport's game. I was motivated and my frame of mind remained positive. I was ready for my meeting, but not the surprise of seeing someone I recognised.

Chapter 8
Surprise Recognition

I made my way to the office I would share with other international tutors. It was pleasant to walk across the campus, while passing small garden areas planted with colourful shrubs and trees. The campus was on the side of a hill, with paths which became quite steep in places. All around were distant views of Dalian. The pleasant garden and open spaces put me in a good mood. My steps felt light as I strode along.

The paths led to the slab-sided office building of the management school. The large windows and architecture were of utility design. Along the road, beside the buildings, were a number of faded flags on stainless steel poles. I looked up and noticed the flag of China in a central higher position, blocking out some of the other flags. I recognised several EU country flags, but a couple of other ones were unknown to me. Behind the fluttering flags was an ugly concrete building. The building's design could be described, without exaggeration, as heavy brutalism. Its size and position dominated the landscape. It was full of sharp angles surfaced with grim concrete slabs. The construction materials were lacking in quality as the cheap outer fabric of the building was in decay. Black mould stains dappled the walls like a battleship with its camouflage. It didn't appear to be the type of environment to give students a sense of creativity or learning.

A small balcony sat perched above two double doors to the entrance. Two people were standing on the balcony talking and smoking. I made my way down steps to the entrance. Young students scurried in and out in chattering groups. I left the brightness of the day for the gloom of the building. The entrance gave way to an interior with high ceilings, large door openings and dated fitments. Posters in English or Chinese were displayed on many of the walls.

I climbed the stairs to the second floor. The place was a maze so I wandered along trying to get my bearings. Dark-brown office doorways stretched out into the distance, each with a number and label as to the occupants. The search for the room was resolved. A voice rang out as I wandered down the corridor looking for the English tutors' room. James must have been following me and seen me assessing each office door number in turn.

"You must be Harry Long. Welcome, I'm James," an English accent sprung from behind.

I turned to face him. "Yes, I'm, Harry. Nice to meet you."

I was impressed he knew my name without my needing to tell him. I'd been expected. James approached me, closing the distance between us. We shook hands politely and he introduced himself as the head of English language. In my usual way, I tried to gain some insight about an individual from my initial impression. I noticed James was dressed in old-fashioned clothes and seemed to be a heavy smoker. Cigarette smoke clung to his clothes. He was shabby but formal, as he dressed in a dark-blue suit with wide lapels. The look was finished off with a cream shirt and green tie. I noticed his jacket pocket had two pens, as if indicating his role. He looked like a timeworn headmaster but was possibly no older than fifty. His taught face portrayed a look that seemed to indicate he was worried over something. He raised his hand and pointed a finger in a prodding way to indicate we needed to walk back the way I'd come.

He led me back along the corridor and opened a door to reveal a large open office space. The space was a mess with papers spilling across a number of the desks and in piles on the floor. So this was my base to work from. Five faces looked up and turned in my direction as we entered.

"This is Harry. He's our new English tutor." I felt reassured as everyone welcomed me warmly with 'hi' or 'hello'.

There was a face in the crowd, which generated a deja vu moment. One person who said 'hi' sent my senses into overdrive. A man's face had caught my attention due to its familiarity. My mind raced to recall him. Face recognition senses were whirling while scanning the people in the room. The face proportions, eyes, nose and mouth were a match. The clothes were a match. My eyes widened a little, but I was careful to ensure my surprise wouldn't be noted. Rather than focus on him, I gazed around the room. I was now certain it was him. The image of one man was the same as the person exiting from the

Institute of Technology building. It was easy to decide as there was no mistaking he was that person.

I was introduced to Ian, Geoff, Matt, Maria and Amanda by James, who was taking it upon himself to make the introductions. I could now match the face to a name. So it was Matt who was the person I'd seen earlier. My curiosity was aroused.

The introductions continued. I'd already placed James as being English. He was obviously from the south of England due to a clipped accent with clear and precise enunciation. James's speech wasn't formal, but certainly one of exaggerating his English vowels. I find it interesting how some foreigners when abroad often exaggerate their natural regional accents.

I noticed Matt wore the same light grey jacket and trousers I'd seen him wearing at the Institute of Technology. I tried to assess his nationality, but he was a little more difficult to place. He was possibly American or Canadian. Matt had a relaxed, easy way about him and his body movements were slow yet deliberate. He had the twang of a North American accent, with an over-friendly tone to his voice. Although the tone was friendly, he was assertive in what he said. He was well built, and his clothes were neutral in colour and taste. I thought the colours of his clothes didn't reflect his personality, as he seemed quite strong in character.

From their accents, I was able to place the backgrounds of other members of the staff. Ian sounded Scottish and was possibly from Edinburgh. Ian had an open, engaging personality. He sported a fine black moustache that highlighted his pleasing smile. The second noticeable thing about him was the moussed-up hair that seemed out of place amongst the other tutors. He was tall and wore casual clothes selected from leading brands. His jumper had a Hugo Boss emblem, a company not to my liking due to its tailoring history. Ian cut a fine figure, but he wasn't in the category of good-looking.

Geoff was probably from Essex or the Thames Estuary area. He had the appearance of a dedicated teacher as he portrayed a more academic look. His personality didn't have the strength of character of Matt or Ian, as he seemed a more quiet type. Geoff was slim and looked like he cared about his appearance. He was well groomed and wore a pair of blue corduroy trousers, a button-down shirt and brogue shoes.

"Can I get you a mug of cha?" Maria asked me, while making her way to pick up a mug.

"Great, but I would prefer a cup and saucer." Noting her reaction, I added, "…if you have them?"

"We don't. You can always buy some though," she answered nonchalantly.

"A mug'll do for now. Thanks."

Maria sounded like she came from a Midlands city. She looked a homely earth mother type, not too worried about her appearance. She was clothed in loose fitting natural fibres, which flowed as she moved. She wore sandals and they accentuated her heavy-footed walk. She obviously dressed for comfort rather than style. Maria smiled in my direction while continuing to make a mug of tea for me. She projected the image of a friendly, mature woman at ease with herself. It was easy to visualise her being pleasant to others.

Amanda was the last person to meet. She'd stayed at her desk during the introductions and was busy with her computer. I decided to go over to say hello. As I walked to her, she waited until the last moment to look away from her computer screen. Amanda smiled, but it was a more nervous than shy smile. She picked up her pen, looked pensively at James and started to fiddle with it. Though seated, it was obvious Amanda was a tall woman. I was struck by her slender arms, small face and soft eyes. Her make-up was lightly applied and enhanced her features. A tight purple top made the most of her shapely figure, which probably equated to a perfect BMI score. Amanda put down the pen and ran a hand through her hair. She finally gave me a reserved smile of welcome. Then, her gaze flitted between her computer screen, James and me, as if she would sooner be occupied in work. James did most of the talking and the few words Amanda uttered placed her from London.

I was welcomed in different degrees by each person. Handshakes and smiles were generously provided, but thankfully no one wanted to overdo the welcoming process. Ian squeezed my hand harder than expected and I applied a polite grip in response. He seemed the most self-assured of the group.

"Your desk is the one in the corner," said James, pointing to a desk away from the light of the window.

"Fine. I'll sort my things out."

The desks were obviously part of a territorial realignment after someone left. This meant as the newcomer, I was last in any pecking order. I made my way to the desk to see what was awaiting me. It was a mess. A Lenovo screen and dirty keyboard, plus the course handbook, a timetable, some pens, pad and office equipment were piled on the desk. I sat down, but the chair wasn't designed for someone of my build or height. A few adjustments and it became more comfortable. I examined my materials and started to sort them into logical order.

James perched himself on the edge of a desk, watching the proceedings. I caught his eye and he stood and addressed the group, but the emphasis was on me. "I'm glad most of you are here. It's normal for new staff to go out with us for a meal. Okay everyone for this evening then?" He turned to me. "You need to get to know us and to find out about this place. So you will need to join us for dinner tonight, and," he looked round the room. "*NO* excuses from anyone," he delivered this in an assertive manner.

I put down the papers I'd sorted through. "That's a nice gesture. Thanks." I nodded in approval but didn't like the *no excuses* line.

"Okay, right." He straightened his small frame. "I'll expect us outside here at six."

I felt pressurised by these commands rather than being asked if I was available to join my new colleagues. Perhaps he was asserting himself over me as my new boss. It didn't matter. I felt calm as it was a good idea to be welcomed as a member of the group. So far things were going well; the meal would be a good way to meet everyone as a start to my investigation. The students and Matt would be of special interest. I couldn't have thought of a more ideal way to learn about the people and events in the school. It made things easy. Everyone had seemed friendly enough and open in their conversations. This helped me feel confident they would reveal useful information at some point.

Amanda's chair creaked. A clacking of stiletto heels on the wooden floor signalled her walking across the room to get something from a cupboard. Amanda flicked her eyes to me and back but never smiled. She clack clacked without any worry about the attention the sound created. She was wearing high heels and a short skirt. James and Matt followed Amanda with their eyes scanning her body as she moved. I was watching intelligent men becoming distracted in the presence of an attractive woman. Amanda didn't seem to worry about the reaction she was generating.

A new noise of someone entering the room led me to look round. I caught a glimpse of a blue, floral print dress. It was Lily Wang who entered the office. She strolled in, put something on her desk and then placed a wad of papers in a rack near the door. She went about her work quietly without acknowledging us.

I turned to look, but she seemed busy with her work. She caught my gaze and I smiled to her, thinking it the right thing to do.

"Hello, Harry. Settling in okay?" asked Lily.

"I'm trying to organise everything. But there's nothing pressing to do yet," I responded.

"That's not going to last."

"You're so right." I reflected on my task in China rather than the office work.

"They're a nice group." Her eyes glanced from me to the others in the room. Then she returned to sorting out and signing papers at her desk.

"I feel good, as James has arranged a welcome for me. We're all having a meal later."

She looked up. "That's good. It'll be nice for you to share a meal with everyone. You'll have the chance to get to know them," her voice was subdued.

"Yes. It gives me a perfect start to meet the team."

"I'll not be there, but I'm sure you'll have a good time." James turned to her with a pensive glance, but she was looking down at her paperwork. Maria interpreted James's facial message and seemed to understand the awkwardness of the moment. Maria went over to Lily's desk to speak to her.

"Lily, will you come with us for the meal?" encouraged Maria. "Please do come, as I love your company. It would be such a shame if you didn't join us."

"I'm a little tired, but I suppose I should join for a while. It will be good to welcome Harry."

Maria looked pleased, and was just about to say something when James cut in, "Fine. It's at six, Lily. And we're all meeting outside this building."

I glanced at my watch and saw it was already five.

Chapter 9
Restaurant Conversations

All eight of us arrived around the same time outside the building. We all stood around James, who'd arrived a little earlier than the group. He took the lead. "Somewhere local for Harry I think."

The conversation circled around what restaurant to go to. It was an easy group as they were enthusiastic about which place to choose. There was no need for small talk or the filling of silences. The final decision was between hot tasting Sichuan food and sweeter Shanghai cuisine. I felt confused about the different choices so remained quiet. The others were well informed about Chinese food and they discussed the possibilities of where to go with great passion. Maria thought it may be a good idea to consider the need to order only medium-spiced dishes, but Ian told her she was being too cautious. The discussion wasn't prolonged as the spicy Sichuan restaurant was agreed upon. I was happy there was no delay with the decision, as an evening chill was in the air. We moved off at a rapid pace and in good spirits.

After a short walk, we arrived. James pointed up at the name of the restaurant. "This is it," he said.

We had arrived at a restaurant festooned on the outside with red lanterns and a frontage in need of renewal. I'd no idea why it had been chosen as it looked similar to the other restaurants we'd walked past. Nothing about the look of the restaurant appealed to me, so I felt grateful that the group had made the selection.

The restaurant staff welcomed us in and seemed to know most of the group. A tired-looking waiter organised a space for us near the window. We all crowded around two tables that were pushed together. There was not much space. Rather than using chairs, we squatted on red plastic stools. In fact, chairs would be too large for the available space, so stools were the only option. I looked around and wondered if there were food safety standards in China. The place would have been good training for the environmental health inspectors from my first impression. The walls and floor had a fine covering of dirt, making me feel I needed to wipe the table before the meal arrived. It was obvious the unhygienic surroundings didn't discourage custom, as the restaurant was crowded with local people.

Lily was given the task of ordering what the group decided upon. A number of dishes, plus rice and Tsingtao beer, were ordered. Amanda joined the men in having the beer, while Lily and Maria had hot wheat drinks in earthenware cups. The place, while small, was full of loud people enthusiastically plunging chopsticks in and out of communal food dishes. It was reminiscent of a small flock of starlings dipping their beaks into the ground. The clicking chopsticks dug in and out of the food in rapid movements. People could be seen slurping at their food, eating with open mouths and enjoying everything.

"Can we shuffle up?" asked Maria politely, to enable us to fit round the small tables.

The group complied, and we all managed to squeeze around the combined tables. Maria put down her bag on the table and it made a loud clunk. Ian raised his eyes at the clunk noise.

"What on earth do women carry in their bags?" was Ian's general question.

Maria frowned. "Essentials, Ian. I'm sure a man of your experience would understand that!"

"Ouchhhh. Touché," replied Ian.

"Where's the toilet?" I asked, thinking it a good idea to wash my hands before eating the meal. Several of the group looked in the direction of a piece of cloth over a narrow opening.

"It's over there. Good luck," said Maria. "If you need a tissue, I've got some."

Moving across the restaurant, I passed other customers. The surrounding air carried a pungent odour of clothes in need of laundering.

The toilet consisted of one cubicle for either men or women. I entered the cubicle and used a small bolt to lock the door. It was symbolic rather than functional as any reasonable force could easily open the door. My nostrils reacted to the new odours as soon as I entered. A bad stench of sewers led me to breathe with shallow breaths. The smell was coming from a dry hole in the middle of a flat-stained china surround. It was as if a toilet had been removed and only the hole remained. Next to the hole was a bin. Tissues were placed in it rather than being flushed away. As I'd been told, there was no toilet paper provided.

Like the restaurant, the toilet area lacked any form of cleanliness. Thankfully, I only wanted to pee. A lever on the wall flushed a torrent of water into the brown hole and beyond. I realised things were not going to get better. Outside the cubicle was a small stained sink with a single cold tap. Perhaps it was good luck that a small bar of soap was on the sink top. I believed there was never more of a need to wash my hands than now. I took my time to feel the water and soap working before shaking my hands vigorously. This was preferable to the small, thin towel skewered on a hook at the side of the sink. I returned to the others and the food was already being served.

"Here, sit next to me," Maria beckoned on seeing me. She'd already arranged a stool beside her that distanced her from Ian by one seat. "You're softer on the eyes than Ian," she joked. When I sat down next to her, she patted the back of my hand. I imagined Maria as a favourite aunt figure, whose presence would always provide for a calming influence. I was struck by her caring character.

The waiter unceremoniously placed several bowls of food onto our table. I could see slivers of red peppers and seeds amongst the first dishes. We started to eat without waiting for all the dishes to arrive. Immediately, my mouth suffered an intense burning sensation. This was different to my idea of a curry. Rather than eating with abandon, I paced the number of different peppers and garlic attacking my taste buds. Some rice helped pacify the effect. I found the unrecognisable dishes had a similar consistency and an over-spiced taste. Thankfully, the beers arrived. The cold beer acted as a soothing balm. It worked to reduce the spice-laden heat of the meal. I took a long draft of the beer. The taste and quality of the beer was good so I mentioned this to the group.

Ian looked at the Tsingtao label, then put down his bottle. "Yes, it's really good. This beer was developed by German settlers in North East China over one hundred years ago. It has a great pedigree."

"I'll drink to that," Geoff lifted his bottle, then added "…so that I can order another bottle. I'm a bit low and getting drunk could be the answer." He gave a weak mimic of a drunken person's eyes rolling.

James looked across at Geoff and with a flourish of his chopsticks retorted, "Come on, Geoff. There's no strength in it to get drunk. You're just processing it before pissing it out. There's only a mild effect."

"Well, it works for me. But I'm a lightweight," said Geoff.

Ian responded. "Hear, hear, motion carried. But I notice you drink more these days."

James chuckled. "Well, the beer is as cheap as the water… AND, while it has the same effect, it tastes better. So cheers." He gulped his beer.

At this, Ian emptied his bottle, placed it on the table and rotated it in front of him to get people's attention. "Another everyone?" He slid his fingers along the condensation formed on the bottle, then lifted it. He beckoned the waiter and another round of drinks arrived. Everyone seemed to enjoy the evening in a relaxed way.

Ian twirled his new bottle of beer while he gazed at Amanda. "Now, as you're single," he waved a finger in her direction, "…and our Harry here is new," his finger switched to my direction, "it'll be good if you look after him in the next few days."

"You never matured beyond student life," said Maria, trying to stifle his approach.

Amanda's cheeks flushed and she responded, "Don't be embarrassing, Ian. I'm sure Harry will be taken care of by us." She dipped her chopsticks into her bowl and left them there as if she'd lost her appetite.

"Ah, but a NEW, new friend is available – and you two look a good match." He moved the bottle aside and intertwined his fingers, as if to emphasise a match.

Amanda looked vacantly at me, then Ian. "You're a pain, Ian. Harry can ask me if he needs my help."

It was clear Ian liked to organise things. Perhaps this was his normal approach. I remained quiet while James weighed in, "I'll put your match-making down to fatherly concern, Ian. Otherwise we'll get Amanda to neuter you in order to calm you down."

"Don't bother with him," Amanda said curtly, "he's the group bully."

Maria tactfully changed the subject. "It'll be nice to have a picture of the new team," she offered, while holding up a small camera.

"Then let me," responded Matt, putting out his hand for the camera.

"Thanks, but I'll get the waiter to take it." Maria called out, "Fuwuyuan." The waiter, seeing the camera, moved to our table to take the picture. As the camera clicked, Matt turned his head toward Maria and pulled a face.

Maria sighed, "Ohhh, please stop it! That's another picture ruined."

"Burrrp. Oh dear, beg your pardon," said Ian, due to a loud belch that was over emphasised.

"Being annoying, I see," said James, asserting himself.

"Peace man," Ian sarcastically responded. "Get the beer down you and relax, James. We're not in the office now."

"This meal is different in taste." I straightened on my stool. "But I hope I'm not eating dog or something else I would feel bad about."

"Well, it's not often dog is on Chinese restaurant menus. But it's often on Korean ones," responded Geoff.

Lily took up the explanation. "Well, to be clear, the dogs are a special breed and bred just for their meat; the menu doesn't have any dog," she delivered this in a flat tone.

Matt weighed in, "We're funny when it comes to food. Horse meat is eaten in many countries, yet often the press treat it as unnatural or cruel." He gave a measured nod.

"Well, it seems you like the spicy bull frog you're eating," said Geoff, looking into the different parts of his meal.

We used wooden chopsticks, but I wasn't as quick as the others in filling my bowl from the main dishes. Lily and Maria noticed this. Both took turns in filling my bowl, so I could have as much to eat as they did. I leant back and looked around. The question of hygiene crossed my mind. There was no serving spoon for each dish, yet no one worried about each other's chopsticks being dipped into the main dishes. Several more beers were ordered as we progressed with the meal. Ian pointed his beer bottle in my direction. The bottle began wagging at me before he spoke.

"Where you from, Harry? Are you from the south, possibly Surrey? Got you down as a private school boy. Right?" Just as I was about to answer Ian stated, "I'm sure you're one of the southern privileged classes."

I would've sooner told Ian he was a waste of space and floored him but was happy keeping things amicable. "You sound biased. Well, I'm privileged to live in a multi-cultural world. That's my privilege." Ian's eyes widened. "I'm a citizen of the world. I judge other people by what they add to society." I looked around trying to gauge everyone's reaction.

"Seems the right way to look at things," said James.

"Emm. Yes, I agree," added Maria.

I could have left it there, but found it hard to hold back. Ian's directness triggered my own. "I've moved on from questioning why there's regional bigotry from people like Ian."

"My dear, Harry, I never meant to belittle your background." Ian may not have realised it, but I didn't find his words formed an apology. I found his patronising character wasn't to my liking. Maria was responsive to the seriousness in my facial expression.

"Cool it, boys. We're all the same – all come from Storks, don't you agree?" said Maria, providing some lightness. "All of us sucked on similar mothers' milk." The remark by Ian had created an interest in my background and Maria went on, "Do tell us about you, Harry?"

A discussion developed. It was easy to tell them about my childhood and that I was brought up in Surrey. Ian smiled, nodded at the mention of Surrey and acted like he'd won a quiz night competition. The group talked of Surrey. They knew the towns and countryside such as the Devil's Punch Bowl area and Gibbet's hill. None of the questions caught me off guard as nothing was confidential to my cover story. Soon the conversation slowed as people tired of reminisces regarding places they had visited. The conversation switched to help me know about the Dalian area of China and the students they taught. Maria was the most helpful and wanted to tell me as much as possible. Ian and Matt looked bored and spoke in a separate conversation to Lily and Amanda, while James, Geoff and Maria told me more about Donghai. They went over the number of students, the teaching and the needs of administration.

The time was right to change the subject. "There's something else I need to know. I picked up a story about two student deaths. What happened?"

There were sideways glances and a pause. Most glances were directed at James. Not Lily though, as her eyes fixed on me. She seemed relieved that someone was raising questions about the students. She switched her gaze to James and appeared more alert.

"Harry should know about the problems with the two deaths, James," insisted Maria. The atmosphere amongst the group changed and became tangibly heavier.

James paused a moment, "We've had a sad time recently. A couple of the students died while on a medical experiment programme. It's caused a lot of upset around here."

"What's happened to make people sad?" I asked.

"Their deaths," was all he responded. Others nodded, but no other information was volunteered.

I wanted to obtain more information without arousing undue concern, so pressed for more detail as casually as possible. "On my way through Beijing, I had to call in to the British Council to arrange my paperwork. An official mentioned he'd heard that a couple of students had died from medical trials. I'm interested in what's happened, as I may need to know if they contact me."

"Nothing known yet," James offered. He then changed the direction of the conversation from my enquiry to talk about the mundane aspects of the job. The conversation reverted to the information from a few minutes ago. It became boring. He told me about the level of the students' English abilities or, more accurately, lack of them. I listened without interest to negative attitudes about the acquisition of language by the students. James complained the boys or Chinese kids, as he called them, did far worse than the girls at English. I felt frustrated at not steering the conversation in the direction I wanted.

"Many of these kids think they can get through the course without any hard work. Don't let them get away with laziness," he insisted.

I failed to get the conversation back to the main reason for my assignment. I had tried to find a way to ask about the deaths of the students, but James had switched to other topics. The conversation moved on to describe Xinghai Square, the coastal area and the best restaurants to go to. The group chose lighter subjects, such as insisting I should visit the coast near Tiger Beach as it was a special area. Maria had it in her mind to tell me about shopping in Dalian, and Amanda helped by adding details of large shopping malls. As the evening wore on, I found the Chinese names began to merge into each other. James insisted Maria was a veteran expat and shopping could be her chosen subject for any quiz, but when it came to bars, Matt should be consulted.

The discussion had moved on from details of my background to local Dalian details. Everything was superficial. This allowed me to relax as I felt sure they had bought my cover story and accepted me as a member of the team. The group became quieter. I sensed I was able to continue with my quest to gain more information. Everyone was in a happy, relaxed mood. The mild opiate effect of the release of endorphins, due to the hot spices plus alcohol, was kicking in. Maria started fussing over arranging the empty dishes on top of each other. Calm came over the group so I took this as my chance to reopen the earlier discussion.

"Thanks for the welcome. You've told me a great deal." I smiled at James. "I'm still wondering about the student deaths though. Perhaps you can tell me what happened?"

No reaction for a moment, then Lily said, "It's very sad to talk about." She stared at James. "We should discuss it."

Amanda surprised me by stating, "Come on, James. You've more to share with us on this. We need to understand what the management people know."

James took his time to collect his thoughts. "It's better if we do what the dean wants. He wants it to blow over without problems."

"Yes, he would. He doesn't realise how well we knew them. We feel it's a tragic loss, but our dean wouldn't understand that," said a disconsolate Maria.

Geoff dropped his head and said quietly, "We knew them both and liked them, so let's not reopen any bad feelings of the events. The shock of it has upset me."

"Yes, it's sad, but it's over now," commented James. "We're under strict instructions not to discuss any details of the deaths outside the school."

I wanted to open up discussion. "Okay, but we're the school people; I'm in the school. So it would be better if I knew some details."

"I think you should know what's public," offered Matt. "Both the students were in some kind of medical trial programme. The harsh fact is both were earning money and trials can go wrong."

"Yes. Their deaths must be connected to that medical trial," said Lily.

"In what way?" I asked.

Ian had flashed his smile around the room most of the evening, but now his lips formed a pensive shape. "The students asked me if large magnets can be dangerous. I asked senior university people why some peculiar magnetic equipment was part of the experiment. They made it clear if I wanted to renew my visa, I shouldn't speak to anyone outside the university. Or ask questions."

James looked around the table, stopping a moment to capture the group's attention, before offering, "Well, in China, lots of news is supressed. We know this country isn't open. They said it was patient confidentiality about the students that mattered. So we have to respect that." He looked me straight in the eye. "It's not that simple. The government has admitted over two million people are employed to monitor and police the Internet? Trust is in short supply here, especially over these deaths." His eyes never wavered. "We need to say and do nothing until this blows over. All of you need to just get on with your work." It was a clear message not to make a fuss.

"You're right, James, but we should find out more," said Matt.

Maria started with, "It's all too much..." Her voice drifted off into silence when James sent her a stern look of reproach.

Lily became more spirited and spoke. She'd not talked much all evening and now there was concern in her voice. "I know you want us to let the deaths pass unnoticed, James. That's not good enough. We should have cared enough to ask more questions." Lily looked down at the table and across the remains of our meal. "I want to find out more, given that experiment has killed Cheng and Bao. Perhaps it could kill others. We really do need to know."

She continued to look vacantly at the meal's leftovers, which was starting to congeal or dry out. I followed her eyes to the bowls and raffia baskets littering our table. It was a mess with items of dropped food and left-over debris. I fixed back on Lily, who seemed upset at James's shutting down of the conversation. She shuffled on her stool and didn't look at ease. I guessed his obdurate approach motivated her to want to leave.

Lily stood and said she had to go. Amanda looked in her direction and indicated she would leave as well. I asked if I could accompany them back to Donghai as I'd many things to sort out. "Do that," said James, "I'll take care of the bill."

"Must run as well," added Matt, seeing we were leaving. "Amanda, can I have a word with you on the way back?" he asked.

We stood up and as our stools moved backwards they screeched on the bare floor. I was hoping to learn more about the dead students from Lily and Amanda on the way back. It wasn't difficult to realise some of the staff were more open than others, and it seemed Lily could be helpful. It was clear that others, like James, would be more reluctant to provide details. James probably knew more but he was deferring to his dean.

Lily caught my eye. "Let's go." She obviously wanted to get away, but I was delayed by James who came to say his farewell, "It was good to meet you. I think you'll fit in here." I noticed that Lily waited by the door for me while I said my farewells.

"Goes for me too. I'm glad you've joined us," said Maria. The others made no comment and I followed Lily into the street.

Chapter 10
Knowing Lily

Outside, the air was fresh and the sky full of stars as if sequins were glinting above us. It formed a dome of familiar, universally recognisable stars. I looked back through the grime of the restaurant window to see what was happening. Ian, James and Geoff were still seated and had started on another beer, while the others were getting ready to leave. The clacking of Amanda's heels sounded, which signalled she was following us. I turned to see Matt with her. Her bare legs below her short hem stepped out like a model on a catwalk. I slowed wondering if we should wait for them. They were making conversation, and she was talking earnestly in a friendly manner. The situation changed when Matt attempted to link arms with Amanda, as she wasn't pleased with this. She moved away from his attempt to be close, but continued chatting with him.

"We can leave them to walk back together," said Lily, seeing what was happening. She set off at a brisk pace through the night streets. It was good to have left the confines of the restaurant, as it felt pleasing to be moving again after sitting on the low stool.

"Is, Matt the office Romeo?" I asked, having seen his approach to Amanda.

"He has a reputation in dating young Chinese girls, and this is not liked. He has different moral standards to the rest of us."

"Amanda probably realises this, as she wasn't going to let him hold her arm."

"I worry about Amanda, as she has a number of concerns."

"Am I right in thinking she seems to be rather nervous?"

We took a couple of steps before she said, "Amanda told Maria and me about her difficult history. She told us how she suffered problems in her early years from an over-demanding father." Two more steps before she added, "She thought China would be a fresh start for her. After she arrived in China, she met James; it didn't work out."

"I notice she's rather nervous, especially in front of James. I find that interesting, as he's not the sort of person I would think women are easily attracted to."

"I think she seeks approval from older figures like James."

"Interesting."

"I can identify with Amanda. My early life wasn't straightforward either."

I tried to build bridges with her. "Childhood can be challenging. We're vulnerable then."

"It's not only childhood that causes problems." She stopped talking and stared ahead with a thoughtful expression. We walked a couple of paces in silence. "Well, Amanda needs to trust people again. She's just finished an upsetting relationship."

"I see. That's possibly the reason."

"I try to support her. When she first arrived in China, nothing worked out well. As I'm Chinese, I helped her sort things out. Some people require a second chance in life, whereas Amanda probably needs a third one. I've done what I can to help her."

I didn't want to continue with Amanda's problems as there were more important topics I needed to concentrate on. Lily seemed matter of fact in talking about problem relationships. Perhaps she'd suffered as well but I didn't want to pursue that topic. It was time to change the subject, so I tried to find a common theme. "Did you think it was a good meal and discussion?"

"Think so. It helped clear some air over the two students. I was happy that you helped us discuss the problem."

"Oh – I noticed you seemed upset that no one has asked enough about the student deaths. I had the impression that you were angry about people remaining quiet," I decided on a direct approach given Lily's feelings in the restaurant.

"I was." There was a tangible pained look. "Tonight was the first time we raised questions about the students."

"Did anyone try to find out what happened?"

"In China, we say you never put two feet in a river to see how deep it is." She frowned. "I try to be careful."

"I find that Chinese saying very interesting. It's expressive and helps in understanding Chinese peoples' attitudes and values. Perhaps you know something about the students though."

"Well, I know both students were taken away by government people after becoming ill. So I guessed this was a special medical case." She paused and took a breath. "Then more government people arrived to see our dean. He said there was to be an official enquiry."

"Did they start one?"

"No. We had no news given to us. And we were told not to discuss the deaths as the enquiry could be compromised due to rumours." I remained silent hoping Lily would say more. She went on, "It was obvious the deaths were not normal because of the high number of officials who turned up. It's sometimes difficult to find out things here."

"No one did anything and it's like they didn't understand how serious it was."

"Do you know about the story of the two small fishes swimming along in the river?" I looked lost. "Well, they meet an older, larger fish swimming the opposite way who asks 'How's the water?' 'What's water?' asks one of the small fishes."

"What's all that mean?"

"They never knew how important the water was for them. Because, they never questioned it."

We walked on, and given her remarks about questioning things, I asked, "Would you like China to have a free press... are you in favour of a more open China?"

"Bad things happen here if someone wants to create an open China...an open society."

"Like what?"

"My father is a good example." She breathed in. "Well, my father was placed in a laogai, that's a prison labour camp, because he wrote articles critical of the government. They placed him in a re-education laogai in Shenyang." Her voice slowed. "They attempted to retrain him with reform through labour."

"What sort of reform?"

"Reform seems simple, but it's based on hard labour and agreeing to the charges against you. He had to work long hours in a factory inside the prison. When you celebrate Christmas, you may not know that many of the home decorations are made in these prisons. Western enjoyment of Christmas is sometimes based upon their hard labour. It didn't end there. After finishing work, he had to endure two hours of indoctrination to change his views."

She paused and took some steps. "Go on." I wanted to know more.

"Well, they tried to break his will," Lily stiffened. "He didn't worry about sleeping on the floor, using a bucket for a toilet or surviving on meagre rations. He just couldn't agree that he was at fault in wanting a more honest, open government. It would have gone well if he'd agreed to change his personal beliefs, but he retained his views."

"What does that mean?" She obviously felt upset about the way he'd been treated.

"Other inmates were sometimes ordered to encourage him to change his views. He didn't find this easy. Finally, his dignity was destroyed. He gave in and decided to sign a confession that he was an anti-revolutionary – yet he loved his country. My mother also had to follow party lines. In the Cultural Revolution, my mother needed to hide her make-up, or she would be seen as too bourgeoisie. She had no personal choice about her appearance as it was mandatory for females' hair to be bobbed above the shoulder. Simple things in life can be viewed as bad if those in power want to control them." With a sad look she asked, "Do the bad people always end up with power?"

"Individuals are not simply corrupted by power, as they are often corrupted by the politics of power. What I mean is, people do things to please those in power just to get what they want."

"I worry about these things as well." It seemed we were bonding on this point.

"I think you probably do, Lily." I realised her strong values. It was becoming clear Lily was a social campaigner, like her father. "It's difficult to have change. I think good people should be strong at times, like your father." She nodded. "Or be brave enough to ensure the rule of bad people is broken." My words about good and bad were flying around in my mind. My assumption was my government was the good one when confronted by communism. I could realise that Lily's father was right in his campaign. The clarity for me was that Lily had confirmed how communism is oppressive.

We walked a few more steps. "The answer is to have more campaigners in the world, trying to obtain justice," she added.

"Unlike many others, your father had conviction and also action. One thing I'm clear about is claiming to have conviction without action is meaningless." Her eyes brightened and she became animated. "When it's right to do something, we should act and not simply debate," I stressed.

There was a reaction in her body language. I think she'd recognised a kindred spirit in me. I knew for me it was only in spirit, not politics. Little did she know how politically different we were as campaigners. It was always my country first. I wasn't naïve though. I realised I wasn't allowed free will in my role and was reliant on taking my orders from politicians.

"You seem a good man," she said cheerfully, "but big fish are always the ones that eat the smaller ones. In China, you need to be aware of this, as those in power use that power. So remember to be careful." Her mysterious seriousness melted away. It seemed I'd broken the ice with her. Perhaps the inscrutable appearance of the Asian face was a sign of being careful. I felt her reserve had evaporated and she'd started to like me.

"Well, I like to make the world a better place. Just like your father, I care about doing the right thing. I don't like to suffer regret by doing unacceptable things."

Her face remained alive. "Yes. We have to take a stand. Obtaining freedom for one may end in freedom for all. Lots of people want to improve things but it's not easy. In China, we say wet clay requires turning to make beautiful pots. Nothing happens overnight as we need to strive to improve things."

"People are not as easy as clay but we can shape them. Education is important as it's easier with young people."

"I suppose we chose to be teachers because we want to influence others, and especially the young. That must be a reflection of our character." She paused. "Perhaps after the deaths, the teachers needed to do more. We knew something was wrong with what happened."

"How do you mean?"

"Cheng, one of the boys who died, was a special student. As with all my students, I cared about him. I spent time with him as we had a mutual respect for each other. I was in a position to support him and should have done more, as he relied on me. Perhaps you would've been more active than me?"

"Well. I'm probably not as good as you think."

"But you seem it. I like your character," she said this with conviction. But Lily had no idea about my real role in life. I wasn't able to tell her what I did to make the world a better place. I'd been trained to lie and to deceive. This was part of being a field agent. She would have to remain in ignorance.

"Making the world better may mean doing harmful things to others. No choice is easy," I said, while reflecting on my covert operations in Europe.

"Harmful – that surprises me. Being good may help the outcome," said Lily. "I wish I'd helped Cheng as he was special." She paused. "My Confucius teachings should have led me to use more Ren."

"Ren. What's that?"

"More mercy, love and humanity to his situation."

I took a strategy of showing personal concern to uncover more detail. "I'm worried that the cause of the student deaths could have been related to something contagious."

"That's never been a worry."

"What was the condition of the students leading up to the illness?" I asked.

"Monday was the first sign of a problem. When I saw them, they both had difficulties in seeing, so they went to the sick room. Their vision was blurred at the time. They also complained of being thirsty but couldn't swallow the drinks they were given."

"Were you told anything else?"

"I tried to get help, but was told not to interfere. It was obvious someone made things happen as they were taken away. The officials told James they would be looked after in the hospital. Unfortunately we heard on the Wednesday they were both dead." Lily raised her head. "Yes. Dead in three days; both in the same way."

"Sounds suspicious?"

"I question why the two of them died at the same time?" She looked tense.

"Have you any idea why?" I wanted Lily to open up.

"Yes. It had no reason unless it was due to the medical experiments. Others are also in that trial."

I tried to soften my tone, "Did you speak to them about the medical trial?"

"No, not in any detail. There's one thing that stays in my mind though. Cheng told me they were lucky in the trial as on one occasion a large transformer exploded in the next room. I told him I thought this was strange as it didn't seem like medical equipment. He explained that special equipment was part of the treatment they received."

"Emm. What kind of equipment?"

"He said powerful magnetics were used in the trial. I didn't ask more as both students told me they had signed a confidentiality document. I tried to find out more facts when they were first ill. They said they couldn't tell me anything in case they got into trouble."

Lily tilted her head to one side and looked away. I decided not to prolong the questions as she'd become quite emotional about the students' plight. She became calmer and turned to see what had happened with Amanda. Amanda was walking on her own, so Lily stood still and waved for her to catch us up.

Lily looked back to me. "Before Amanda gets here, I just want you to know I'm not clear why I told you so much about my life. Anyway, I'm not sorry I told you as much as I did."

Amanda clattered toward us without any rush. "You both seemed in deep conversation," Amanda commented. "It's sweet of you to wait for me."

"We must have been busy talking as I didn't notice Matt leave," said Lily.

"He asked me to go to a bar, but I didn't want to. Then he took a phone call and went off in a taxi."

"Well, Harry gave me the third degree over the student deaths." Lily caught Amanda's eyes. "I've let him have my account."

I judged it was best to change the subject. "What do you both do for relaxation?" I asked.

A silence then Lily said, "The Kung Fu classes and motor-biking help me relax."

"Ohh, I love the thrill of a bike ride, especially on a bike like the Shadow," I said.

"I feel the same way about my bike." A smile broke across Lily's face and her teeth sparkled against the dimness of the night. "I feel lucky to have my Shadow as motorbikes are not sold in Dalian."

"And for you, Amanda?" I enquired.

"Nothing as fast as a motorbike." She looked at Lily. "I enjoy walking at weekends along the coastal roads."

"Lower on the adrenaline than a super bike, but relaxing," I offered.

"I like to go to Bangchui Island or stroll along the boardwalk of Binhai Road when life closes in around me. It offers fresh air from the sea and complete escape from everything." Her expression seemed much more relaxed than earlier in the office. Both these women caught my attention, as both had an air of mystery surrounding them.

"I'll leave you here," said Lily as we arrived back at Donghai University.

It was a pity the walk was over. I was pleased to have walked back with Lily. It enabled me to gather some interesting information on her, as well as the student deaths. I stopped to shake hands, but Lily strode on with simply a smile to say goodbye. The smile, while modest, had an assured openness about it. I watched her stride away and disappear into the night. I took a couple more paces. "I'll leave as well," said Amanda. She held out her slim hand. We shook hands politely, and at the same time, I felt a piece of paper had been left in my palm. "There's my number. Ring me." She gave me a warm smile and no more was said. She swept off into the night.

I walked in through the dimly lit grounds below a pink moon. Young student couples were walking along holding hands, or close together in the shadows sitting on low walls. While ascending the stairs to my room, I unfolded the scrap of paper from Amanda. Written carefully in elegant flourishes was her mobile number along with a message: 'We should talk about the students'. My initial instinct was to question why she'd given me this just after meeting me. Perhaps, she had information that she wouldn't share with others. But why me?

I entered my room and my priority was to check recent communications. After what I'd learnt at the meal, I felt a need to move forward on the project. I flipped open my computer. The screen on my encrypted system read:

Hope you have all the plans you need. Arranged 4pm pick up for the installation visit – contact us if you have any special requirements.

It was important to find out more about the people I'd met. The more detail I could obtain, the easier it would be to assess them. I logged into the Donghai University website to get the full names and qualifications of the English teachers. Most qualifications were of quite a low level. However, I noticed a couple of tutors, including Lily Wang and Geoff Flounder, had been educated at good universities. Lily had an MA in education studies from Bath University, and Geoff had a science MSc from UCL. This reinforced my initial impression that Lily was an intelligent, capable person. The other staff had various first degrees but from less prestigious universities.

In the quiet of my room, I could consider matters calmly. I mused over the contacts I'd made. From what I'd observed, James was a compliant head, who exercised control over his staff. Unfortunately, he was unlikely to give me more than an official line on the deaths. The other men showed an interest in what had happened but seemed happy with what they already knew. Outside the office, the men acted like they needed to let off steam. The females were far more interested in uncovering the facts and were a better group to concentrate on. Maria's character was clearly that of a harmless auntie type, while Lily and Amanda were more puzzling. Lily identified with Amanda in terms of unhappy feelings, and both showed signs of tenacity when talking to me. Their behaviour indicated interesting characteristics, which I would keep in mind.

Now I'd met all the group the next step was to get more details on each of their backgrounds. It was sensible to get the field base people to do further checks on the whole teaching group.

I pinged off a message: *made contact with English teacher colleagues, which gave me some interesting background information – one point that requires research is our need to know how magnetic fields can be used in medical trials. Also, can you find out anything important about the people I am working with here? Need to screen their history and backgrounds. They are Ian Clarke, Maria Donnington, James Davis, Geoff Flounder, Matt Groom, Lily Wang and Amanda Coe. Do a deep search on Matt Groom as he seems to have some link to the Institute. I saw him when he made a visit to some officials.*

I identified the things I wanted for the next day's mission. A detailed list was sent, based upon the plan of entry into the Institute of Technology. I set my alarm and tried to enter into a positive visualisation of what I was going to do. The plan was risky, but everything had been worked out as thoroughly as possible. I became clear about what I was going to do, which slowed my thoughts and calmed me. I fell into sleep feeling relaxed, as I was ready to deal with whatever the next day may bring.

Chapter 11
Important Information

As soon as I was fully awake I sat up in bed and checked my text messages.

Following your request:

No known medical applications, or improvements to medical research by way of magnetic fields that can be identified to date. Even powerful MRI equipment has little effect on any type of medical condition or trial.

Nothing significant on the people's names provided after we accessed CV details from the Donghai University system to make follow up enquiries. Everything on Lily Wang and Geoff Flounder shows they have claimed the correct cv detail and are well-qualified. However, Matt Groom is of concern. His birth place looks correct. We accessed Canadian documents and a postal code check of his parents reveals he was born in, and grew up in Vancouver, in a predominately Eastern European community environment. Cross checks of his credit cards and places of work on his CV show no trace of a correlation. We think he had part-time jobs in and around the Vancouver area, and while he has a first degree in English he does not have the teaching experience he claims on his CV. Neither does Maria, James and Amanda, but it's not unusual to embellish CVs to get work in China.

We've just identified an official message from the Institute requesting the Chinese MSS to gather information on the Canadian, Matt Groom after he made contact with their officials. It seems there's a need for us to watch him closely.

The field base response, on the possible magnet related applications, gave no clue as to what may have taken place in the trials. Of more interest was the profile of the staff members, which provided some background evidence and left a question mark over Matt Groom. Perhaps a meeting with Amanda could give me more insight about him.

I decided to phone Amanda early, given she'd been keen to arrange a meeting. I didn't want to leave it until later, as it was possible she could change her mind. I checked the note she had given me and phoned the number. She answered immediately and sounded full of good spirits. We shared a few pleasantries about the previous evening's meal, and then agreed to see each other in Starbucks for coffee. I felt it was a worthwhile call, as she seemed eager for us to meet.

After dressing, I made my way to Starbucks, but there was no sign of Amanda. I looked around to find an area which was quiet and without other customers. I chose a corner seat with a small round table, which offered a good place to talk openly. Amanda arrived soon after me and I ordered two coffees. She arrived wearing a lightweight, cotton dress, which captured the essence of the spring weather.

"How are you today?" I decided to make small talk. This wasn't required as Amanda was ready to discuss what was on her mind.

She held out her hand and we shook. "Hi, I'm good." She put down her bag and settled herself. "I've not long, but I want to let you know about the students. I need to catch a meeting later." I saw the coffees were ready, so went to get them and brought them back. I waited while she added saccharine to her coffee and stirred the mug. She looked down into the swirls of the coffee rather than looking directly at me. "What happened here was upsetting for us, and I want you to understand what I know."

"I'm glad you feel you can trust me, and that you'll let me know what you can."

"Well, it's important that anything I tell you is treated in strict confidence. Experience of life has taught me to be careful about what I say, or do." She caught my eye, "Can I rely on you?"

"Of course. This will all be in confidence."

"I don't mix too much with the others, but I keep in contact with James. This enables me to keep informed of anything interesting that's going on." I wondered if this was to get his attention and approval. "I'm careful about mixing now as I may have made mistakes in the past."

"As James is head of school, he must have given you some interesting information."

"James told me he was impressed that your reference had come from the UK ambassador to China. So, this suggests you are well connected. I also heard what you said about being at the British Council in Beijing when you first arrived in China. That gives me confidence to talk like this, as I realise those contacts mean you will take things seriously." It was clear she'd tried to assess my credentials. She took a sip of coffee. "I recognised you wanted to know more about the students. You asked a number of questions last night, so I know you want to obtain more details."

"I do." I thought I'd better explain about my references as she'd mentioned them. "It's beneficial to know someone like the UK ambassador. Having the right contacts is good if it oils the wheels of getting things done."

I took a gulp of coffee and savoured the taste. I wanted to find a common theme, so continued, "Like you, I think it's beneficial to keep in touch with senior people, especially when living abroad."

"Yes. James is certainly someone you should get to know."

"I agree, but I'm not sure that I got off on the right foot with Ian. Perhaps, I should have tried harder to get on with him last night. I didn't do my best to build a relationship with him."

Amanda straightened her back, leant forward and gave me her full attention. This gave her a more imposing appearance. "I don't think it matters. You'll find out that China really bores him. And he thinks he's too good to work here. Ian is the sort of person who gets fed up easily, and then creates little scenes for his own pleasure." She looked thoughtful. "But he's the serious type and would be furious if he knew I was talking about him."

"Interesting."

"It's okay. We understand him, as we all know he can be arrogant at times."

"I'd like to know if your colleagues discuss the deaths of the students." She looked toward the window, which made me pause to allow her to think. I went on, "After all, most people don't like unsolved mysteries. I assumed there would be a high level of interest created by the mystery over the deaths."

"There was concern, but we didn't talk much." She scanned the customers before saying, "Some of the English teachers are duller than you may think."

"I'm surprised."

"There's also a fear factor. You'll find China is a totalitarian state like Oceania in Orwell's 1984 book. You must have seen the posters of the Chinese president plastered everywhere. It's an authoritarian regime. Big brother, in China, is definitely watching people and keeping tabs on them."

"Should foreign nationals care about surveillance?"

"When it comes to a problem involving the government, the officials suppress everything and everyone. The officials can be bloody frightening whether you're foreign or not."

"How?"

"I'll give an example. Students tell me horror stories about relations disappearing into black prisons. They're called black as it's impossible to trace where the relations are being held or what the charge may be."

I decided to raise my concerns. "Staff may worry about their jobs, but surely it's important to have more openness. Those student deaths worry me. If people asked more questions, it could stop the same thing happening again. Perhaps you can tell me what you know?"

"Okay, I'll tell you some important things." Amanda sat back and didn't seem in such a hurry to leave. "There was a problem with the medical trials for sure. Bao wanted to leave them as he'd been there when part of the equipment blew up. He was worried about taking part and asked my advice."

"Yes. Lily mentioned about the equipment explosion last night."

"Something else amazed me. He also told me about something he overheard a scientist say. His worry was he heard the scientist telling a senior person, 'This student, Bao, is a hero working for the good of the military.' Bao was confused about this and assumed the trial involved some military purpose."

"Did he ask them about that?"

"No. Chinese people don't question senior people." She gave a slight shake of her head to add emphasis. "It's all about saving the face of the other person. You'll experience it when you're teaching. You'll find Chinese students don't ask questions."

"I'm thankful for this information."

Amanda then shared something interesting about Cheng. "The other problem was with Cheng. Matt said he knew something personal about him that required solving. He said he needed to help him leave the university, as Cheng was under emotional pressure."

"Did you find out what sort of pressure?"

"I tried to ask Matt about the emotional pressure Cheng was under. He didn't want to tell me more about it. He explained it was a serious personal matter that he was dealing with."

"Well, that certainly sounds serious. I wonder if he solved it."

"I don't know. Our concern was to get both boys released from that terrible trial. Matt helped me write letters, which we sent to the institute where the trials were taking place." She seemed more animated. "We indicated their equipment must have been at fault, but the institute insisted both boys had to continue with the trial. We knew it must have been dangerous if it was for a military purpose."

"Anything else?"

She paused and I waited until she continued, "Lily had already tried to do something for Cheng before our letter, but didn't manage to get him removed from the trial." Amanda took a breath. "Lily has been upset at what happened and has become unhappy since the time of the deaths. It could be that she cared too much about the dead Chinese students. That may explain why it's taking a while for her to recover."

"Did she try to help both of them leave the institute trials?"

"I'm not sure exactly what went on," she said slowly as if trying to recall events. "Cheng was her main concern, as they were often seen together in and out of the office before he died. I told her I was trying to help them as well."

"Has anything official been reported?"

"No. Nothing. I think that's strange as two students dying in a trial should be part of an official investigation. They're not carrying out an investigation, and that could mean the authorities are at fault."

"Have the students families been involved?"

"It seems the families have applied for some compensation but James told me this has been held up. It seems there's been no news as to the official cause of the deaths. I don't know why. It may be that the authorities want to deflect blame on others rather than the trial."

"Before you go, how do you find Matt as a person?"

"Well, he's pretty forthright, and he chases the local Chinese girls. He's not bad though, as he's willing to help out with things. For example, he was happy to be involved with letters to the Institute of Technology."

"Is there anything else you think we should discuss?"

Amanda paused, looked away and then responded, "Nothing I know right now."

"Well, thanks for seeing me and sharing what you know."

"I'm telling you more about the deaths because I've the feeling you care and want to help."

"Thanks. If I can help, I will." I felt Amanda had become an ally. "If you find out anything more, ring me. Then, we can meet again."

She crossed her legs and composed herself. "As Ian isn't here to embarrass me, like he did last night, it's true I'm single. Therefore, I'd be happy if you wanted to contact me."

"I'm pleased with your offer to meet, thanks." Our meeting had certainly been informative, but I was aware I needed to handle this situation carefully. I felt it more of an invitation for us to see each other than for an exchange of information.

"Okay. We should keep in touch, Harry." I nodded in response. "I'm sure you'll have something you can share with me."

"Sure. Let's do that."

"Perhaps we could meet up to enjoy a walk along Binhai road. I think you would like it there."

"Good. I'm happy with that idea." She reminded me of her meeting and that she needed to rush off. She opened her bag, applied some lip-gloss, stood and left with the regular clacking of heels. I remained sitting, trying to think through what she'd said. She was the last person in the office whom I suspected would want to meet me to share information. I got the feeling it was just to string me along in order to develop a closer friendship. I was happy to embrace this and leave our keeping in contact as an open possibility. Any exchange of information could be beneficial.

I went directly from Starbucks and walked across the university to the teacher's office. My luck was in as Matt was already there. He was alone in the office and sitting at his desk. As I entered, he looked across at me and wished me a good morning. I noticed he seemed a little worse for wear. Perhaps his drained look was due to the stubble, which gave his face a darker appearance.

"Morning, Matt," I greeted. "Was it a good night?"

"I've a girlfriend downtown and it was a great night. Things got good." He smirked and rubbed one of his eyes. "You should experience a Chinese girlfriend. The girls here have great bodies and look gorgeous. Perhaps I can introduce you to one."

"That's not for me. I'm the more traditional type when meeting someone."

He ignored my remark. "Keep an open mind while here, Harry."

I felt we were not in sync with each other. "I will, as many things are new to me."

"Good man," he continued with the type of line I'd come to expect from his previous comment. "Well, Amanda is at a loose end now she's finished with James. She's a beauty and ripe for picking."

"I'm not sure if I'm happy with remarks like that about our colleague. Do you think it's right to describe her as fruit in this age of equality?"

"Relax. There's no offence as all us ex-pats are quite friendly. That keeps the place liveable. It's important we get on with each other."

I tried to soften my approach. "Sorry to be blunt. I don't want to create an unpleasant atmosphere between us."

"There's a lot to learn here. And you'll need time to adjust to the differences of China."

"I suppose so."

"Well, one word of warning is to understand the Chinese are an unscrupulous race. They're a crafty people, who are greedy to get what they can out of life. Don't be taken in by them."

"It's not surprising given their recent history of needing to survive under Mao."

"Yes, they certainly have had a long troubled history. There were many deaths from past famines and rebellions before Mao. The whole history has been a tough one until the last twenty years."

"I suppose the emphasis on communism caused a lot of problems?"

"Communism is a farce. They've always attacked capitalism, but now it's capitalism that's used to strengthen their economy. Old ideas from the past all changed under Deng Xiaoping, who rebuilt the economy on capitalist ideas. They just hide behind being communist. The gaps between, rich and poor, wealth and privilege is creating tensions, but they insist it's a communist country."

"Are all old ideas dead? Isn't Confucius important in creating passive relationships?"

He laughed in a deprecating way and shook his head. "They talk a good line about deference to the old, and their superiors – but will push you out the way to get on a bus!"

This discussion seemed to be drifting into unimportant areas. Given I'd seen Matt at the Institute of Technology, I wanted to find out about his activities. I needed to find a way to throw light on why he was there. "While I'm in Donghai, are there ways to earn extra money with local companies?" I enquired.

"A few English language people here do consultancy work. It's not just English language training though, because that's basic low-paid work. They help with service training improvements and especially in hotels."

"Do they get involved in anything else that may be of interest?"

"Yer, they help with cultural awareness, which allows the Chinese workers to understand Western requirements. That's a major need here." He paused in thought. "Poor quality is a big problem. China is like Japan was in the early stages of its development. Recommending quality improvements to service and manufacturing businesses gives the English teaching staff a top-up to their income."

"Have you personal experience of that kind of work?"

"Oh. It's not for me. I don't like consultancy work."

So much for that line of enquiry as it led nowhere. It left me wondering about the reason for his presence at the institute. This remained a mystery. "You seem more interested in the local culture than extra work?"

"Yer. As I said, I went off to a bar downtown and met my friends. Sometimes I go to a South Korean Spa." His eyes came alive. "I love those slim girls walking on my back."

"I suppose this could be one way to relax to forget what's going on with the student deaths. What do you think?" I saw Matt's reaction and realised this wasn't a good way to change the topic.

"LOOK, Harry, don't get me wrong." He threw down his papers and stared at me. "I think you should get away from worrying about people dying. It happens."

"Sorry, but I find it difficult to understand why staff aren't more worried."

"It's obvious you need to relax more. Why don't you join me and my friends downtown?"

I moved over to my desk. "Possibly, but suppressing information annoys me."

"Didn't you hear me – you have to relax." I listened to his words but ignored them. I realised he wasn't going to open up with any further information.

Just then, Ian arrived. He carried some books and papers, which he dropped on his desk with a loud thump. "Ohh, I don't want this sort of exercise in the morning," he exclaimed.

There was no immediate reaction from us. "Morning, chaps," he said, moving toward the tea making area. We greeted him; he caught my eye and looked as if he wanted something. He vacillated between making his tea and looking in my direction.

Matt was clicking away on the keys of his computer, with his back to me, when Ian slipped a piece of paper onto my desk. Ian half lifted his finger toward his mouth and I got his meaning. I knew it was important to keep quiet and not ask questions. The paper was folded in half. I left it there, while Ian sat at his desk and switched on his computer.

I opened the folded page. It was an email sent to Ian that he'd printed:

Subject: Worried
Ian Clarke reply: We need to wait for the authorities to inform us with more details. See me if you are still worried, or your academic work is affected.
From He-Ping
We trust you to help us with our work as we cannot work. Bao and Cheng were friends and now they're dead. We know they were not just having a medical treatment but had been going for tests for long time. Others too. Now with the don't speak about it messages we all have big worries. I cannot work well now. I'm studying badly. Can you help with telling us what's going on?
I cannot do my work unless you help it. Tks.

Ian had scribbled a note on the bottom of the page informing me He-Ping was coming in at 9.30 am, and I may be interested in attending. The note indicated the small meeting room at the end of our office was the place to meet. It was obvious Ian didn't want Matt to be aware of the meeting, but on the other hand, he was including me. I was puzzled, but it offered a chance to learn more about the deaths from a student who knew them. There was the possibility it would provide more knowledge surrounding the events, and background to the deaths.

The meeting room was small. Ian arranged chairs for the two of us on one side of a table, while He-Ping would sit on the other side. When He-Ping arrived, Ian indicated for him to sit down. He-Ping arrived looking as if he came from a well-off family. He wore a brightly coloured blue sweater over an immaculate white shirt. A pair of black, tight jeans was finished with ankle-length leather boots. He-Ping sat down and placed an expensive mobile phone on the table. His action of sitting resembled a balletic lowering of his body. He looked across at us and then leant forward with his arms resting on the table. His smart appearance was in stark contrast to the room.

The surroundings of the meeting room were bleak. Poor quality dark-brown chairs and a table furnished the room. It was similar to a police interrogation room. Given my feelings about Ian's character, I smiled at the thought of him keeping a rubber hose in his pocket or a polygraph machine in the drawer. Bright neon tubes gave a glare to everything. The walls were bare apart from a big mass-produced clock that scratched away the seconds. There was nothing about the room that was relaxing.

On sitting, He-Ping looked back into the office at Matt and I noticed a strange look. I thought I identified a look of dislike cross He-Ping's face. Ian closed the door and took control of the meeting. I was introduced as the new tutor. There was no further delay as Ian immediately asked what problems He-Ping suffered with his work.

Ian didn't get a direct answer.

"You were all close to my friends. We think there's something you all know we don't. It's like hell now unless you tell," said He-Ping, leaning further across the table toward Ian.

Ian's body language became quite stiff, and he spoke in an officious way, "You must know the medical trial was secret. We have been told not to discuss the details. So, that's the final word, which is, NO details." He exhibited a veneer of self-importance I wanted to crush.

"What do you think happened, please?"

"It was just made clear that Mr Long and I are not at liberty to discuss this." Perhaps he wanted to keep the odds of two to one, and that's why I'd been invited to the meeting.

"Could bad things have been used in the medical trial?" the student enquired.

All went quiet and Ian started to doodle on a piece of paper in front of him. He drew circles with squares in. He-Ping followed Ian's pen strokes with his eyes before asking, "I heard their family was told they could get good monies. Is it to keep them quiet?"

"Yes. Compensation may have been offered," said Ian, improving on He-Ping's English. But he never answered the first question about the medical trial.

"Can you let me know things?" he requested, then picked up his mobile and began to fiddle with it. He turned it over and over in his hand, while looking at Ian.

Ian was probably contemplating the risk of his visa being cancelled and didn't answer. He bit his bottom lip and was lost in thought for a few moments. "I'm not sure what happened. I did know regular blood samples were taken from Cheng. I've no idea why. I'm sure taking blood wouldn't be the reason though."

"But why did it seem their brains have been infected?" asked the student.

"Did you see Bao or Cheng on the Monday or Tuesday?" I asked, believing this was my best chance to gather more information. Ian looked annoyed that I'd directed the conversation in this way.

He-Ping wrinkled his brow and put his phone down. "Emmm, on Monday, they ill and had difficult speaking. Then, Tuesday it's a difference. They go to hospital and couldn't be breathing properly. They're not making sense when talking. It was bad. They were the best in our school. They won prizes for their work."

"Do you know where they went for the medical trials?"

"We're off to institute they would say. I know it's Institute of Technology."

"Who was the person who looked after them before they were taken away to hospital?" I asked.

He-Ping at first didn't answer. He looked left, then right, as if looking for a way to get away from the room to free his mind. "Miss Amanda did things and Lily Wang cared for Cheng lots. She had big worry over him, big one. She wanted to help. When we met on Tuesday, she was crying. I saw her try to phone the hospital about my friends. She—"

Ian interjected. "Well, we can discuss these details all morning but that does not help you with your work problem. We need to support your work."

"Oh!" he said and picked up his mobile from the table as if about to leave.

Ian sensed this and continued, "I have asked Mr Long to be here so he can see how we deal with pastoral care." He-Ping looked confused at the term. Ian simply sat back in his chair and enquired, "Perhaps you can tell us what are the specific problems you think you're having?"

The question sent He-Ping into floods of tears. It was obvious He-Ping didn't think he had problems – he knew he had them. Ian looked lost for a second, then threw down his pen and reached into his pocket to pull out some tissues.

"Now, now. There's no need for tears, use these." Ian looked at He-Ping and his face showed an unexpected sign of sympathy. He then assumed a more relaxed pose and launched into an explanation of how death affects other people. "I'll provide you with some counselling about death."

He provided a long monologue as to how death makes others feel not only sad but also guilty. This was followed by ways He-Ping could refocus on his work by utilising time management. It became a mini-lecture not a counselling meeting. I believed He-Ping needed better reassurance given his blank expression. Ian trotted out theory of how to plan and complete work but never involved He-Ping in meaningful discussion. He never asked He-Ping if he felt better for seeing us or needed further counselling. The experience with Ian led me to believe his world was game play, rather than having seriousness of purpose.

"That's all we can cover today," he asserted. It seemed he'd become bored with the whole exercise and so decided to conclude the meeting.

We finalised the meeting with Ian reminding us the meeting's details were to remain confidential. He told He-Ping to email me or him if he required further counselling.

"Can you give He-Ping your email address, Harry?"

I had the feeling I'd been invited along to the meeting in order for Ian to pass on his work. I wrote down my email address but wasn't comfortable about it. He-Ping kicked back his chair, picked up the paper with the address on and left. His body language was more downcast than when he'd arrived.

Ian sat looking at the door closing, before switching his gaze to the chair He-Ping had vacated. "What a waste of time these students are. They need to 'man up'."

I was left thinking Ian was devoid of compassion. I realised he had not been worried about the stress He-Ping was suffering. He picked up his doodle, screwed it up and threw it without accuracy in the direction of a waste paper bin. The clock continued to scratch off the seconds. I'd never understood why wall clocks required measures of seconds. After my meeting, this belief became reinforced. I felt that each scratch had been a negative reminder of time wasted.

Ian turned to me. "Had a few over the eight last night when we were eating – Sorry if I said anything out of turn."

I looked at him, nodded and left the room without speaking. Another member of staff had arrived as Maria was now at her desk.

"Hello. How's your day?" I asked.

"Same old same. Hope you're settling in okay."

"Did you download the pictures from last night?"

"I've loads on my computer. Would you like to see some?"

"I would love to see them, as it'll be interesting to see what you all get up to."

"I'll open my rogue's gallery then," Maria responded happily to my request. I moved to Maria's desk and scrutinised the different images as she scrolled through her picture library. Maria stopped at one picture, gave a sigh. She told me I was looking at the students who'd died. Another scroll and I saw Lily, Geoff and Maria were pictured with Cheng and Bao in different restaurant settings. I noted the absence of Matt and James. Some pictures of interest were of Geoff and Ian looking a little intoxicated and seeming very friendly. Geoff had his arm around Ian's shoulder, or his waist. It seemed strange because Ian didn't seem the sort of person that Geoff would want to mix with. Two more pictures scrolled up. "Oh, they're my children."

"They look like you," I said, seeing a clear resemblance. Both were female, seemed in their late twenties and had Maria's friendly eyes.

"Yes, my wonderful girls. One in America, and one in Australia." She paused to look at the screen and mused, "And their father is god knows where. Pity, but anyway he wasn't father of the year material."

"Seems you may have struggled in the past."

"Yes. It's the past though, and I'm over it. Perhaps it's one reason I came here." She gave a quick look at Matt and Ian and raised her eyes. "You'll meet lots of misfits who've escaped to China." She smiled at me. "Luckily I'm not damaged goods."

"Hi, everyone," it was Lily. She had a pile of student papers and some apples in a plastic bag. We responded positively to her. She gave out the apples to those in the office, while assuring them they were well washed.

I went to my desk to think. I sat quietly trying to figure out the events and motivations that surrounded the student deaths. If there were dots to join up I didn't have enough of them yet. It was difficult to patch together the information especially on Matt and Lily. Nothing was clear. Was Lily involved with a student and is that why she'd become more upset than the others. Matt required more attention as he could be some kind of foreign field agent, or could he have simply falsified his previous work experience. Why did Amanda exhibit a dual personality of appearing nervous or confident depending on the situation? What is Ian doing in China? I wasn't clear about any of them. I looked over at Ian and he was looking aimlessly at his computer screen. Probably doodling in his mind now. Lily spoke, and I was shaken out of my thoughts by her invitation.

"When I've dropped these off, I'm going for walk. Anyone interested?"

"Would you mind if I joined you?" I requested, hoping this would be a good opportunity to find out more from her.

"Yes do. I'm off to Labour Park, as it's good to walk around the lake."

"Anything interesting to see?" I asked.

"Come, and you'll see the Chinese dating system."

"Dating system? What system?"

"There are messages pinned to the trees from people looking for a partner. I'll help you write one if you like," she said, looking amused.

"I'm game for a walk in the park, but I don't need to write a lonely heart message. Not yet anyway."

"Can't see you being lonely," chirped Maria.

"Lonely? There's nothing written about being lonely – it's not about being lonely as it's more about offering a business proposition," added Lily. "You'll see."

"I'm quite happy as I am," I said a little abruptly.

Maria chortled, looked at Lily and said, "Take him. He needs to get out."

Matt shouted across the room, "I told him he needs to relax! So show him some of the culture of Dalian."

Lily picked up both of their threads of thought. "I agree. There's benefit in relaxing, Harry. So, let's go."

"Okay point taken; I get it. I'm happy you're having fun with me. It makes me feel I've been accepted here." I looked and saw Ian and Matt where smiling.

We made our way down the staircase together, passing groups of young students. Some of the students acknowledged Lily with smiles and greetings. I felt happy to be with Lily and looked forward to the walk. I realised we would be away from the pressure of the office and assumed Lily would provide more information for me. I was planning to expand on our conversation that we had following our restaurant meal. But, I didn't realise this walk would also allow me to understand China, and how different it is to the West. My walk through the park was about to introduce a whole new cultural experience. It was about to make me realise how interesting Chinese culture can be.

Chapter 12
Labour Park

"It's not very far to the park," said Lily.

I felt happy to have left the management building. Once outside, the breeze and its cooling currents helped me focus on what I needed to find out. Lily lifted her head and breathed in the air. She had relaxed and I felt this would allow me to steer the conversation in a useful direction. We sauntered along, through the university grounds, on uneven paths flanked by shrubs. The sky was thinly flecked with threads of clouds, and the air was fresh. We passed a magpie pecking at the ground as if tapping out messages. People passed by; some walking small dogs on leads. One dog sniffed at me and wagged its tail in a half-hearted way before having its collar pulled at by the owner.

"I didn't realise there would be so many dog owners in China. Is a cute dog a fashion accessory for some people?" I gave it some thought. "Or, do you think the previous one child policy has led to dogs becoming an extra child?"

"Well, you could be right about dogs being another child. Anyway, the change in law, to allow more children, is sensible. Even though we have a large population, it's for good economic reasons." She went on with some conviction, "This will help to deal with the future problem of too many old people in China and not enough working-age people."

There was logic and clarity in the way Lily thought. We walked on. The pavements were busy with young people, dogs on leads, grandparents or mothers and children. The atmosphere in comparison to the office was bright and relaxing. That was apart from the deliverymen on quiet electric scooters. They weaved dangerously amongst the people on their journey to distribute food or goods.

"I'm pleased we're going to the park after being in our oppressive office environment," I said, trying to get away from politics.

"I agree, as the office can be claustrophobic. It's not good to concentrate on just our work. We constantly use our brains as academics, but we should also balance that with outside interests. You're probably aware of the importance of having a balance to life."

"Are you referring to ideas of yin and yang?"

"Yes. You know about this?"

"Not really. Perhaps you can you explain it?"

"Did you know this is where differing or opposing forces are always in conjunction? One is linked with the other, and they're always acting together."

"You mentioned balance."

"Yin and yang are a balance between things. Well, like good and bad. They exist together and affect each other. Just as the sea comes in and goes out, or light creates a shadow, there are opposites. Yin and yang are the energy forces of life that affect us."

"It sounds very eastern. Is your thinking affected by these concepts?"

"Of course. It's my culture, and that's my thinking. You're Western and I'm Chinese. Chinese act Chinese and try to find balance."

"Give me an example."

"The yin and yang balance is very important for Chinese people. We don't like to have too much or too little of anything. For example, I don't like too many good things."

I was confused. "Not too many good things. Why?"

"We think if we have too many good things, then bad will follow? This expectation is like a wheel when it turns, so that the top becomes the bottom, before the bottom becomes the top. Good things can't last. Bad follows good, as in yin and yang. We believe life is made up of two sides. It's best not to treat them as opposites as they're always part of each other." She looked at me. "Does that make it clearer?"

"Yes, that makes sense, as you explained it with some clear images." I smiled and we continued on our way. I was learning about the way Lily's mind worked and her culture.

The pavement widened as we walked beside a high wall. The wall continued for about 400 metres until we reached an imposing set of ornamental iron gates and railings. I was enjoying the easy way I could discuss things with Lily. However, I realised I needed to choose the right moment to find out more about the student deaths.

"Labour Park," offered Lily.

We walked in. The entrance was flanked on both sides by colourful shrubs and flowers. In front of the flowerbeds were benches that offered resting and eating havens for the local people. The heavy scent of the large oleander bushes slowed our walk as we took in their remarkable fragrance. Our pace kept to a saunter as we passed through an avenue of trees creating shady coolness. The avenue focused the eye on a lake, with a distant dark sheet of water. The sun sparkled and flashed off its surface at each rise of a fish, or ripple of disturbance.

"This is beautiful," I said.

"Yes. I come here to relax when I feel stressed."

On the way to the lake's edge, I could make out the metallic blue swoops and hovers of the dragonflies amongst the bull rushes. The flowing dance of the dragonflies interacted with the darting moves of damselflies. Nature was at its best. Weeping willow trees drooped their leaves into the lake, providing a foil for a white stone bridge with its traditional high-curved arch. Childhood memories flashed before me. I'd walked into a scene reminiscent of the willow design plates I'd seen on my mother's dining room sideboard.

Around the lake, we could see seats and low walls, on which sat groups of older people playing cards or other games. A slapping noise came from their direction. I saw what was making the sound. The cards were thrown down with such force they created the slap noise. Looking across the park, the outline of people could be seen writing on the ground with long brushes. It fascinated me. There were a number of people dipping long handled brushes into metal pots, partly full of water. They took out the brushes from the pots and wrote Chinese characters on the concrete ground. The brushes were like those used for water colouring but about a metre long. The only difference was the hairs of the brush started as fat at the ferrule and ended in a point at the tip.

"There's a crowd being drawn to those writers," I said, wondering what was happening.

"Let's go over there."

We joined the crowd. Local Chinese people looked on with fascination. It seemed they were either admiring or commenting on the attempts of the scribes. Various comments and advice were given to the writer. However, the wet Chinese characters that were brushed on the ground disappeared in the sun's warmth. The people's comments disappeared along with the writing. Keeping as a group, the local people moved to another person's writing to provide a new commentary.

"Calligraphy is an art form in China," said Lily, noting my level of interest. "The amount of water on the brush, the curves of the characters and freedom of the strokes are important."

"I saw this type of calligraphy, done by students, hanging on the Donghai University walls. Is it the same as when we display paintings?"

"It's art – but then it's more than art. It's often calligraphy based upon famous poems. I'll try to explain, yet it's as difficult as trying to describe colours to a blind man. We judge each of the brush strokes."

"Oh. We also analyse people's handwriting," the words spilled out, but I should have waited.

"Well, it's more than that. It has deeper meaning. We expect something aesthetic from the writer. The strokes of each character can be sublime."

"Is that neat writing?" Lily gave me a look which indicated I didn't understand.

"If a character is written with a small inaccuracy of a stroke, it will affect the perceived quality of the writing. Maybe, it would be like you recognising the wrong note on hearing a piece of piano music. Also, the ways the characters are created reveal the writer to us." She looked across at an older man applying his brush with flourishing arm movements. "The writer shows us their inner self. There are differences between the writers. Some writing is complex, some extravagant, some neat but each style shows us who the writer is. It's a display of inner emotion."

"Ohh, it's the quality an artist requires."

"Yes. The brushwork is an extension of the writer's mind. It shows the person's deep mind. The person is showing people their soul."

Lily had softness in her eyes when she said this. This drew me to her eyes. I saw the almond shaped mystery of them. She had captured my interest. I looked away but had become aware of her wide cheekbones and unblemished complexion. I felt drawn to her but was careful in case she thought me too attentive.

I refocussed on the people writing. I realised Lily was taking me into a new world of meaning and thinking. My experience was opening up a more spiritual understanding of life. I realised I was definitely drawn to her and the different world of China and wondered why? Was it this spiritual enlightenment, her features, her personality or what?

I reflected on her words about a person showing their soul through their writing. This wasn't easy and I still remained vague as to the true nature of its art form. "What a fascinating culture you have. I feel I'm a stranger in a strange land." I watched the confident swishes of the brushstrokes. "I'm the simple layman here, as China is so different."

"Okay strange…er man, I'll give you a full tour! Let's go to hear traditional songs."

"That's great! I hope you enjoy being my tour guide," I was upbeat.

We strode off to the back of the park services building. There, among the trees, under pergolas were about thirty older Chinese people singing Chinese songs. A tall Chinese male acted as a conductor. A lady stood beside him. It was a joint effort with both leading the group in the songs. The massed voices sung out. I heard the name Mao a few times but didn't understand what was happening. The people held themselves with an upright posture and were quite intense in their singing. I was hearing and seeing traditional Chinese culture from the past.

"They're singing the old revolutionary songs," said Lily. "They know them off by heart. Enjoy the experience as this is the old China."

"I can see they're happy people."

"The old songs are reassuring for them. They learnt them while fighting for a new way of life." We stopped to watch and listen.

"The cultural revolution was not a way of life I would have fought for."

Lily turned to me. "Are you sure? If you were Chinese, it could be different. All governments use different ways to get what they want. The state apparatus is used to obtain what leaders want. The West used religion from Roman times to provide political stability. We adopted Confucianism over 2,000 years ago in the same way as our preferred set of values for the people."

"What's its place now?"

"It was stronger in the past in affecting Chinese culture. This changed when Maoism and the Cultural Revolution were used to get the country back to stronger socialist ideals. Mao didn't want to follow the more liberal changes in Russia and work with the West. Russia was thought to have given up Marxist ideals and he didn't want China to take a similar path. He created the Cultural Revolution to strengthen ideals of communism. I'm sure you realise different ideologies are used to gain support for every government. These people singing wanted socialism and not a drift to Western ideals."

Lily reminded me my job was linked to a Western political system. I didn't question my role in carrying out orders and realised it involved achieving political ends. I had no questions about this. What I did gave me a purpose in life, and a way to do what was right. It hit me that this was a Rule Britannia moment of understanding where tunes, songs and history reinforced common ideals. I felt I understood my Western roots from what I was experiencing.

"You mentioned Confucius lived over 2,000 years ago. Why were Confucius teachings important for so long?" I asked.

"A lot of it is about creating harmony. Emperors recognised his teachings could create a more harmonious, peaceful society. So, they incorporated his teachings into the state education and examination system."

"What did he stress as important?"

"Confucius wanted to make society more moral. A person leading a proper life each day was seen to inspire others to improve morally. Learning manners from each other could slowly improve the whole of society. People agreed with him that manners, virtue and education were important. Those qualities were required to be demonstrated by those in power from the emperor down. Then, at every level of society, manners needed be shown in relationships and, especially, in the family."

"He stressed the need to be moral? I can relate to that."

"Yes. Through self-cultivation there was a way to become a Junzi or, in English, a superior person, a gentleman. But not just acting well. Bowing isn't good enough unless the person bowing demonstrates the proper emotion while bowing."

The singing faded as we walked on. I saw in the distance what looked like plane trees decorated with hundreds of pieces of paper. As we came closer, the written messages pinned to the trees were noticeable. Some were placed on the ground, with a stone on top to stop them being blown away.

"Here are the proposals from single people. It's a dating system."

"Writing messages in this way looks like an historical enigma in this age of IT and social networks."

"Writing a message is much more personal than a typed message. It's also possible to look at the person's handwriting and characters."

"Have you ever placed a message here or don't you need to?" I asked, looking across the messages.

"No never. I had a partner but we didn't meet by writing a message." She continued to scan the messages. "I'm single now so perhaps I should think about leaving a message," she said with amusement.

"I'm sure you wouldn't need to do that. Have you been single for a while?"

"I had a boyfriend back home when I took my first degree, and then someone else."

"How recently?" I was wondering about Cheng.

"Oh. I don't want to talk about that now." Her gaze drifted to the trees.

"Sorry, I didn't mean to pry." I saw her gaze had wandered. "Hope I've not offended you?"

"Well, I'm surprised you seem so interested in my personal life."

"Perhaps this whole message dating process has captured my interest."

"I see. Well, the truth is I never felt the need to rush into a relationship." She paused as if reflecting. "When I studied in England, there were opportunities but I decided to concentrate on my studies."

"Are you worried about developing relationships then?"

Her face remained expressionless. "Like other young Chinese girls, I'm under lots of pressure to find a husband."

"Well, you're young, so it doesn't matter."

Lily continued to view the messages. "A girl unmarried at thirty is looked down upon. I've three years to go before I will be called, 'a left over woman'. But the others can worry as I don't."

A series of cracking noises could be heard from across the park. Lily told me it was someone giving lessons in the use of a bullwhip. We were drawn back to the many messages. Lily explained they were mainly from women or more likely their parents. She translated directly and the information provided in most cases described the height of the person, their age, salary and telephone number. I asked Lily what else was written. None were providing details of personal qualities, such as a sense of humour or an outgoing personality type. It became obvious that economic details are required in China, whereas lifestyle details are used in Western countries. In China, marriage rather than dating was obviously the main focus.

The scene amongst the trees was of individuals intensely reading messages. People were taking down notes from the messages but this was mostly by the older people. Lily described how they would return home and put pressure on their children to meet someone.

"How can a thirty-year-old woman be thought of as a 'left over'?" I asked.

"You ask more questions than a Chinese person would. We always try to save someone's face by not asking questions that may embarrass a person."

Perhaps my interest in Lily's life was getting the better of me. I deflected the topic. "Perhaps you want to ask me something?"

"All women like to know about the men they meet, and their relationships." Lily brushed her hair back with her fingers and then let the strands drop.

"Well, I've not found someone to share a meaningful relationship with." I became thoughtful. "I find love is the hardest thing in the world to find."

Lily looked bemused. "Well, does respect and compatibility come first and then love develops as time passes? If you look for love first you may never find it."

"I suppose too many people in the West give love a casual meaning."

"This is what many Chinese people would think. Chinese people are more careful about feelings and love." Lily looked directly at me and I assumed she was also careful.

I felt I should explain to her the way love is used by men. "Men use words of love as a way to get women to trust them, and get what they want. They believe all women are romantics."

"You're simply stereotyping the world. Many Chinese women are calculating. They assess the economic benefits of the man, rather than being carried away with emotion." To emphasise this, she turned to point at the messages on the trees. "I'm afraid you're biased from reading Western literature, which stresses romance. And your poets have coloured people's ideas of what love may be."

"How does it work in China then?"

"Chinese people ensure they have control over relationships. But there are other reasons. Their family will need to accept the partner. This will be based on a rational decision. It's because we believe in being pragmatic about partners."

"I wonder if this means young people are less happy."

"Pleasure in the West is sought, but in the East is suppressed to create personal harmony. The harmony of the family is important." She paused.

"Think about your Victorian times. Families would assess the background and prospects of a partner. Chinese parents do this."

I started to understand so added, "This must be about the attitude of deference in China. This means young people defer to parents' wishes."

"Many do, but things are changing." Lily smiled at a young child who passed us playing with a balloon. She continued, "Deference is showing good manners. Chinese people will show it to those who are older or in higher social positions. However, it doesn't mean an individual will bend to other people's wishes."

"Perhaps I've tired you out with all of my questions? Now I need to show good manners to you," I attempted a weak joke.

"It's no problem, as I feel I'm like a teacher today." We smiled and she looked at me with unmistakable happiness.

"I'm thankful for your time. It's all so interesting, and motivates me to learn more about China." I realised China was a fascination for me, and Lily was the font of much of this. "I want to know how I can learn more. But I've no idea where to start?"

"Well, to be honest, if you watch Kung Fu Panda films, there's a lot you will learn about Chinese culture. More than I can tell you," she'd continued with our light joking.

"I've watched it. Do you think I'm the tiger?" I pushed my chest out for affect. "Perhaps I'm the strong and fast tiger who protects people."

"*What*! You're the one who simplifies things. Your character would be female as it's the Tigress not tiger." She was giving a slap to my ego. "Let me think – How about you being Po, The Kung Fu Panda?"

"No more please. You're too well-informed."

"Okay, it's enough. We can go for a coffee and special apple pie in the Eurobake café before we go back."

"That will be good. I think the pie will be a fitting end to our walk." I was not sure if this outing had achieved what I needed to find out. However, it had given me an improved understanding of Chinese culture and a liking for Lily.

Eurobake was a small place hidden away at the edge of the park. It was located within an amusement area below a large Ferris wheel. It looked like a Little Chef outlet with an area at the front furnished with parasols and tables. We went in. I squeezed behind a table and sat facing her with a view along the length of the room. Posters on the walls portrayed a number of iconic films, such as Barefoot in the Park and jazz performers such as the American pianist, Dave Brubeck.

"Order what you want, but make sure to leave room for the apple pie," was the advice from Lily.

Luckily some menus were in English. I asked Lily to order me a Caesar salad, Thai spring rolls and Calamari. When we finished our main meal, Lily asked for the apple pie. There was no denying the apple pie was special. Its aroma and the look of the buttery crust triggered my digestive juices. The waitress served it along with a scoop of vanilla ice cream. We talked about England and Europe as Lily had experienced a number of different regions during her master studies. It was a pleasant discussion and before we departed, I was happy Lily asked to exchange mobile phone numbers with me.

We walked back out of the park, past dog walkers and individuals out for a stroll. Off to one side of the park were shapes against the sky of funfair attractions. We strolled on quietly with our thoughts. Chinese music emanated from the direction of a middle-aged group of women, who were dancing outside the park gates. It took on the appearance of a type of Chinese line dancing. We passed by the group and went to the roadside where Lily waved down a taxi. We clambered in to the back seat and sat close to each other. I felt we had bonded in friendship. There was a feeling of ease in our being together. We drove back to the university with the unwelcome smell from the taxi's natural gas powered engine. I opened the window to let fresher air in.

"I'm very happy you took time to show me so many interesting things. How do I repay you?" I wanted to arrange another meeting, not only to gather further information, but also to spend time with Lily.

"No need. Perhaps we can go downtown one night or to the coast. I'll take you on my Shadow." There was eye contact but nothing more I could discern.

"Let's do it soon. Perhaps you can let me know."

"I've got your number, so I'll contact you when it's convenient." There was a pattern of not making firm arrangements. I had no idea how things would play out. I felt we enjoyed a good rapport and Lily's discussions continued to lead me to wonder about her. She certainly was open, clever and showed a sense of humour. She made me realise my Western beliefs didn't easily match the complexity of Chinese culture. I was learning it was not a simple 'us' and 'them' by seeing China through Lily's eyes. The day gave me lots of new cross-cultural insights to reflect upon. I enjoyed the way it allowed me to question my own perspectives and interpret my different values.

I arrived back at Donghai University in good spirits. I was relaxed and ready to focus on my task ahead. This was good as the objective to obtain information from the Institute of Technology wouldn't be easy. Lily said goodbye and I walked on thinking about the plan for the break in.

Chapter 13
The Break-In

I returned to my room to change into casual clothes. On stepping inside, stagnant air and dowdiness once again hit my senses. The need to change into more appropriate clothing was the main task. This involved changing into jeans, changing my leather shoes for camel boots and my smart shirt to a sports top. The casual clothes were sensible as they allowed for better freedom of movement. They also allowed me to look more informal, like a deliveryman. My mobile phone rang and I recognised the number.

I gave my code, "Hi, Donghai one."

"Hi. I've a recent interception I need to relay. Is it clear to talk about the intel we have?" It was the woman from the British field base in Dalian.

"Yes."

"A Russian communique has been intercepted with a picture of you on it, along with British Council officers. It was taken in Beijing. It is coded but it's probably a message that means you're under close surveillance. We believe they know you're in Dalian, given what happened at the institute. So, watch your back as you're on a Russian watch list."

"Thanks."

"Anything else?"

"Nothing. I'm just getting ready to leave."

"Okay. We don't have more on this right now. Take care and good luck with the mission. Bye."

It was four o'clock and time to meet Leo as arranged. I set off down the apartment steps at a fast pace. As I emerged through the university gate, I could see Leo scanning different people. He was a good timekeeper. I slipped into the taxi and saw a rucksack on the back seat.

"Hi. Have I got what I wanted in here?" I pulled the rucksack onto my lap. We set off and merged into the swarm of traffic. Our taxi was anonymous amongst the multitude of other taxis plying their business along the busy streets.

"Things as wanted it…Yes."

I rummaged through the various things and found everything was correct. I took out the stun gun and placed it in my pocket. "It all looks okay."

"It's good, ah?"

We got to the place we'd arranged quite quickly. Perhaps this was because my mind was focused on my task, not the road. Only the vivid green colours of the passing trees and shrubs formed a background to my thoughts. Our plan was to drive to a delivery depot, to make use of one of the vans that left from there. The delivery van would be the means to smuggle me through the security check and into the institute's building. The goods' area was selected as the easiest route of gaining entry. We knew vans went to the side of the Institute of Technology building, where there was a service bay. It was a good plan as a delivery van, making regular calls, would reduce the level of risk due to its familiarity. The security was located at the gate of the institute's building, which led to the bay. If I could get as far as the bay area, it would be possible to enter unopposed through the open doors. Once inside, the safest route was to use the emergency staircase to get to the upper floor. Dalian had done its job in identifying a delivery van that arrived on a regular basis directly from its depot. It left its depot each day in the afternoon, apart from Sunday. The route included delivering supplies to a number of companies, but always to the institute first.

Leo dropped me off beside the van's depot and we confirmed the later meeting place. His task was to help smuggle me onto the van with a diversionary action. He drove off and parked a short distance away. I placed the rucksack over the front of my body and walked toward the depot. At a sensible distance from the depot, I took out my mobile as if taking a call. My position was beside a small store. From there, I could see across the road and through a chain link fence. All was on time. The driver was loading the van I was going to use. After a few minutes, I saw the swing and shut of the van's doors and heard a reassuring clunk as they locked. This was the pre-arranged time to send a text to Leo.

I sent the text message, '*Time to go.*'

As the delivery van was about to leave its depot, Leo stopped his taxi across the exit lane. He took out his mobile as if making a call. The van needed to stop because the exit to the main road was bared. The driver's attention was taken by Leo, who acted oblivious to the situation. The driver waved and shouted to him. This allowed me to walk to the vehicle's side unnoticed. The delivery van driver gave a couple of blasts on his horn. Leo continued to ignore him and made out he was busy on his phone. I rolled underneath as the van driver blasted more heavily on his horn and cursed Leo. The two suction devices I'd taken out from the rucksack were applied under the chassis. They held the strap supports for my journey. The sound of the suction units attaching were quiet enough against the blasts on the horn not to cause concern. My upper body and legs were supported by the nylon straps attached to two devices. I held on first with my hands on one strap, and then placed my legs through the other one. I was relieved I'd also asked for wrist supports to help brace against the stress on my arms and wrist. It was then possible to move my upper body backwards into the support. The timing was perfect. Leo shouted what sounded an apology to the driver and drove off. The driver drove away turning sharply into the traffic. The driver's manoeuvres swung my body in opposition to whatever way the van moved. I was like a gymnast out of control on a rings exercise routine. But no gymnast would exercise in the unhealthy air I was breathing. This, and the heightened noise of the tyres on the road, made the journey uncomfortable. Thankfully, the journey was short.

The driver followed the regular pattern for the delivery by travelling directly to the institute. On arrival, the van stopped for a few seconds at the security point. Habit and familiarity reduced the level of inspection as the driver and van would be known by the guards. A few words were spoken to the guard, and we moved off. A chill wind rattled some leaves before we moved. The leaves picked up, swirled and danced, and subsided to the ground again.

The van arrived at the loading bay. I felt the van shift as the driver got out, so he must have been heavy. A friendly conversation ensued with someone beside his driver's door. Four stocky legs were visible. I slipped out of my slings, took off the suction devices and rolled to the other side of the van. There was a welcoming creak from the van's hinges. The driver was now at the back of the van opening the doors. I could see the four legs had moved to the back. The van shifted again as the driver stepped into the back, above me. I slipped out into a dark, hard shadow thrown by the van. No one noticed me. I made my rucksack into a barrel shape and put it on my shoulder, so one side of my face wouldn't be seen. I dropped my shoulder to make the rucksack seem heavy. The large loading bay door was open and there were vertical plastic blinds just inside them. Once inside, I would be obscured from view.

I hopped up onto the loading bay and disappeared through the heavy plastic slats. They flapped gently as they shut behind me. Two young people were in the corridor and their chatter subsided when they saw me. There was no lingering eye contact as they didn't pay much attention. It probably looked like I was making a delivery. I walked across the corridor to pass under the CCTV camera, ensuring it only covered part of my body. All was quiet, so I guessed my entrance was acceptable. The corridor had storage rooms off each side before entering into a more open space. The geometry was of sharp horizontals softened by curves. There was a sense of volume and airiness to the building. It matched the visualisation I'd made from the building plans. Next to the open area was a flight of concrete stairs, which acted as the fire escape. This was a welcome sight, as it would be an area less used by the staff. I went through the doors, dropped the rucksack to my hand and made my way up the stairs to the top floor.

I made it to the staircase and texted Leo to give him my progress. He was to phone the institute director's secretary to say a very important package was waiting in reception. His job was to distract the secretary by telling her she needed to sign for an urgent, confidential package for her director.

On exiting the fire escape, the opulence of the interior decoration was a surprise. Chrome, stainless steel and exotic wood created a sense of modernism. This was obviously the executive area of the building. I stopped and listened. A keyboard patter indicated someone working in an office. My breathing was controlled and my senses were at high alert. Stepping quietly along the corridor, I heard a door opening. There was a need to assess what to do before I was seen. My senses reacted. I swivelled round and ducked into a gent's toilet. The steps passed by. I waited and listened. A lift door opened and closed somewhere down the corridor. I emerged from the toilet and made my way to the institute director's office. The door was heavy and impressive. I knocked and placed my hand in my pocket to grip the stun gun. No one called out to enter. Things were going well. Meanwhile downstairs, a small Chinese woman arrived at the reception desk. Leo carried an important looking package with the words confidential in red.

"Are you from Tao Shou's office?"

"Yes."

"Check this package carefully, as it's important. Then sign for it." She examined the document and a frown appeared.

"This is the wrong package. This is not the right address or name." Her gaze was intense and her frown tightened.

"My apologies," said Leo. "The urgent package is in my taxi. Please wait and I'll get it."

I entered the secretary's office. A desk and filing cupboards filled the small room. A door to one side led to the director's office. I touched the seat to move it back and found it remained warm from the secretary's body. Her computer was on and the screen was live. I set about downloading a dump of the files from the computer onto a hard disk. We knew the director attended regular meetings out of the building at this time and day of the week. We had made sure we were careful about timing and access. I moved the secretary's chair back to look for the push button under the desk to open the director's door. My plan indicated the button would unlock the door to the director's office.

"Shit." I was surprised as there were two buttons. One could be an alarm button? I followed where the wires went but they disappeared into the wall. I took a deep breath and pushed the one that looked most used. There was relief when a metallic click indicated it was now possible to access the inner office.

The office was unoccupied. It was spacious with a meeting table and two sofas. Between the sofas was a low table, with traditional Chinese tea making utensils on it. I focussed on the large desk and a safe built into the wall beside it. As it was still normal work hours, no time lock was in operation. However, it was a commercial electronic mechanism, which is more difficult to break into than a combination system. I rummaged in the rucksack and pulled out a strip of plastic, coated with a thin layer of gel. This was placed over the keys to the safe. A special torch fluoresced the surface, so I could analyse the residue left from fingers pushing the buttons. It identified the transfer of sweat and natural oils to only some of the keys. This indicted four of the keys had been in constant use. An electronic device was placed over the keypad and the four numbers keyed in. This reduced the possible combination possibilities. The device delivered high intensity electronic pulses in random combinations. Two beeps signalled the combination was identified. The read out gave me the necessary combination numbers, which I punched into the key pad. This was followed by the metallic sound of the device unlocking. I pulled the central handle down and the door swung heavily open. "Yesss," I whispered.

A number of document folders were piled on each other. Two were in red folders. I'd been requested to take the information from red folders or ones that looked like reports. I sat down behind the desk and searched through the materials. There was a USB and a number of papers. I plugged the USB into my hard disk system to copy it. Then set up my video camera, so I could flick over the pages to copy each page. Once I'd captured the video images nothing else looked important.

I put everything back into the safe in its original place, closed it shut and wiped the keys. The equipment I'd used was scooped up and packed in my rucksack. I retraced my steps to the staircase and made my way down to a rear emergency fire door on the ground floor.

All was going well when Leo returned with a small package. The secretary signed for the package, which contained an expensive watch and no sender's name. The watch would be accepted by the director without question as he would think it a bribe. After receiving it, he would be waiting for some comment about the watch from a supplier. That meant he would expect one of his contacts wanted a favour in return. Perhaps he would guess the source incorrectly and some lucky supplier could benefit. The secretary returned to her office none the wiser to what had happened five minutes earlier. She entered the office and left the package on his desk.

Like a cat with soft, agile strides, I descended the stairs two at a time. I reached the ground floor, knowing the emergency door was alarmed. That was no problem. It was easy to connect the necessary wires together, so when the doors opened, the alarm wouldn't sound. I pushed the bars then gasped. The doors were locked from the outside. I'd not expected a large padlock and chain would be fitted to the doors. It was locked shut. Pushing on the door provided a gap, but it was too narrow to squeeze through. The opening was only wide enough to put a hand through.

There was a need to recall the alternative ways to exit the building. I disconnected the wires on the alarm sensors and made my way to the second floor. I opened the door into the corridor a fraction and listened. Murmurings were somewhere down the corridor. I hesitated, then decided they weren't moving in my direction. Walking out from the staircase coincided with two Chinese staff crossing a T-junction at the end of the corridor. My heart pumped a little faster. There was no need to worry as they never looked in my direction. They were more intent on chatting with each other. Where they passed at the end of the corridor was my chosen exit through a window. My stride lengthened to reach the window as quickly as possible. All senses were on full alert. I could hear sounds coming from the offices, which motivated me to get out before being detected.

The window opened and offered the benefit of a ledge to stand on. I stepped onto the ledge and looked down to assess my drop zone. The outside area below the window was clear of obstacles. Seeing a lightly planted area of box shrubs, I decided to jump. By relaxing my body and keeping my knees bent, the drop to the ground was safe. This absorbed the impact and on landing I knelt down to reduce my outline. Dusk was a welcome cover, as it aided my dash to reach the wall surrounding the grounds. It was a matter of moving forward trying to keep quiet and low. I moved stealthily to a covering of shrubs. I looked around in order to identify the best route to get over the wall. One tree was of the right size and spread to enable my escape. It wasn't difficult as the shrubs and trees enabled speedy climbing, and a way to drop onto the outside pavement. I looked back at the institute and punched the air with joy, bursting with the elation of the moment. Mission accomplished, or so I thought.

Chapter 14
Attempted Abduction

I walked away feeling pleased the mission had gone well. Our plan had achieved the desired outcome without any problems. So, we had accomplished our first objective and could now assess what the Chinese were up to. I set off on a brisk walk to meet up with Leo. The journey took me past a number of new office buildings and different groups of people. I phoned my contact number feeling exhilarated. "I'm outside now with some nice presents for our people."

"That's good. We're looking forward to them."

"I'll get them delivered S-A-P."

"Be careful, as we spotted the Russian's Mercedes back in the area. We're wondering if they have managed to track your movements."

"Will do. I'm off to meet Leo."

"We'll speak when you get to him. Bye." The phone went dead.

Two minutes later, the shock occurred. A large black car came alongside me travelling at about fifteen miles per hour. The force of a blow from the car sent me sprawling. I was knocked to the ground by a car door opening and swiping me across the back. Given the car was moving in my direction, the impact of the door on my body wasn't too powerful. I started to scramble to my feet but was pulled into the back of the car. Someone had set a trap. Two strong hands overpowered me and deflected my forward motion sideways into the now stationary car. The person pulling me in was a familiar figure. It was the guy who should still have sore gonads. This could be bad. Nothing would be worse than the Russians obtaining the materials in my rucksack, nor someone who was intent on revenge because of a past encounter.

The big Russian had me at a disadvantage. I flinched at a blow to the side of my head that sent my senses whirling. The speed of the unexpected events was confusing. There was a need to assess the situation and evaluate a response as quickly as possible. Only two Russians were in the car that had taken me off the street. The driver activated the lock and the door clicked as the car pulled away. At the same time, I saw the Russian beside me was holding a small can. It was an aerosol can being raised up; probably to spray me with a disabling chemical. One of my hands blocked the spray and the other one gripped my stun gun, which I fired from my pocket hoping, rather than knowing, it was aimed correctly. Luckily the gun was resting against my assailant's thigh.

"*Zizzz*." And another. "*Zizzz*." The discharge worked well. The effect was potent as my weapon provided more power than the normal police issue model. The Russian rolled back across the rear seat unable to move as he became immobilised in his muscle functions. The pain from the discharge would be excruciating. His eyes half-closed and his mouth became slack.

I gathered my senses. By now the driver realised how vulnerable he was. He reacted and the car screeched to a stop. Half-turning in his seat, he swung the butt of a gun at me. I guessed they probably wanted me alive or he would have shot me. Seeing the arc of the oncoming blow, I sat higher in the seat. The butt missed my head, but hit me on the side of my shoulder in my deltoid muscle area. Grabbing the gun with one hand, my other hand followed up with a vice like grip on his wrist. His arm was already half-turned due to the angle of his swing. I twisted his hand in a powerful two-handed movement and snatched the gun away from him. Then, demonstrated how a gun should be used. He looked at me with a wide-eyed stare. I pulled him toward me with one hand and brought the gun across to his temple with the other.

"*Thwakkk*," it was a classic pistol whip blow. The force rocked his head sideways and knocked him senseless. The danger subsided, but I felt claustrophobic and just wanted to get out.

Knowing the car door was locked shut, I decided to barge my way out to save time. By leaning back in the seat it was possible to get forward leverage. I charged at the door with the full force of my weight and shoulder. Metal creaked, the lock broke and I spilled out through the car door. It was difficult to stop as the inertia of the force took me across the pavement. I landed next to an unsuspecting pedestrian who gave out a loud gasp. The bewildered-looking Chinese man started to run along the road in panic at the sight of what had happened. I picked up my rucksack and put the gun in my belt. For some unfathomable reason, I walked back to close the car door. It swung uneasily on its hinge and didn't shut properly. It simply banged against the frame and bounced open. The big Russian looked at me but was in a dazed state. He was attempting to sit up properly and steady himself. It was time to leave the scene as quickly as possible. The experience made me far more cautious of road traffic and possible danger. The contents of my rucksack required assessment by our people and no third party. It was important to get everything back without delay. To do this, it was important to take the quickest route to Leo, so I checked on my google map for the directions. I crossed the road and started jogging along the side of the road facing oncoming traffic.

I spotted the Volkswagen Santana taxi waiting in a quiet side road as agreed. It was dark, but I could make out the outline of Leo in the taxi. He was slumped across the steering wheel. Was he okay? Was this where the Russians had been before attacking me? I needed to concentrate and decide on priorities. I looked around, took the gun from my belt and hid it from view using the rucksack. Everything seemed normal, but to be sure, I put a bullet in the chamber and released the safety. It felt reassuring to be vigilant. My eyes scanned the inside of the taxi for clues as to what may have happened. There was no staining on his shirt or head and the inside of the taxi seemed normal. I took my time and checked under the car in case it was booby-trapped. It could have been suicidal to open the door.

"Leo, you okay?" I called loudly.

No answer.

There was a need to be methodical. I wondered if the side door's glass was bulletproof. There was one way to find out. I knocked the butt of the gun on the door window in a couple of places, deciding on where to strike it with a harder force. The top of the window near the doorpost seemed the weakest area to break, and a better alternative than opening the door.

Leo heard the tapping. He sat upright with a jolting two-stage movement. His head lifted before he raised his upper body to sit upright. I stepped back a pace startled by his swift movement. He wasn't aware of my concern for him. He simply yawned, leant across and opened the door for me to get in.

"How'd it go?" asked Leo, looking inquisitively at the gun.

I was about to say as right as rain but stopped myself... "It went to plan. But after leaving the building, I met those Russians again. They don't seem to want to leave me alone."

"What's happened, ah?"

"I kicked more bottoms." I didn't want to recount all the detail.

"Ha ha. That's good. They always seem to be in your area." He looked around, and then drove off. "I'm sure you kicked good bottom again, ah!"

"Yes. Not an unusual thing in my job, Leo."

We drove on with headlights picking out the silhouettes of pedestrians. They appeared as dark clothed figures crossing the road oblivious to all sense of danger. There was little contrast between them and the road.

"It's all in here, Leo." I gave a debriefing to Leo on the materials collected from the institute. He drove for a while, doubling back on himself to check no one was following. I was beginning to trust Leo more. He was carrying out standard manoeuvres to keep us safe. More of a worry was I couldn't resolve the reason the Russians kept finding me.

My phone rang. "Are you with Leo?" it was the same female.

"Just left with him."

"Did you get everything?"

I answered in a coded response, "Yes, and our pictures will be with you soon."

"Any problems?"

"None, apart from having to deal with two Russians. They never got the better of me though."

"That's a relief. Leo can bring the materials in. Bye for now." The phone went dead and Leo distracted my thoughts.

"It funny what you say. Why pictures, ah?" asked Leo.

I looked downward and showed a blank expression. Leo got the message. As normal, I didn't see the worth of entering into discussion on the colloquial points of the English language or on coded responses. He must have been getting used to my irritation as a reaction to his irrelevant questions.

We stopped at the lights just as another taxi screeched to a stop beside us. The driver opened his door. I gripped my gun in anticipation of his next move. Leo looked relaxed but I got ready for a confrontation. The taxi driver made a guttural noise in clearing his throat, leant forward, spat on the ground and then closed his door. After my earlier encounter, I remained on edge at every unusual movements, especially from watching other cars. Time passed and we arrived back to Donghai. Leo dropped me in front of the university so I could go to my accommodation.

I was going to warn him to be vigilant, but then changed my choice of words to, "Be careful, Leo," as I'd anticipated a hooded eye expression response.

"Okay, no problem."

"You need to get going, bye." He drove off to deliver the Jinying materials for detailed study.

I made my way into the university, wondering what I should concentrate on. However, there was little need for planning as circumstance provided my next move. It would be a chance meeting that would help me understand more about the student deaths. Things were about to become a little clearer.

Chapter 15
Further Insights

I walked to my room against the tide of students leaving the university. I stepped aside once or twice and was careful moving through the hordes of students coming in the opposite direction. The flow was the evening exodus of students seeking out their evening meals. In amongst the students, I saw the figure of He-Ping, who was still wearing his bright-coloured jumper and tight jeans.

I called out and that caught his attention. He-Ping recognised me, stopped and shuffled toward me between a mass of students.

"Why are so many students leaving the university now?" I asked.

"Well, perhaps you don't re'lise how those in university rooms aren't allowed to do cooking in case of fire. They not allowed cooking in rooms and up to four in room are with each other. Lectures are finishing so all very hungry. Many are rushing to make sure they get table in local place to eat."

"Do you want to have a meal with me? I would like to have a talk with you."

"Okay. What you want to eat? Perhaps pizza? We can go to Francis place."

He led me to the traffic lights, where we could cross more safely. Luckily, he pulled me back by the arm when I stepped off the kerb after seeing the green to cross sign. I'd not realised traffic could turn right when the lights were red. Francis place was a small fast food outlet. It was reasonably clean with plastic surfaces and a tiled floor. Against one wall, there was a long eating counter, with stools under. In the centre of the room were small plastic tables. He-Ping chose the counter seats. We ordered the combination meal of a Francis pizza special, a bottle of coke and a salad. There was a relief in seeing my pizza being prepared and cooked freshly. The pizza topping was half as fish and half as sausage meat. The restaurant had an interesting environment. The walls caught my interest with several pictures of cycling, and photographs of the customers. I assumed cycling was an interest of whoever Francis may be. Our meal arrived with the salad looking a little sad. I wondered if it was better not to eat the salad and to just enjoy the pizza. The sight of a knife and fork on my tray relaxed me. He-Ping ate quickly and managed to eat more than I did. Once he had cut his pizza, he picked it up with his fingers. His way of eating was off-putting as he kept his mouth open and made slurping noises. This was followed by a gulping noise when he took his drink.

"How are you feeling now? I realise you must have found the meeting with myself and Ian quite distressing." I wanted to start by showing some sympathy about his difficulties.

"Still not good – but okay. I accept more the things about the deaths." He continued to gulp his drink.

"I'm relieved to hear that. Also, I noticed that when you saw Matt Groom in the office, you didn't look happy to see him. Perhaps Mr Groom did something to upset you? Perhaps I can help there."

"Matt Groom is not nice teacher to us. He put lot pressure on my friends."

"Do you mean the ones who died?" I put down my drink in order to give He-Ping my attention.

"Yes. Bao and Cheng. He wanted to know too much from them. It was kind of blackmail I think. He asked many questions about their personal things."

"Was it the medical trials he was asking about?"

"Yes. It everything. He's pushy man. I think he's no good to my friends."

"Pushy. What do you mean?" I asked, probing him to explain.

"Well. All Westerners strong to us students. All need softer way of asking." He gave me a severe look. Perhaps I was also asking too many direct questions but he went on, "He asked silly questions to Cheng. He question twice if it was good idea Cheng be in relationship with someone older. It upset Cheng who didn't want to talk about these things."

"Who was the person having the affair that Mr Groom was asking about?"

"Cheng never told us. We never ask as he can tell if he want. In China we save other's face. We don't ask anything to embarrass others."

It was important to move on to find out about the deaths and keep He-Ping calm. I wanted to concentrate on key facts. "Tell me what you think happened with the death of Bao and Cheng. Or is that information upsetting?"

"No one I know has idea of what happened. We in darkness, you see."

"A mystery then? I think it will calm people down if there is an explanation of the events."

"Yes. That's it. Cos this situation is big worry to us. Perhaps they have illness we'll catch."

"Has anyone spoken about what happened?"

"No. Lily Wang is kind person but not say anything. Or, Mr Ian never told anything."

I waited for him to say more but he remained quiet. He changed the focus by talking about his future plans. On some of his questions, I needed to be evasive. He asked me about the strengths and weaknesses of UK universities. My knowledge in these areas wasn't adequate and it was obvious He-Ping had discussed this matter with others. He must have realised that I couldn't help in the area as he lost faith in my ramblings. He changed the subject to football and the problems of Manchester United. I was surprised that I could have such a well-informed conversation about football and the premier league with a Chinese student.

"My English name is Manchester. Chinese people like to have a Western name as well from the Chinese one. It's Chinese thing as Japanese people hardly have English name as well."

"So, you called yourself Manchester because of your favourite football team?"

"No. The English professor for marketing who teach me. It's him. I talking lots about Manchester United to him when break time. Then, he asked all class tell what's your English name. Two of us told him they never use one. He said alright for me I now need be named Manchester. After whole class call me Manchester. So it keep with me all time after this."

The story made me smile, and this led He-Ping to smile as well. We got ready to leave. He-Ping asked for a takeaway of the salad and a slice of pizza that hadn't been eaten. I noticed he never paid any money for the takeaway packaging it was put in, or tipped for it.

"Do you ever give a tip in China?" I asked seeing the box and bag being given free for the takeaway.

"No, we don't give tip to taxi driver or restaurant. Price is price."

"It may encourage better service in restaurants if there were tips as incentives."

"We're used to get our normal service. So with us, it's not a big worry. We get what we want by asking or telling. We finished kowtow many years ago. It's you foreigners who want recognition or smile."

"I see," I said, as pleasantly as possible.

"It's like a need of power or good feeling. We don't need it. Tips are not fair – it makes other person second-class. They need to lose their real face to get money."

"That's some more interesting cultural differences I need to learn about. There seems to be many differences here."

"It'll take time to understand Chinese culture. You start with study Kong Qiu teaching. Oh. He's called Confucius in your language. He's teacher as you. We treat each other with respect cos of him."

We left Francis place and walked toward the university. Coming along the road, I saw Maria walking toward us.

"Hi. Meeting our students already I see."

"It's one way to get to know the best local places to eat," I answered jovially.

"I'm glad to see you as I wanted to have a talk." She'd taken up a position between us, sending out a message for He-Ping to leave. I never thought Maria would show anguish but her body language suggested this.

"Okay, I'm not busy," I told her. He-Ping said goodbye and walked on. I stood with Maria, knowing she wanted to discuss something. "You seem a little worried."

"Well, it's regarding Lily. She's been to see me, and became tearful about the student deaths."

"I picked up her feelings when we walked back from the restaurant."

"Yes. At the meal, she was reminded that no one had bothered about the situation of Cheng and Bao."

"Why is she upset enough to cry?"

"She cares about the students who died. As a Chinese national, she was closer than us Westerners and often spent time to help them. I would like her to put it all behind her, so please be sensitive with anything you discuss."

"I'll do my best. I'll be careful to remember that she's a caring person and may get upset," I said this while already understanding Lily's personality. I wondered if there was more to Maria's concern over Lily's feelings.

"Lily has one side that is strong, and another that is more sensitive. I like her character and wouldn't want anything to hurt her."

"I'm sure you want her to be happy. I realise you're a caring sort of person."

"You're right, I'm a mother hen type, but I also speak my mind." She changed her weight from one foot to the other. "Lily also mentioned your walk in Labour Park when we met. It seems she likes you."

"Ohh."

"As a friend, she asked me if she'd been too open with you." She caught my eye trying to read my reaction.

"I like her openness and find her thoughts interesting," I gave an honest response.

"It's good mixing with as many different locals as you can. Knowing Lily will be a good introduction to China for you."

"Yes. She must have noticed how new to China and how Western I am. She's articulate and smart, so I'm sure she noticed I was interested in everything Chinese. I enjoyed going to Labour Park."

"She's certainly an interesting and sharp-minded lady. My feeling is you will get on well, then who knows – anything can happen between you two."

I nodded but couldn't think of an appropriate response. I already knew I admired Lily for the qualities she demonstrated.

Maria went on, "There's one more thing before I leave." She fixed on me. "You are a man with strong values. Don't judge things here too quickly. China can question our Western values and play havoc with our British beliefs."

I wanted to speak more to find out what she was getting at, but it was obvious Maria was intent on leaving. We said our farewells and I walked back toward the university. I was musing on her words when I saw He-Ping emerge from a shop.

"Hi." There was now a second bag of what looked like more food. "I come back with you," he sounded in good spirit.

On the way back, we crossed the wide road again. This was quite an experience for me. He-Ping could see I needed a lot of coaching in how to use my body in a standoff with the drivers. The logic was if enough people left the kerb, the traffic would slow and allow pedestrians to cross. We crossed the road when the traffic was still moving using this approach. On crossing, I almost collided with a student stepping from the kerb in my wish to avoid the traffic. It seemed a game of chance and one that wasn't a skill I valued. We arrived back on the university campus as dusk was falling.

I'd promised Maria I would be careful with Lily. But sometimes fate takes the lead. I'd no idea that Lily would be subjected to one of the most traumatic episodes in her life. The next day's events would change everything between us.

Chapter 16
Having to Tell

I opened the door to my room and switched on the light. The low energy bulb lit the room in a dismal glow of sickening unfriendly light. Each time I entered the room, my mood was affected by the depressing palette of colour. The room was overflowing with gloomy, melancholy hues. I switched off the light and it made things seem better. I found it was far better to move around in the failing light from the window. A TV set was in the corner and I decided to see what programmes it offered. There were lots of channels to choose from. However, every channel was in Chinese, and rather than watch the soap, war or costume dramas, I chose the channel that played music. This was preferable to the building's dull noises of toilets flushing or people moving around. The TV served to muffle the sounds being transmitted through the building's concrete walls. TV music filled the room and lightened my mood. I moved to the tunes, while undressing in a slow-motion dance. Finally, I relaxed in the shower, which provided a tranquil state of mind. It was like a double helping of Horlicks. After the shower, I put on shorts and T-shirt, switched off the TV, got into bed and attempted to get comfortable on the hard pillow. The relaxing shower had ensured a smooth entrance into a deep, deep sleep.

I woke to another fine day. My eyes opened and my head was clear. The sun cut through the sides and top of the curtains though it was still early. I felt an energy and spirit, which propelled me out of bed ready to face another day's quest to solve the Jinying situation. This wasn't what I needed to decide right away though. The initial question was where I should go to get a decent breakfast. I'd noticed a Pizza Hut on my way back to the university. This seemed a good place, as I wasn't ready for Chinese food for breakfast. There was need for a clean, safe place to eat. So, Pizza Hut it would be.

A short, brisk walk brought me to the restaurant. I looked at the familiar Pizza Hut branding and it felt reassuring. This could be because I was accustomed to the quality of its food. A young person welcomed me at the door, and I raised one finger indicating I wanted a table for one. It was not busy as only about three other tables were occupied in the whole place. The menu lay on the table in English, as well as Chinese. There were pictures of the food, which made it easy to point to the choice for my order. The omelette and toast looked good, so became my first choice. I noticed the possibility to get free refills for my coffee, so went through three mugs before becoming happy with my coffee fix intake. I thought about the discussion from the previous evening with He-Ping. Matt was a person showing on my personal radar as a man who needed watching. He was not liked by He-Ping and I wondered what was meant by the pressure Matt had given to others.

I enjoyed the breakfast, feeling it would prepare me to start my day. I paid and left to make my way back to the room. The sky was offering a fresh start, as it was another pleasant day without the pollution that had been affecting many Chinese cities. An abundance of the sights and sounds of nature accompanied me on the way back. The birds, the rustle of the trees and the chatter of people provided a pleasant background to the start of my day. Everything felt happy in the newness of the morning. However, the calmness wasn't about to last.

There was no clue that such a good start to a day would change like it did. Soon things were to become far more complicated. I walked into the lobby area of my accommodation building and climbed a few steps. There was an ominous sense of foreboding but it was too late. To one side, there was a recognisable click. I spun toward the click. In the semi-darkness, I glimpsed the outline of two men. Two guns were levelled at me from a side corridor. I felt as if I were caught on flypaper without any route of escape.

"Be calm and you will be safe," came a dangerous sounding voice from the gloom of the corridor.

My eyes adjusted to the light as the rush of blood and neurochemicals piled in. Hormone levels spiked and mental focus increased. Turning to face the sound, I saw the two men more clearly. Both appeared to be trained professionals and were holding guns. One had a Steyr machine pistol and the other, a handgun with silencer. The men wore dark suits with an indiscernible lapel pin badge and, by size, resembled bodyguards. I could see they moved well and knew what they were doing. The man nearest me was pointing a handgun at my heart. Not a good feeling. It's only when someone has had a gun trained on them that they can know what it feels like. It heightens the senses of mortal vulnerability and near death. It's an out-of-body sensation where death is simply a trigger pull away. But if the men wanted me dead, it was beyond that point already. What should I do? I wondered how tense their trigger fingers were.

"Okay Freeze." This was difficult to agree to as the instinct to act becomes so strong. The danger was fuelling my instinct to fight or take flight. "Take us to your room – Now!" I had no alternative and needed to obey. These two were surely friends of my previous Russian assailants. The one with the handgun used close contact, and the other with the machine pistol hung back. I felt I wasn't able to defend myself.

"Don't look round. Just move to your room," snarled the one with the handgun.

I assumed they wanted me to help them search my room, so it seemed better to wait before going onto the offensive. I moved forwards trying to assess the situation. I decided on a plan to take advantage of passing through the narrowness of the door to my room to react. It would offer the chance to attack the man behind me. In an instant, none of this mattered. Everything spiralled into confusion. That plan was wiped out, due to the interruption of a major new event.

Both my assailants were following me and didn't notice a person approaching quietly from behind them. The person creeping up on them made no sound. Their silence allowed for the element of complete surprise. The man with the machine pistol was attacked from the back. His leg was kicked down from a strike to the back of his knee joint, which made him fall forward. His pistol went up in the air, looped in a circle and fell to the floor. I looked round, as did the man behind me with the handgun. There was a thud of a strike and a clang as the machine pistol bounced off the floor. A female was raining a series of blows on the man's kidneys and neck. The strike movements were similar to those I'd seen when Lily was in the sport's hall. In the mayhem, I could see it was her; she'd come to help me. I couldn't immediately get to grips with what was going on, as Lily had appeared so suddenly.

The man with the handgun momentarily froze. He was deciding whether to continue facing me or to turn and shoot Lily, who was attacking his comrade.

He decided to turn to stop the attack on his companion. The decision gave me an advantage, given he spun around to look toward Lily. There was little advantage though. I could see he was too far away from me to strike him easily. His gun levelled in the direction of Lily. He was beading in on his target. I had to act quickly so made a flying tackle to the back of his thighs. He flew forward with the force of my dive. His gun fired a single muffled shot, but the shot went harmlessly into the floor. He sprawled forward and the impact of the fall on his wrist dislodged the gun. I was fully stretched out on the floor and felt helpless as I still couldn't strike him. Things were becoming more desperate.

He scrambled to his knees to raise his body and looked round for his gun. It was against the wall. We were both racing to get an advantage. He moved and stooped forward to pick up the gun. I'd crawled forward and ended up eye to eye with him beside the gun. He paused along with me. We made our move for the gun; I sprang forward and picked it up first. He was able to jump on me and pin my arms to my chest. I didn't want to be under him. We rolled over together, struggling for advantage. As I rolled to the top, I got the benefit of being able to move my hand. I angled the gun toward him as far as I could and shot him in the chest. The momentum of our struggle and the shot to his chest carried him across the floor. He released his grip, struggled to sit, went down on his side and rolled to face me. My aggressor was now limp and done for. His mouth filled with blood and he stared vacantly at me. I watched his lifeblood ebbing away.

Lily was having problems with the man she'd knocked to the ground. He twisted away from her, then spun round like a break-dancer and kicked her leg away. She toppled over. I sat up and caught sight of his eyes, which were bulging with rage. He'd looked in my direction and saw I'd acquired a gun. Time was ticking and there was a need to decide something quickly. I raised my gun but Lily was between us attempting to stand, which made it impossible to get a clean shot. He realised this, jumped up and ran down the corridor to escape. There were a number of heavy thumps and claps of heels, as he ran down the stairs and out the building.

"Let him go!" I shouted. My request wasn't needed. Lily sat down and placed her head between her legs. She looked drained and didn't respond. Training kicked in. My senses were heightened and it was necessary to secure the situation. An acrid smell of the gunshot held in the air and all was quiet.

There was no sound of doors opening in the building. It meant the fight noises had blended in with day-to-day activity. The silencer had muffled the gunshot.

"You okay?" Lily said nothing. "You surprised me, but thank goodness you helped me."

Lily raised her head. She was breathing heavily. "He looks dead."

I checked the neck pulse of the man, while knowing he would be dead. "Yes. He's dead I'm afraid." A tear rolled down her face. "It was him or us in that fight."

"I had no idea it would end like this – I'll phone the police."

"No. You musn't." My eyes tightened.

"What? We need to ring the police."

"Don't. This is my business. I can't have the police here!" it was an assertive, straight into Lily's face delivery. I needed to take control of the situation.

"Your business?" She paused. "What business? You're a teacher!"

"Leave it. We need to deal with him."

She wasn't backing down. Lily continued, "You said your business… What business are you in that would make those Russians come here?" she was insistent.

"My business here is confidential."

"Confidential? …Why?" She glared at me before shouting, "What's this secret?" Her constant questioning was making things difficult. I couldn't tell her my secret as it could compromise the mission. She repeated her question, "Why confidential?"

Lily waited, but I didn't answer her question. I wanted to change the subject. So I asked, "How on earth did you know I needed help?"

"I'd just arrived when I saw Matt. I made my way toward him to say hello, but before I could speak, the two Russians spoke to him."

"Spoke to Matt?"

"Yes. Only a few words," her ponderous tone indicated her frustration.

She rubbed her temple before explaining. "I heard them use your name. Matt pointed in the direction of your room, so I guessed it was to find out where you lived. They spoke in a language that sounded Russian. That seemed weird, so I watched them and saw one put his hand inside his jacket to take out something that looked like a gun," her words were flat. "That was it. He had a gun, so I decided you were probably in trouble. At first, I walked away as I was going to phone the police but decided to follow them to find out what was happening."

"They were two Russian hitmen." I looked at the dead Russian and then Lily.

Lily wasn't giving up. She gazed at me. "Why would Russians want to kill you? What's the reason? I don't understand any of it. Why do you say you have confidential business here?" her questions spilled out. She looked lost and then snapped, "Tell me!"

She was insistent and had become involved, so I felt I had no choice but to tell her something. "Okay, I need to bring you into the loop. First, let's drag this body into my room."

Lily looked at the body, then back at me. "Show the way."

"I'm hoping you can cope with this."

"Uhhh, cope? My world's been turned upside down." She stared at the body. "Tell me why they were here. Were they going to hurt you for some reason?"

"I promise I'll tell you about these bad guys. But, let's deal with this." I was desperate to move the body from the hallway. "I need to clean up this mess." The pungent smell of nitro-glycerine from the gun's discharge was already dispersing and a pool of blood was forming around the body. We dragged the body the short distance into my room. There was no noticeable exit wound, which surprised me given the closeness of the fatal shot.

I couldn't find a cloth to clean up the blood so I took two of my shirts from the wardrobe. Lily watched without speaking, while I removed the blood from the hallway floor. Luckily the hall floor was tiled and not carpeted. Blood in large quantity has a peculiar smell and a tacky viscose nature. Wiping it up when it's had time to congeal is more like wiping treacle than water. I found a plastic bag and put the shirts inside it. I returned to the room, washed my hands and sat on the bed. Lily stood by the window that overlooked the sport's hall. She gazed out with her back to the body.

"Life is normal out there," her voice drifted down in volume as she stared through the window. "What's happening here is madness." Nothing made sense to her.

I handed a bottle of water to her. "Why not drink this?" Lily held the bottle and looked back at me. There was a question of what Lily may say or do, given what she'd seen? I needed to decide if I could trust her. It wasn't clear if I could rely on her with what had happened. I knew little about Lily, apart from her having an independent character and strong values. Those had become obvious from our discussions. My overall assessment was I'd no alternative but to trust her, yet at the same time, I would need to watch her. I decided it important to gain her trust and make her believe I was doing what was right.

"Okay, Lily. I owe you an explanation, given you may have saved my life today."

"I think you do." The assertion was clear. She wasn't going to give up asking, so I decided on my story.

"I can't tell you too much. What I can tell is I'm here to see if the deaths of the students were natural or not."

"I don't get it. Why someone from Britain? That's weird." She thought for a while. "Why's this your responsibility? It should be James not you." She put down the bottle without having drunk anything.

"I told you I can't tell you too much. I found out that the medical trials had many secrets related to them. At the moment, I don't know anything more, but each day things become clearer."

"An old saying here is, 'involve me, then I will understand'. So, who are you working for?" She turned, resumed staring out the window and looked up at the sky.

I grimaced. "I'm working for good people." There was no way I could tell her the truth. "Look, in this situation, you need to realise I know best."

"Okay. But why were the Russians here?"

"They would've hurt me if I didn't tell them what I know."

"Secrets that you know?" Lily had a mind of her own. She wasn't going to relax and trust me until she found out more. She was intent on my divulging more.

"Yes. Look – I know you want more information about the student deaths. Trust me. I'll find out what happened. Those Russians think I know more. But I don't yet."

"I want to trust you. I don't know why, but I do." She turned to look at me. "Can you find out more about Cheng and Bao?"

"Just like you, I want to know what happened. So work with me on this." I wasn't authorised to ask Lily to work with me so I knew I was taking a risk. I'd decided it was acceptable.

"Okay. So how can we work together?"

"Let's start by you telling me something about the personal details of the students."

Lily bit her lip, then responded, "I knew the students well. There were serious emotional problems I tried to deal with. Cheng wanted me to organise a transfer to another university as he was having personal relationship problems. I was involved in trying to help him move on."

"What emotional problems? Were they caused by the trial, a staff member or another student?"

"Some things are not talked about publicly in China. Those boys had some personal worries they needed to deal with. It's upsetting, but that's all I can tell you."

I wondered if she was keeping some things in confidence, so I focused on what needed doing. "Look, I'm going to get things sorted out here. I can get this body taken away without anyone knowing."

"Okay. Do what you have to." She seemed willing to help.

I made a call on my mobile to explain there was a special laundry bundle to be taken away. I gave details of where to come and asked for an urgent service. A check to the hallway indicated no obvious signs were left of the fight. Lily decided to stay with me until the cleaning service arrived. She kept watch from my window for a laundry van. Within the hour, a small van with two Chinese men in overalls arrived. They came to my room and seemed surprised to see Lily. A few words were spoken to her in Chinese.

"We'll take this one, then clean all the evidence." They wasted no time in dealing with the situation.

As they worked, I noticed the Dalian base was well organised and prepared for any eventuality. I was struck by the English words, 'specialist carpet cleaning', written on the back of their overalls under a few Chinese characters. The two men folded over the dead Russian. A crack and grinding noise sounded as the body was bent in half. The body was placed in a padded roll, in a more compact shape than a normal body. The roll covering, with the doubled up Russian in it, had the same words on as the overalls. In ten minutes, my room was back to normal.

"We leave now," said the one lifting the front of the bundle.

"Thanks guys."

My cover had been compromised, so I needed to leave. Before I said anything, Lily spoke. "I can't believe what's gone on here. It's like it didn't happen." Her eyes circled my empty room.

"There's no way I can stay here. It's too dangerous with the Russians knowing where to find me. I'll have to move out to operate from somewhere else."

"Yes, you need to move out. The chances are they'll come back to get what they're looking for."

Chapter 17
Moving Out

My mobile phone bleeped a message. I took it from my pocket and viewed it:

We are now code red active. Cleaners reported they saw a girl who was with you and the body. So the question is whether she should be eliminated. We want to send in a cleaning team if you think she compromises our situation. Also, your cover is not safe as the Russians are on to us. We suggest you move out. Contact SAP.

I was now faced with a dilemma. Lily had possibly saved my life yet my controllers would see her as a threat and would want her eliminated to protect the mission. It was obvious they would want everything to remain confidential, but they didn't know her. My decision wasn't an easy one. The question was what threat level did she pose? If the assignment was in danger of being compromised, this would be deemed unacceptable. I knew it was important to have no loose ends. The Dalian field base could be right in wanting her eliminated given the importance of our mission and her lack of security clearance. I placed my phone in my pocket and Lily walked toward me.

She stopped close to me, slipped her hand in mine and held it quite firmly. "I need to put this behind me," she said. I loosened her grip on my hand and let go.

I was still trying to deal with the text message. Her involvement had complicated the situation, and Lily had no idea how much danger she was in. The text message asked if she would compromise our mission. I needed to decide on what to do. There was a need to move things forward quickly, but should I follow my instincts or orders?

I stepped back. "Give me a moment; I need to think things through."

I realised a team is only as strong as its weakest member. Was she strong enough, or were we vulnerable? I recounted she told me many things after our Chinese restaurant meal. She was for good people, not bad and had witnessed the wrongs to her father. The final decision was simply a question of could I trust Lily? My resolve was strong and I made my decision based upon logic, not emotion. She'd already demonstrated what it takes – so my assessment was she could be recruited.

"You look serious. I can see you're having deep thoughts." She'd no idea about the reason for my seriousness.

I tried to take control. "That's not surprising," I replied at once. "I need to find out more about why Matt was talking to those Russian men."

"What do you mean?"

I was curious about Matt so told her, "I've got to see Matt, to understand what has gone on. He needs to give me an explanation."

"I've no idea why was he talking with those Russians today."

"I'll find out," I insisted.

"One thing I know is that he's good at Eastern European languages," she offered.

"I'll find out as much as possible about him."

"I feel relieved that we have the chance to find out more about what happened."

I smiled trying to reassure her, "You'll need to trust me. I'll get to the bottom of this no matter what it takes."

"Yes. I know I'll have to trust you if we're going to find out what happened to the students," she said with confidence. "There are times in my life when things seem right, and someone else can take control of my destiny."

It seemed she would cooperate and I'd made the right decision. Her character was as stubborn and tough as mine in getting things done. There was little doubt she would work with me, as she also wanted to solve the mystery of the student deaths.

"Can we leave?"

"Not so fast, as I need to talk to someone."

My thoughts were filled with a need to deal with the text message I'd received about sending a cleaning team to eliminate Lily. Within earshot of Lily, I took out my mobile phone and made a call to my Dalian contact. It was important for her to listen to the language of my field office to understand the true danger of what was happening. It was obvious they would ask questions about the security of the operation now Lily was involved. I was ready to back her, as I now felt more confidence in her loyalty. If she heard the conversation, she would hear my positive attitude and be able to understand the situation.

"Everything is clean here," I confirmed. "I'll move out and stay in a quieter location."

The female asked, "Hold on… Is everything clean – What about the Chinese woman?"

"I'll vouch for her. She's on our side in this." Then, more assertively, "I'm recruiting her as our new asset." I nodded at Lily confirming the point. "She's Lily Wang from the Donghai Management School."

"Right. Not what we expected, but we'll check on her to see if we can validate her credentials."

"That's fine."

"All right. I'll get her checked out and let you know what we find. Bye." The phone cut off. It was clear Lily would be vetted as to her background and potential risk to the operation. My vouching for her would be a short-term reprieve.

Lily looked at me. "New asset! That's an impersonal role. I've never been an asset before so do your people think they own me?" I smiled at her remark, but her face stayed serious. "Okay. So that voice and the way things are being controlled means there's a big organisation backing you up."

"Please don't try to figure out anything connected to me. You said you trust me, and I promise I'll find out about the dead students."

"That's good. But I know you aren't alone in this."

"I've things to sort out even though others are involved. First, I need to get my things and move to a hotel. It's not safe here." I started to walk around collecting things to put in the rucksack.

"This all seems dangerous and must put you under lots of pressure."

"You don't understand, Lily…I actually enjoy this job."

"You do?" An inflexion showed her surprise. "You enjoy this. What's that supposed to mean?"

"I feel good doing my job. There's satisfaction in it." Once I'd said this, I knew it was crass. So I tried to be clearer about my job. "What I do gives me reason and purpose to make things better."

There was a silence before she asked, "How can you feel good? Someone died."

"Yes, but that was from self-defence. It was me or them – and I won."

"Sorry, that just sounds like you're numb and not sensitive." Lily could make remarks that were difficult to answer.

Did she think me remorseless? I searched for a common link. "Think about our martial arts. We both train expecting to use our skills to overcome others."

"I never thought someone could die from what I do."

"There was no choice. Any alternative action wasn't an option." I was struggling to convince her.

I detected some compromise. "True," she voiced after some hesitation.

"Like it or not, we have a bond from what happened." I nodded gently and Lily mirrored my movements.

There wasn't anything else said. It was now a matter of packing all the important things that could be fitted into a briefcase and rucksack. Before leaving, I looked back in the room to ensure nothing important was being left. The cleaners had taken the Steyr machine pistol, but I'd retained the handgun and spare clip of ammunition. Lily insisted on carrying the heavy rucksack, and I took the briefcase with the computer.

"All right with that rucksack?" I asked.

"I need to eat." She put one arm through the two loops of the rucksack, settled it on her shoulder and said, "I think we should find somewhere to have a light meal."

"You're right. We probably don't have an appetite after what's happened, so a light meal will be fine."

"Do you want a Baozi meal?" I opened my arms up not knowing what she meant. "Oh, they're steamed buns with fillings. Like a sweet dumpling. They originated here in North China."

Lily led me to a small place, which sold dumplings filled with pork, prawns or vegetables. It was near the university in an area where students ate. The place was the first step up from a roadside stall, as it could only seat about ten people. There were no menus and the choice was made from faded pictures on the wall. We ended by choosing a selection of each dumpling.

Lily ordered the meal, and then looked across the table at me. "I realise I've put you in a difficult situation and am thankful you protected me from your organisation."

"I want you to understand the risks of what's happening here."

"I think I'm aware. Don't worry I'm strong enough to handle this."

"I'm glad you're like me in the way you react. We have something in common." I paused and looked at Lily. "If you want to understand me, it's important to realise I'll use all my power to do what is required."

A waiter in dirty beige clothes delivered the meal to our table. The dumplings arrived in the bamboo baskets they'd been steamed in. When the lid was raised, there was an appealing aroma. Some of that aroma was coming from the cabbage leaf base. We added soya and vinegar to improve the flavours, but this made the dumplings hard to grab with my chopsticks. Lily spotted this and smiled at my poor attempts to pick up the slippery round dumplings.

"Ha ha. Give up, Harry. I'll get you a spoon."

It was good as her amusement deflected our thoughts from the earlier encounter. We both smiled as nothing I did improved my attempts. At least I'd succeeded in calming her. I'd become the source of entertainment with my constant dropping of the dumplings before I could get them to my mouth. She laughed again. The owner of the place heard the mirth and started watching my difficulties. He came over to our table, provided a china spoon and smiled. He then discussed the joke with Lily.

Our appetites weren't large, so we left a few dumplings in the bamboo baskets. The owner said something in Chinese as we left, and Lily told me the person had said, "Walk carefully." It was good advice given the recent events and what was happening. This short relaxed period came to an end with the recognisable sound of my phone.

My phone beeped and I opened a text: *Be careful. We think Russians are back watching your room and may check on your movements.*

I looked from my phone screen to Lily. "I've been warned the Russians may be watching out for me. I need to find somewhere safe."

"Let's go to my place. This will be safer than anywhere else right now," there was concern in her voice.

"I'm not sure if it's a good idea."

"It's no trouble for me. The best solution is to stay in my room, as it's the easiest place for now." She looked at me trying to read my face. "You'll be safer there."

"But, is it best to stay in your place? It's good of you, but I worry there may be no room for me."

"You're right, it's a small place. We'll be together, and while it's not perfect, it's the best alternative. Just to be clear, I'm not expecting anything by you being there," she took control.

"We understand the situation that we'll be sharing your place. I'm happy as it's the best alternative at the moment." I'd no idea what else to say.

On the way back, it was important to be vigilant. I watched for anything that may signal danger. Lily led me to her motorbike, and we left accompanied by the thumping roar of its engine. I placed the rucksack on my back and held the briefcase by my side. My free arm went round Lily's waist and it gave me a warm, intimate feeling. I held on enjoying the power of the bike and thinking it a match to Lily's strength of character. Her character and Asian charm had developed feelings that made it difficult for me to retain control. I could feel the emotion of the moment as it swept throughout my body.

It was not long before we arrived at the apartment block where Lily stayed. Her building was a tall, modern block. She parked her bike in front of the building between two cars, and I followed her in. While relatively new, the interior décor was damaged. Wallpaper was pulled off the wall in places, and the wood and tiled areas were scuffed or broken. The waste bins in the entrance area were overflowing with empty cartons from take away food. She led me across the large hall area, past a reception desk and to the lifts. Three lifts served the different floors. We travelled to the eighteenth floor by means of Lily's security card, which controlled the lift. I noted the benefit of the security this provided.

"Here we are." Lily's front door was a high security metal door, which clanged open to reveal a bedsit studio of about forty square metres. It was certainly a compact place. We entered and put down my belongings in the hallway. Lily shut the door behind us and locked it. Apart from the small square room, there was a separate bathroom and shower off to the left of the entrance. There was no question whether Lily lived here. The room smelt of her perfume.

"Don't judge the furniture or room as being my taste. It's a furnished place that I rent."

I scanned her studio room. "I think the size is the main problem."

"Anything bigger is too expensive."

"Well, it's certainly compact." The room had the effect of making me feel large.

The furniture was mainly built-in units with cream wardrobes and a small desk come dressing table along one wall. A small kitchen area with a microwave and two electric rings was part of the entrance space. I could see that no oven was available. The only other items were two chairs, a flat-screen TV and double bed pushed against the wall. Boxes for shoes were against one wall, and other boxes were scattered around the room. I noticed the colour of the bedding as it brightened the room. The bedspread was a pastel blue with small yellow flowers, which matched the curtains. A number of colourful soft cushions were on the bed. Although small and cramped, the room felt comfortable and suited to Lily.

I was drawn to the view from the window. Due to the height of Lily's room, being on the eighteenth floor, it allowed expansive sea views. Distant large ships and small boats could be seen on an azure blue sea. The vessels sitting on the sea were toy-like due to the distance between us. It seemed unreal. It was like an oversized sapphire dotted with small grey vessels.

"Do you want some cha?" Lily broke my contemplation of the seascape.

"Sure do…please."

"I'll put the kettle on. I'm having one as I need it."

"The views from these high-rise buildings are spectacular."

"Dalian sits on a long promontory, which means lots of the buildings have those sea views."

It was better to sit on a chair as the only other place was the bed. I figured Lily probably sat on the bed and used the cushions, placed against the wall, for her back. Lily busied herself with the tea things, and then played music from her iPad. I was happy that her music included Adele. I picked up one of her books which pictured Chinese art. Everything felt relaxing. She sat on the bed, looked over at me and remained quiet. I offered some comments about the number of horses and fish depicted throughout her art book. She kept her silence, so I made comment about the power of the images created from just a few brush strokes.

Her look became more intense, and her words came out slowly. "Sometimes simple things are the most beautiful."

Lily slid off the bed and knelt before my chair. She removed the book from me and laid it on the floor. I saw the warm emotion in her eyes. Then, she took my hand and held it a moment. She studied it before raising it to her lips. I knew I liked Lily, but this was not a situation I wanted us to be in. I tried to gently remove my hand without causing offence. "Wait, there's no need to be so affectionate with me," I whispered, but Lily sensed my concern.

"Are you afraid of showing your feelings? Affection is good at times." Lily held onto my hand and gazed into my eyes. "You must sense my feelings." The music continued with emotional ballads while the kettle started to rumble.

The beauty of her eyes melted my resolve and I sensed we shared something special. Her gentle approach went under my radar. I stopped any idea of removing my hand, took Lily's other hand and mirrored the way she'd kissed mine. Holding hands created a warm and alive feeling, but I knew it was making me feel weak. There was no need to escalate the feeling, so I held back from taking a further step. Thankfully, the spell of the moment was broken by the kettle making a loud boiling sound. Lily smiled, stood up and moved across the room to make the tea.

"Things can get a little crazy sometimes," I said, relieved at the excuse for a change in emotion.

"No, we're not crazy – it's simply you. You make sure you keep your distance."

"It's just my way."

"Let's relax. I can understand your reservations." I was grateful that Lily understood how I felt. She passed over a mug, along with a bowing motion and smile. "It's jasmine tea. Hope you like it?"

"I do. It's comforting." She watched as I sipped the tea.

"I think you're enjoying jasmine tea, and perhaps what you're experiencing in China."

I tried to reflect on Lily's views of what I'd experienced. I'd entered China without any uncertainties of who I was and what I stood for. At first, the detail of Lily's backstory, of her father and mother's experiences, of being supressed to suit the politics of communism all reinforced my ideals. However, our discussions about doing right and wrong, and the link between power and politics had confused my beliefs.

"I was thinking about what you've shown me about your culture and the discussions we've had. They seem to have made me reconsider what I've taken for granted."

"That's good, as you already know my culture stresses a need to have harmony. Perhaps you will expand and broaden your views by being in China."

Her words about harmony resonated with me. I started to realise I could be too principled and needed more balance. Perhaps I was an unquestioning political cog while working as an agent. My role didn't involve asking questions, but my experience of China had made me more aware of the bias of national politics. I realised my thinking was simple symbolism where I treated issues as good and bad, them and us, communists and democrats. I could now understand there were grey areas that weren't simply black and white. This was the first time I'd considered if there should be a better balance to my life. I think it developed from new insight into yin and yang, understanding the inner soul of the calligraphy writers and the passion of the choir singers in their political beliefs. It was igniting a spiritual awakening. China had allowed a pause in time, a long enough moment to ask questions of life. I felt confused as to where all this may lead or how it may fit into my life.

"I need to thank you for expanding my thoughts about what's important in life. Our talks and what I experienced in Labour Park has had an impact on me. It may sound silly, but I think I'm becoming more philosophical."

"As long as you're happy with your new thoughts, then everything's good," she said.

Lily began looking at her mobile phone. I held my mug of tea and looked at her. I had thoughts about her but needed to fight my feelings to keep things sane. There was a need for me to relax and take control of the emotion between us. My reason for being in China was to carry out my mission, and that shouldn't take long. Once it was finished, I would be moved onto a new assignment. I didn't want Lily, or both of us, to be heartbroken at my departure. Lily looked at me, and I noticed she didn't look concerned over what was happening. Perhaps Lily knew my careful approach hid far deeper feelings. It was obvious she was no fool. Lily sat back on the bed, and we both sipped our tea. Calmness descended on us, but the situation wasn't an easy one.

Chapter 18
Clarifying Things

"Tea is an important ritual in China. We make it into a ceremony and serve it to show respect for others or to strengthen friendships." Her words allowed me to understand why serving tea was connected to giving a bow. She added, "The hand movements, the tasting and the ceremony of making the tea facilitate deep thought processes."

"Yes, drinking tea offers a good opportunity to reflect, and talk." I was reminded about my mother who often insisted we should have a nice cup of tea. A cherished memory flashed back of my home as a boy when my mother served us tea and cake on a tray in front of a fire. I now realised she'd always created a pleasant ceremony for us.

Lily brought me back to reality. "I feel we're circling each other, Harry. I want you to know our short time together has been important for me. How about you?"

"That's a direct question. Well, we've done a lot of flirting."

"Flirt...ting?" commented Lily in a drawn-out way. "Is that all you can say?" she added, with a flat tone.

I felt a need to reinforce my reason for being in China. "I'm here to find out about the students and that's my priority. So we're not meant to get involved." My tone became gentle, "I worry about the feelings we could develop before I go home."

"You're complicated in many ways."

"Yes," I said, pulling a face. "Perhaps we can find a way to deal with this?"

"It's okay. But I would like to think we could be friends. Don't worry about the difficulties of being involved. Just be my good friend."

"That's like a Facebook request. Well, we're already good friends." We both smiled at my remark.

"Yes, but this is a friendship that involves me in so many other complicated things. We're never going to be Facebook friends sending trivial details to each other. So what important thing do you want to do next…friend?"

I listened and realised I'd definitely made complications for her. Another sip of tea and I said, "It's confusing and nothing is clear yet. First, there's Matt Groom to consider. I saw him going into the Institute of Technology building, but I don't know why. Whatever comes next, I'm sure you're prepared to do what is needed."

"Oh, I can help with Matt. He told me he was going to the institute to find out about the students. He felt the people there were answerable to us in the school and needed to be clearer about what had happened."

"That's interesting. It means he wasn't trying to cover up his visit."

"No. Because he discussed it with me."

"I assumed he was prying around for details of what was going on with the medical aspects of the experiment. But you're right. He didn't need to say anything if he wanted to keep his visit secret."

"Well, that's not all. He told me a couple of days ago, before we went out for the evening meal, that the deaths were becoming a police matter."

"Why a police matter?"

"He was told an autopsy of both bodies identified other causes. He said the medical experiments may have had nothing to do with the deaths."

"That's interesting. Perhaps he only told a few of the staff like you, in case it became general knowledge that he'd exceeded his authority. It was obvious you would never say anything, as you realise it could have negative consequences, especially for his visa."

"Given the autopsy findings didn't place blame on the experiments, it could be a cover up. What he was told was possibly the institute's way of hiding the truth."

"Interesting thought. Where can we find him?"

"Well, in the evening, he meets people in a bar called 'Comrade's' in a downtown area. Or he goes to a South Korean spa near there."

My phone rang and I gave my code. "We have you positioned in the Central Dalian area," said my female contact from the Dalian base. "What are your plans?"

"I've moved out as agreed to a safer place. It's difficult now with the Russians onto me, as they'll know I've killed one of their men."

"How long will you be there?"

"This is my new location until tomorrow."

"Right."

"I'm going to find Matt Groom as he was talking to the two Russians who jumped me. I've a number of questions he will have to answer."

"We need to see you here first thing. The analysis has revealed a number of interesting developments. HQ London is agreeing strategies with senior government people before we activate new responses."

"I'll be meeting with you tomorrow morning. I'll see you then."

"Yes. It'll give London time to rubberstamp the plans. We see you're near the Carrefour supermarket. Be outside the main entrance at nine, and Leo will make a pick up."

"Okay."

"I look forward to our meeting. You've done well. See you soon, bye."

It was the first time I'd received a friendly goodbye. However, it was still like a speaking text message system rather than a real person. Lily had gone over to the kitchen area to wash up the mugs and tidy up. She turned to me. "So you will meet with Matt to find out more?"

I was about to answer when my phone rang again. "Hello, Harry. It's Amanda."

"Hi, Amanda, it's nice of you to ring."

"Well, it was just a quick call to see if you want to join me on a walk along the coastal road."

"I'm a bit tied up right now. That's a nice offer, but I'll need to delay things until I'm less busy."

"No problem. We'll keep in touch then."

"Yes. Let's do that as we can go another time." I wanted to keep an open link with her.

"Sure, I'll be leaving for my walk soon. Bye."

"Bye."

I could see Lily had an intense look. "I feel a little upset about that call. Amanda is quite forward in developing relationships. You need to be careful with her."

"It's not a problem as I understand her."

"You're questioning Matt soon. Well, Amanda had some dealings with him before he went to the institute. Make sure you can trust her."

"It won't be a problem," I assured her.

"Harry, I'm not feeling relaxed at the moment. I think we could both do with getting away from here for a while? I'll take you for a bike ride along the coastal road."

"There's the Tiger Beach you mentioned." Once I said this, Lily raised her spirits from her earlier feelings about Amanda. I thought I could judge her change in mood, as well as its reason.

"Perhaps we can go on that bike ride right now? I'm sure we'll enjoy it."

I wanted to have a break from Lily's room, and this was the ideal opportunity. "Okay. Let's do it. The freedom of a bike ride will be a great release."

"Well, it'll be more than a freedom feeling." Lily's eyes became excited. "I'll ride fast. What do you think?"

"I'll enjoy that. But when you're taking, risks clear thinking is required," I warned her. "Sorry to go on about risks, but it's best to assess them."

"Me too. I worry about physical risks." Then she gave me a knowing look, "…but with you, I realise you won't take a risk with your emotional feelings."

"You're too clever. You realise too much about my risk taking," I admitted.

Lily's eyes became fuller at my confession, and her face relaxed into a broad smile. I picked up the gun and unscrewed the silencer. I put the silencer in my pocket and pushed the gun into the back of my trousers. I wasn't going to travel around Dalian unarmed now I was a target.

Chapter 19
Tiger Beach

I helped tidy the room before we made our way down to the ground floor. While cleaning up may seem mundane, I enjoyed the more organised look of things as we left. We took the lift and went out to Lily's bike. Once again, it caught my attention due to its inspiring lines. The angle of the front shock absorbers from the frame gave the Shadow a ready to fly look. This, and the glint from the front wheel made it seem ready for motion.

"Let's leave," said Lily. She mounted her bike and perched on the low seat. I followed.

The V-twin cylinders came to life, and created a symphony of raw sound. We sat astride locked together ready for the off. Reverberations from the engine increased. Lily looked round and gave me a look which indicated I would enjoy the ride.

"You ready?" she shouted. I nodded.

One twist of the throttle and the inertia sat me back on the seat. I held Lily gently by the waist, but tightened my grip as we started flying by cars. The world went whizzing past. We were soon on a coastal road and everything changed. My inside thighs gripped Lily and pressed harder against her as we swooped in unison round the many bends. The bike's engine noise echoed off the cliffs and road surface. Bursts of noise were in unison with bends and straights as the throttle opened and closed.

The scenes were of sea, beaches, cliffs, forests and open roads. There was freedom in the experience. We didn't wear helmets, which led to numerous sensations and louder sound. I enjoyed the force of wind against my face and in my hair. Being higher than Lily I looked out over her head, experiencing the full force of the wind. I was forever squinting with eyes watering, then drying. The engine softened, then roared as Lily unleashed the throttle. We leaned into and out of the corners in never ending angled movements. It was a fun-fair experience. This was escapism from China, from my mission, from normality.

"Tiger Beach," announced Lily, after pulling into a small car park. "Out there is the Yellow Sea."

The bike stopped in a dust-laden mist. The silence of the bike was accompanied by the sensation of ringing noises in my ears. I got off, still feeling the vibrations in my legs. I looked around. A new development of buildings surrounded the hills around this beauty spot. Turning and looking out to sea provided a vista of small islands, each like an aircraft carrier for bird life. Sea birds landed and took off or whirled around in the slipstream of the ocean breezes.

"How's this?" asked Lily.

"It's so different."

Distant seagull cries surrounded us. Out at sea, small fishing boats were flying triangular red flags. They bobbed gracefully against the rise and fall of the water, each flag fluttering against the different blue and green hues of the sea. We strolled down to the peacefulness of the water's edge. Here wave after small wave ebbed and flowed in rhythmic patterns. At each swirl of water, aromas of both sea and beach filled my senses.

The adrenaline flow subsided and calmness replaced the surge of excitement from the earlier bike ride. This had to be a yin-yang moment. We were fully relaxed as we walked together toward the beach. We were so close that we kept bumping into each other. Shoulders, hips and hands were contact points. We were like magnets with an invisible magnetic field, whose attraction pulled us together. We brushed, touched and moved together as we walked along. It was gravitational as the power was drawing us in and finding a way to repeat the process. The source of the force was mutual. Our hands finally met, and we gently clasped on to each other. This released a surge of emotion. One that felt right. I had no worry about it being the wrong thing to do. We gazed out to sea while Lily leant against my chest.

"This is relaxing," I said. Lily looked at me with a look of serenity and warmth.

I slipped my arm around Lily's back and pulled her into me. We stood there enjoying the moment. It seemed natural without any desire for us to pull away. I felt liberated as my body took over from my mind. There was a gentle flame of feeling in what was happening. Senses whirled. Then, something snapped in my thoughts. There was a stubborn urge not to yield to the emotion of the moment, not to change the arc of my life.

I struggled to know what to say. "I wasn't expecting this."

"Is this more flirt-ting?" asked a sarcastic Lily, repeating her earlier joke. "I just wonder what goes on with you. I sense you don't open up with your emotions. There's always control when you're with me."

"What's wrong with control?"

"It limits a person."

"Are you like some of the women who believe a man requires changing to suit what they want from them?" I paused as I could see her reaction. "Have you considered we have little motivation to change, because we believe our actions are logical? Frankly, it may be that men aren't willing to change."

"Pity. There's no benefit in living in a freezer with a cold heart."

"That's a bit much. I'm not cold. If you care about someone…well, you protect that person's emotions." I could be leaving China in a few days, or weeks? I wanted to balance my emotion and not risk escalating our relationship. Lily looked out to sea and I followed her gaze, noticing how full and clear the moon was. Lily's words repeated in my mind, *You don't open up with your emotions.*

She breathed in the sea air before saying, "I accept who you are. There's no real problem between us."

"If there is a problem, I realise the problem is me trying to control everything," I said softly. Moments passed in a maze of thoughts. There was vagueness in knowing what to say. I searched for the right words. "Look. The sea out there will only reflect the moon if the water is calm."

"Is that how you feel? You must realise the power of a sea cannot be tamed."

"Well. It would be different if I felt calm about us. I need to have more control. It's wrong to seek pleasure for pleasure's sake." There was a sense of being powerless over my inner emotions. There was a strange disconnect between my thoughts, feelings and actions. We'd reached a stalemate and I realised the stress I felt over controlling my emotion.

"You're weird." The 'you're' was elongated. "I've no idea how you got so messed up. You like everything to be right and in its proper place." Lily pulled away a little but her eyes stayed fixed on me.

I studied her expression before saying, "That's true. I've always liked things neat and tidy."

"It's noticeable." Lily made me feel transparent.

"You see things clearly. I like neatness. My mother told me she seldom needed to clear up after me. Yes, it's good to have things as they should be." I'd babbled on. "You're a special person, but we shouldn't be blinded by emotion."

Lily pulled a face. "Yes, you're weird, but I understand where you're coming from. It's okay with me. You're not like those men trying to get close for the sake of it."

The air started to chill. The wind had increased and was blowing from the sea onto the land. Leaves in the trees picked up the breeze and were starting to whisper. A change of day was happening. Looking to the horizon, the large red sun's light was failing. The last of the sunset, with its blood-red hue, was swiftly dimming. I decided to pull Lily back closer as I was losing the strength to control my emotion. In an instant, I felt increased comfort and peace of mind.

"I'm glad you understand me…it's not clear to me who I am, or…why I do what I do," I stumbled over my words. "But my reasons are simple enough. Doing my best gives me satisfaction."

"The psychologists would identify that you act like a little boy scout at times. You always want to do good deeds." She was measured.

"Maybe," I confessed.

"Perhaps we should leave the psychology until another time. We're all different in one way or another."

"Good idea. Let's not deal in psychobabble." She didn't react. "We should return before the weather changes and it gets darker."

I expected we would return but Lily was keen to show me more. "Okay, but I want us to see the famous sculpture of the tigers before we leave."

After a short stroll along the beach, we arrived. My eyes widened on seeing the sculpture. I liked the arrangement and intensity of the tiger group. There was a fluidness of movement. The sculptor had caught the spirit of big cats going off on a prowl after seeing something that attracted their attention. The intelligence and grace of movement pleased my senses. I insisted Lily was pictured in front of the sculpture. She backed toward the tigers and did something typical of her fun character. She raised her two hands in a claw-like pose. I caught the special moment on my mobile.

"Label the picture, Laohu," she said. "It means tiger."

I looked at my phone. "Yes. You certainly look a tiger. That's so…good."

Lily came over to look at her image. "Meooow, or should it be purr?" She was like a child with a natural flair to make things fun.

"I never realised Chinese people could be funny."

"Bigot." She then switched to poetry. "Watch out as I'll be burning bright in the forests of the night."

My lips were forming a response but then I changed to, "I lack your quick wittedness."

"Well, I could always *growl* at your seriousness."

My eyes lifted. "See. You know how to get the better of me."

"Is that the best platitude I will get?" We walked off grinning from the banter of our exchanges.

We picked our way back across the pot-holed car park. Lily looked radiant in the last glows of the dying sun. I looked at her and felt a bond had been developed between us. The wind died and the sun fell below the sea's horizon. We mounted the bike to set off back to the city centre. The gear was engaged and the clutch let out slowly. This time we rode in a more leisurely way. We swayed around corners rather than dipping low at break neck speed. The shroud of the evening dusk was descending and blotting out the beauty seen earlier in the day.

"I'm stopping for food," she shouted above the engine noise.

We stopped at a vegetarian restaurant that offered a choice of healthy-looking dishes. We sat on plastic chairs in front of a table with a well-used plastic cloth. I used a serviette to wipe the bowl and chopsticks. I could see the bowl was stained and didn't look hygienic. Lily watched my actions and reacted, "I'll order hot tea and you can dip your chopsticks in it if you're worried."

Without discussing the menu, Lily ordered the food. It arrived quite quickly. The mixed mushrooms were the most delicious. She explained the black ones grew on trees, and were good for the lungs. The talk drifted to the time when Lily first started teaching. She explained there was the need to show she had a strong character or the Chinese students would have pressurised her into making things easier for them. I judged it wouldn't have been difficult for Lily to assert her authority over the students.

"Because I'm Chinese, the students thought I would be easy on them."

"Probably by your being Chinese, it motivated you to want more from your students."

"You understand."

It was good to let her relate the memories of her teaching. It allowed me to understand her resolve to do well in anything she judged important. The time passed quickly and when we left it was quite dark. I wanted to ask Lily to do one more thing. I was focussed on sorting out the mystery surrounding Matt.

"Can you take me into town?" Lily simply nodded. "Okay, take me to the bar where Matt goes."

"He'll wonder why we're together."

"I'll see him alone. I don't want to complicate things."

"What do you want me to do?"

"Give me his mobile phone number. No need to take chances. I'll only call him if I can't find him in the bar."

We set off into town. Lily continued to ride her bike in a less thrilling way than earlier in the day. But my excitement level was rising in spite of this. The nearer we got to Comrade's bar, the more eager I got at the prospect of meeting Matt.

Chapter 20
Comrade's Bar

We parked the bike a short distance from the bar and Lily passed me Matt's mobile number. I punched it into my phone in case it was needed.

"I'll find out what Matt knows. I'll work it out."

Lily wished me good luck, and we high-fived each other. I walked toward the bar, while Lily waited a couple of blocks away out of sight. It was time to get down to the serious business of checking out Matt.

Dark clouds were chasing each other across the night sky. It seemed the moon was being battered by waves of black clouds. I ducked into an alley beside the bar's entrance, screwed on the gun's silencer and concealed it under my leather jacket. I surprised a rat that stopped to look at me, raised itself up and then scurried away. The alley was full of the mess of empty bottles and rubbish bins. Some overfull metal bins were located around a side emergency-door to the bar. I noted the side door thinking it offered the availability of another exit if required. The alley gave way to a deep pavement area and the front of Comrade's bar. A neon-sign flashed above the main front door and reflected off the plate glass windows.

I entered Comrade's and went over to order a beer at the bar. A line of barstools, most occupied, fronted the length of the bar. Across the back, above shelves stacked with bottles of drink, some colourful neon-signs spelt out *'cocktails, relax to the beat'* and *'cool it'*. The place resembled a European style bar, as Ibiza techno-music pumped out to enhance the ambience. This seemed the type of place that would suit Matt. A pleasant-looking barmaid approached me and said, *"Ni hao,"* to welcome me, before asking in English what I wanted.

The place was busy and a number of people were sat, drinking at the bar. Some nodded at me in a gesture of welcome before going back to what they were doing. Looking around I saw a few European faces, including Matt, in the corner with a Chinese girl. She was wearing hardly anything to cover her legs and body. A skimpy shoestring top exaggerated her fragile shoulders. I noted the tight-fitting clothes cheapened the look of her and detracted from her attractive features. She leaned over to Matt and I'm sure she nibbled his ear and then kissed it. Matt seemed happy with the attention he was getting, but little did he know how things may change given my arrival. It was good that no other people were sitting with him. Looking around, I could see a high number of expatriate individuals were scattered around the place, drinking and eating. It was going to be interesting to gauge Matt's reaction when he saw me. I didn't acknowledge him but watched him in my peripheral vision. An English guy at the bar said "hello". I took the opportunity to give myself an alibi for being there by buying him a drink. He introduced himself as Gary. We chatted about his job in the harbour area, which was mainly about the poor standards of work from his contractors. I positioned myself to watch Matt's activities, while speaking to Gary. After a short while, Matt made his way toward the bar to get another drink.

"Why, it's you. Hi, Harry," he said, with a welcoming tone on noticing me. "What're you doing here?" He patted my shoulder. "Did those two tough-looking Russian guys find you this morning? What did they want?"

I was confused. Matt showed no signs of stress, nor used language that covered up what had happened. This wasn't expected.

"How did you know I met some Russians?"

"Ohh, I recognised the accents when they were asking for you. As I speak a little Russian, it was enjoyable to try out a few words." His approach was quite natural and not scripted in any way. "Glad to see you relaxing, Harry. I should introduce both of you to a girlfriend who's with me." He smiled at Gary thinking him my friend.

"It could be better if your girlfriend came over here. There's something important I want to talk about. It's personal, so it's better if we're alone. Perhaps she could speak with my friend Gary while we do that."

The concern shown on my face may have prompted Matt to agree. He called the girl over and I introduced Gary and myself to her. "Tell you what, Matt," I said when she arrived, "how about if I buy some drinks now and then we both sit in the corner. I want to discuss something privately with you. Is that okay?"

"If you want." His confirmation was a relief.

The girl had poor English, but I got the impression he wasn't with her for conversational purposes. I asked her if she minded waiting while I spoke to Matt, but she didn't understand my meaning. That didn't matter. Matt's girlfriend didn't seem to worry about whom she spoke to and was happy to meet Gary. Matt came with me and we carried our beers to the corner seat. I waited a moment to let him relax to enjoy his drink before becoming more serious.

"I'm going to level with you, Matt. I'm here in Dalian to find out about the students' deaths. I know you've information about them." Matt didn't show any surprise or tension.

"I've thought you're different, Harry. So that's your game."

"You're right. I'm finding out things. I wanted to see you because I know you had some involvement." I wanted to be clear. "I'm here because you can help me. How about starting from your story of what happened?"

He responded calmly, "Relax, nothing is easy about what happens in China."

I tried to escalate the situation. "I don't want to relax. You can make it easier for me. Tell me what you know about the student deaths!" My knuckles tightened and I had my bad cop face expression. I assumed it would create the right effect, but he just looked like he was considering my question. He then took a long draught of his beer. I kept my tensed look.

"Piss off, Harry. You English are far too serious at times." His tone was stronger than expected, so perhaps my approach wasn't working.

"I'm acting with authority – so of course I take it seriously." I checked Matt's reaction to judge if he would react well to my new approach. "Two students have died which makes it serious."

"What are you getting at?" Matt didn't look worried. "You've authority? Who do you think you are asking me these questions?" He then went from calm to angry. "You're acting like an asshole."

I answered in a measured way. "Look, Matt, I'm here on official business representing those students from a legal perspective. An important group has asked me to help," I lied but needed a cover story. I hoped he believed this story as he never bothered to ask who I was working with or why James hadn't been given the task.

"Official business? I guessed you were asking too many questions for a newcomer." Another draught of beer was consumed. I wasn't sure why he drank so quickly, but perhaps he always drank like this.

"I said it was serious. That's why I have to ask these questions."

"I don't know what you want. Why question me?" He put down his drink and folded his arms.

"You wrote letters with Amanda to help the dead students who were in the trial. You tried to get their release from the experiments."

"Well, everyone in the office writes letters for students for one reason or another. But the thing is, none of us know what went on in that trial."

"You were more involved than others."

"What do you mean?" he was unhurried in responding. "You're clutching at straws, Harry."

"We know you went to the Institute of Technology without permission. So tell me why, as news of that wouldn't sit well with James, your head of school."

He unfolded his arms. "Okay. Let's get this over with. To start with, there are the secrets about the way the students died. There's also another secret about a member of staff having an affair with a student. The letters were because the students wanted to get away from the trial. For one of the students, it was more pressing, as he wanted to escape the affair and the university." I said nothing to let the quietness of the moment encourage Matt to open up. "Well, I went to the Institute of Technology to find out what was happening. They were our students and that's how much I cared. No one else would chance talking to the officials."

"What did you hear?" I relaxed my look once he seemed more willing to tell me what I wanted.

"I heard something you may find interesting. They reported the post-mortems had shown the deaths weren't related to the medical trials but probably to food poisoning. If that's right, there's no link to the medical trials."

"What – food poisoning?" My eyes widened and my head moved backward. "Are you sure this is not a simple cover up?"

"There's no cover up. The hospital forwarded details to the police in case it was a local restaurant that caused it. The police didn't follow it up because no one else got ill at that time. Food poisoning here is not unusual. I'm sure you realise that it's a regular problem in China." He looked anxiously over at his girlfriend, who was getting on well with Gary. "Emm, did you know about the rice wine that killed people because it had industrial alcohol in it or the pesticides in the ham that killed people? Or the way authorities allow markets to sell wildlife animals that can lead to SARS or other viral infections? It's kept low key here, as China doesn't want bad publicity. That should allow you to understand how food quality is a big issue."

"The other secret – about staff having affairs. Tell me those secrets?" Matt stalled at this question and put down his drink.

He rubbed his lips with his thumb and forefinger. "Damn you. Why ask about that? It's personal matter about a colleague."

"I already know there was an affair going on between a member of staff and Cheng, the student who died." There was a short period of silence but I couldn't wait any longer.

"And…" I elongated the 'and'.

"Well, I tried to stop it as it wasn't right. I pressurised the student to stop and told the member of staff I would expose the whole story if they continued with the affair."

"Did SHE stop the affair?" I interjected, to get to the point.

Matt's brow creased. "She? Why she? … No him. It was Geoff." My mouth opened in surprise. I had lost concentration for a moment. I refocussed in an attempt to get things straight in my head. Matt went on, "Geoff went mad when I told him I knew. Soon after this, the student came to me to say he'd broken off the relationship. But apparently, Geoff threatened he would let the boy's parents know about the boy being gay if he finished their affair."

"What did Cheng say about you asking Geoff to stop the affair?"

"Cheng told me Geoff didn't want the relationship to end. He told Geoff he was seeing another boy and it had to stop. Geoff wouldn't listen to him. All of this is why Cheng was desperate to leave Donghai to be at another university."

"Another student told me you put pressure on Cheng?"

"No. I didn't need to. My knowing about the affair was enough. Being gay in China is unacceptable, so I assumed Cheng would not tell others. Knowing this, I promised him I wouldn't tell anyone, and he should do what he thought was for the best. He stopped seeing Geoff. After that, I noticed Geoff drank far more and became distant." At the finish of this, Matt picked up his glass and downed his remaining beer. We both became quiet for a moment.

"That's about it," said Matt. He gave a weak smile.

I looked down at his empty glass. "You deserve a drink after that. Let me get another in."

"I trust this has all been in confidence, as I haven't shared these details and I went to the institute without permission."

"Don't worry, I'll not share any of these details."

"What's your real background then?" He fixed his eyes on me. "British Council?"

"I've important contacts and they wanted to use me to get to the truth. I can't say more than this."

He didn't question me more and said, "Well, it was nice finding out about you. Perhaps we can get together more often."

We made our way toward the bar. Matt pulled out his mobile. "I've a call to make."

He stopped short of the bar, looking at his girlfriend. The girl was perched on a high stool, which raised her short dress to the top of her thighs. She had a trill voice and was speaking more English than earlier. Gary was exchanging phone numbers or WeChat accounts with her. She'd obviously got on well with Gary. I stood at the bar waiting for the drinks and took the time to reflect on what Matt had told me. It was like functioning in two parallel worlds. I was concentrating on paying for the drinks but then paused and stopped. *Eureka*, a flash of memory struck me. I remembered the qualifications of the staff I'd seen when checking on their backgrounds.

I visualised the one person who had the practical skills to make a poison. Geoff Flounder had taken a master degree in microbiology and a first degree in chemistry from good universities. The knowledge he had would make it more likely that he created a poison. Perhaps there was a logical link to his reaction to Cheng's rejection of him. Things were clearer now, and the dots were being joined in the right way. I was pleased I'd waited to check on Matt as it seemed he was one of the good guys trying to help. His actions showed he cared enough about the students to risk going in person to the institute. He'd also tried to stop the affair and had done this without breaking any confidences of what was going on. The breakthroughs were coming. At last, there was something more concrete to work with.

Comrade's bar was starting to get quite busy. I could see customers lining up behind me at the bar, some holding out money trying to get served. Matt was still making his phone call and I made my apologies to leave. He was in deep conversation and raised a hand as if to say goodbye. I wanted to get back to Lily to talk about Geoff. As I left, there was the tell-tale look of warm feeling from Gary to Matt's girlfriend. They were both leaning forward to each other and laughing. In the bustle of people at the bar, I saw the girl squeeze Gary's thigh. She obviously didn't give two shits about her relationship with Matt. At the time, I had no idea about the trauma and tragic things that were about to occur at Comrade's bar. I exited onto the wide pavement and quickened my pace to get back to Lily, to share the revelations I'd uncovered.

Chapter 21
How They Died

I left the noise of Comrade's bar and walked along the dark streets. As I made my way back to Lily, I realised my head was spinning from what I'd learnt. Lily was sitting astride her motorbike, looking at her mobile phone. The light from its small screen glowed in the darkened street. She caught sight of me, shut down the phone and watched me approach. Her eyes followed my every step as I moved toward her. I held her gaze while feeling pleased to see her.

"I was worried, so was thinking of coming to the bar," she said, before I got within four metres. "Did you get what you wanted?"

"It went well. I know more about what happened with Cheng." I looked at Lily, realising the mistake I'd made about her. "I've figured out who may have killed those students."

"Did you find out how Matt was involved?" She saw my eyes open wider. "...was he?"

"No, not at all. Matt's totally innocent as far as I can judge."

"But you said you know more about Cheng and who may have killed the students."

"This may sound crazy. Would you believe that Geoff may have poisoned those students?"

She looked confused and became silent for a moment. She leant forward on her bike. "Geoff, No... Poisoned them? Why?"

"We could be dealing with a crime of passion. Cheng was Geoff's boyfriend before he died."

"My god, that's awful." She closed her eyes to think. Her hands came together on her lap. After a moment's thought, she opened her eyes. "*Shui luo shi chu*. Oh yes. It's clearer now. Cheng told me a tutor was giving him so much pressure it was making him ill. I thought it was work pressure."

"Who was Bao and Cheng's close friends?"

"He-Ping and Tao Zhang."

"I need to speak to He-Ping. He'll remember me as I spoke to him in the office."

She nodded. "I'll call him."

Lily rang a number and gave me the phone. "Hi. Is that He-Ping?" I asked.

"Yes. Who this?"

"It's Harry Long. You met with me recently in the office with Ian Clarke and also for a meal." He-Ping remembered me so I continued, "I want to ask you about the day the two students became ill."

"Ahh huh?"

"Did you see Geoff Flounder, the English tutor, give any presents or food to the students who died? Possibly he gave it on the weekend before they died?"

A short silence then, "I remember one thing. We were in big coffee shop when Mr Geoff came in. He said hello to Cheng." He paused. "Emm. They went to other table and Mr Geoff argued about things. But not loudly. I watched to know what was argued but never knew what."

"Okay, good. Did he give Cheng anything?"

"He did. When leaving, he give mushroom and beef take away from restaurant he's not taking home. He gave this to Cheng." There was another pause. "Emm. Mr Geoff left and Bao came to see us. Bao and Cheng talked. I saw they eat mushroom dish together before leaving."

"Do you think it made both of them ill?"

"It's hot cooked. I don't think it's food problems." He paused. "It's all I remember."

"Thanks. You've been a good help to me."

We both said goodbye and I gave the phone back to Lily.

"Can you do an internet search on poisonous mushrooms on your phone? Also, for ones that have been cooked but can still be poisonous?" Lily opened her Safari page. After a few minutes, she looked at me.

"Got it. There's a poisonous substance called a mycotoxin that can be developed in mushrooms as a mould. It appears cooking does not get rid of the toxicity for the more powerful types."

"That's it then. Geoff could have developed a mould on a mushroom using his knowledge of chemistry. Cheng had met someone else so Geoff may have been insanely jealous and this possibly turned to anger. Perhaps he decided to kill Cheng but didn't realise Bao would die as well."

"That's terrible." She gasped.

"He knew enough to grow a mould that would be lethal if ingested. He must have thought he wouldn't be linked to the death. He wanted its effect to seem like a natural form of food poisoning."

"I can't get my head around this," said Lily, still looking at the details on her phone.

I nodded. "It's clever as no questions would be asked. Unfortunately, Bao must have been unintentionally involved as well. So, it's this situation that has complicated the whole story surrounding their deaths."

"Well, I would never have guessed it."

"Then, the authorities weighed in, thinking it was linked to the medical experiments."

"Need to make a call of my own now." I phoned my Dalian contact number to get confirmation evidence of my suspicions over Geoff. I asked if they could check on emails from Geoff Flounder to see what he wrote to either Bao or Cheng. I also requested them to look at his private email accounts, as well as the Donghai University one. I was sure he wouldn't have compromised himself on the university email system but wanted every possibility checked. I also asked for analysis of the phone calls he'd made.

I looked at Lily. "If this was a crime of passion, the emails will identify the motive. Once my people check on the messages from him, we'll get the full picture."

"Well done, Harry. You're people will help us to finally solve it."

"Well, one part only."

"Emm. One part? The motive is clear." She frowned. "We can treat this as poisoning now. It means the medical trials weren't what we needed to worry about."

"I'm afraid the medical trials aren't straightforward. They involve something that is probably for dangerous military reasons. It's why the Russians are intent on finding out about it."

"Now I've got the feeling you haven't finished your investigations. I think you owe me a full explanation of who you are."

I felt I couldn't lie or deceive Lily any longer. She'd already become heavily involved in my mission. She'd seen the way I operated and we'd been through a lot together. It may not have been what my people would want me to do, but I felt it was right to give her the truth. So I told her. "I'm working for a foreign government. I'm an agent." There was a silence. "I've put my life in your hands telling you this, but I trust you. There's a lot more to do and you need to decide if you want to join me. If you do, we need to check if the medical experiments will lead to terrible new weapons."

Lily studied me as if letting everything sink in. She then simply started the bike and leant forward for me to get on. She turned to me. "I'm with you on this…all the way. Let's go back to my place."

"Okay. Nothing more to do here."

"Will you be able to find out more about the experiments?"

"Yes. I expect to."

"Good. We can find out what dangers these experiments are leading to."

My phone rang. "We have broken into Geoff Flounder's emails but need time to scan for keywords and any important messages. I'll ring you if anything turns up." I tried to concentrate on the caller's words, but it was difficult as what sounded like muffled gun noises were coming from the direction of Comrade's bar.

"I think I hear gunshots."

"Okay. Phone back when you can. Bye."

Lily's bike moved stealthily forward and turned into the road where Comrade's bar was located. The night was dark from black clouds partly obscuring the moon. As we neared the bar, we passed Matt's girlfriend being half carried and dragged to a side turning. It looked like two Russians were taking Matt's girlfriend away. She was distraught and was trying to look back toward the bar. Before she disappeared down the side turning, she screamed out some garbled words. Seconds later, we arrived opposite the door to the bar and things became obvious. On the floor was Matt's body being intermittently highlighted in the flashing lights from the neon sign. Blood was pouring from a wound to his head and running in rivulets along the pavement. It had been a fatal shooting. His man-bag lay open and nothing could be seen inside it. The window of the bar was broken and it looked like a submachine gun had raked along the wall. Perhaps people in the bar had also been injured, but Matt was the obvious target for some reason. It looked a hopeless situation. I decided it was better for us to keep going rather than stop.

"What the… Oh no…" Lily said in breathless pauses. She slowed the bike, then stopped. The engine idled sending out thudding sounds.

"Go! Don't stop!! It's Matt!" I shouted.

"Let's help Matt," she begged.

"Go!"

She hesitated and continued to look at the scene. I pushed at her back. "Go – now!"

Her fingers released the brake and twisted the throttle. We sped up again before she braked. There was a screech of tyres as a shiny black Chrysler SUV emerged from a road in front of us. My instinct kicked in as everything pointed to them being the killers. The black SUV must have been parked out of sight before getting away at speed. Perhaps Matt's girlfriend was inside. Did she work for them or had she seen too much? I noted the number of the SUV but didn't intend to follow it given it might compromise Lily. The worry was they could trace her through her licence plate number if they spotted us. I decided it would be too risky to follow them.

I dragged the mobile from my pocket and input the SUV's licence number. It was difficult to punch in the details while still on the bike. I forwarded it with a simple, *'trace this number'* request. The SUV roared away into the night's other traffic. There was no benefit in trying to follow it.

My mobile vibrated and pinged:

'The licence plate is related to FSB as all checks indicate this is the highest probability.'

"The killers were FSB, so keep going!" I shouted. I had no time to discuss this as there was another clear ping. I took a while to read it as the bike vibrated at low speeds:

'Flounder's private Hotmail account and phone call pattern compromises him in a relationship with Cheng. He intimates his love for him in the text and begs him to come back to him. There is nothing to indicate any form of blackmail or threat in the correspondences, from either Cheng or Flounder. No other people are mentioned.

The information closed the circle on what had happened to the students. I made a call to the field agent base.

"Donghai one."

"Hi, Harry. Was the information useful?" my usual female contact now sounded pleased.

"Yes. Thanks for details on Cheng and Flounder. I've some information that ties up with the texts you hacked into. It indicates Geoff Flounder could have poisoned both students."

"Poisoned! Their deaths are not involved with Eagle then?"

"No. It's nothing to do with the medical experiments. It could be a murder. I'll let you know more when we meet."

"You've figured it out?"

"Think so, as it's got to be poisoning." I stared forward at the road, hoping I'd solved one part of the puzzle.

"Seems like you're doing well. I'm sure there will be phone records to show their contact pattern with each other, but the evidence from the texts looks to be enough."

"Yes, the motive was probably old-fashioned passion."

"What happened with the gunshots?"

"The Russians just killed Matt Groom. I'm now wondering if they got him mixed up with me."

Her voice became more assertive. "We'll catch up on the detail at our meeting. We'll see you then."

"Sure thing." The call ended.

There was a tension in the way Lily drove. It was less fluid and quite deliberate with each turn and manoeuvre. She was obviously feeling some unease at seeing Matt's body. I guessed this reflected sadness in her mood. It wouldn't be long before her emotion from the past events spilled out in a wave of memory, remorse and grief.

Chapter 22
Lily's Place

Lily drove more carefully after seeing the body of Matt outside Comrade's bar. We arrived and she stopped at the side of her apartment building without speaking. I watched her put the bike on its centre stand. She pulled the bike smoothly back keeping silent. She remained quiet and it was hard to tell what she was thinking. I felt I needed to understand what was worrying her about Matt. She seemed hurt and distant. To console her, I tried to gain her attention by putting my hand out to her. That didn't work, as she anticipated my approach.

"No, no... No. Don't try to comfort me," her directness threw me. It was obvious Matt's death had affected her.

"Is this becoming too much, Lily?" We stood facing each other. She was on one side of the bike, while I was on the other.

"We should have stopped, Harry. Should've stopped."

"No need." Lily looked bemused at my words. I repeated my message. "Lily, you must understand that Matt didn't need us."

"Yes, he did. We should have stayed to see if we were needed." She frowned and bit her lip.

"It was dangerous, so we had to keep safe. The gunmen could've been trying to kill me. Have you thought that perhaps I was the target rather than Matt?"

"I needed to be there." She looked at me. "You don't understand what's going on inside me."

"Try me."

"It's not good for me to go there." Her eyes looked tearful.

"It will be easier if you tell me."

"I was reminded…" she choked on her words and her tears formed. Lily put her hand over her mouth as if to stop her words. "When my mother died of cancer I was studying in the UK. She needed me with her. You know – in those last hours of life. But no one insisted I went home. It became a weight that has been dragging me down."

"We had to leave Matt because it wasn't safe."

"Are you listening? I wasn't there for my mother or Cheng and now Matt." She looked at me and tried to explain more, "In the UK, I felt my mum wanted me to keep studying. At the time, I didn't feel like I do now." She looked sideways and thought for a second. "Here, a person's relations are expected to feed and look after the sick. It's a duty to care." She gave a loud sniff. "When I came back to China, I had no mother. I felt guilty and it was like a bottomless pit."

I tried to deflect her thoughts of guilt. "Grief for a mother is normal."

"The feeling has lasted a long time. There was no closure and I'm left with this hollow feeling." I walked around the bike and stood near her. The bike made soft metallic crackling noises as it cooled.

"Don't punish yourself. Guilt is a stage of bereavement."

"You don't get it?" she stiffened. "You're so matter of fact telling me about stages of grief."

My mouth went dry. "I'm trying to get you to see things in a clear light."

Lily shook her head. "My father told me he kept looking at the empty bed after my mother's body had been wrapped in the bed sheets and removed. He couldn't bear to talk about it," her voice dropped to a whisper. "If I'd a brother or sister, we would've shared the pain. I wanted comfort. Do you know fathers seldom hug their daughters in China?"

I inhaled, wondering what to say. "I understand your pain." I moved closer to Lily. Perhaps she needed a hug, but there was just a strained silence.

"I've been hurt before, and I'll be hurt again. I think you're the next person to hurt me. I don't want that."

We looked at each other, trying to find a way to resolve the discussion. "Having regrets isn't logical. I move on." Lily looked unhappy at my words, so perhaps I should have said something else.

"Well, I suffer more than you then, as I don't move on." Pain showed across her brow. "I feel empty. I want to feel full of love, not pain. You'll move on, but I'll be here missing you. No one will comfort me then." I was hoping the dam would break and she would release her emotion. I wanted an opportunity to cradle her against me to let it all out.

I reached out and took Lily's hand. There was warmth from her small hand. "Life's not perfect. We're human, and our bad fortune stays with us."

"I know the world is all about happiness and sorrow." Her eyes drifted to the sky and fixed on the brightness of the moon. "The rainbow has to have rain and clouds. It's the yin and yang we talked about in the park."

"Good. Try to find the balance. Perhaps you can then move on." I increased the grip on her hand. "Sorrow will depress you unless you get rid of it."

"I'm not sure if you've a soft side, Harry. I don't want any more talk about a person moving on."

"It's about coping with what life throws you. Everything needs time, so don't make yourself a victim."

"How do you deal with suffering?"

"I've conditioned myself. I don't have self-doubt about what's happened in life. Decisions I've made were right at the time. So, I never beat myself up over what I've decided or done." I opened and closed my mouth without continuing. My mind drifted back to some of the dispassionate actions I'd carried out as an agent. "My strong mind protects me from pain." My expression was non-apologetic.

"Are you serious? Don't you feel pain or emotion?" She pulled her hand away from mine and there was a tension in her. Her emotional scars were deep. "I'm just more sensitive than you."

"In life, we have to make decisions and live with them. I'm careful when I make my mind up – but when I do, I live with it."

"Shit, Harry. Things suck here with all that's gone on. If I wasn't trying to help you, this would be the time for my goodbye. You've certainly made up your mind about us, and the way things should be. You want to control everything. Perhaps you're too cold for me?"

"Look. I want to free up our feelings, but it would lead to future pain. While I'm in China, this is no game; I'm on a mission. I killed a man and more shit is bound to happen." A car's headlamps swept across us as it manoeuvred to park.

Lily closed her eyes and opened them, as if rebooting her emotions. "Okay. We understand each other better now. I feel this was our first quarrel together." She looked at me as if trying to judge my reaction. "It allowed us to know each other and how we feel differently about life." She smiled and became more relaxed. "Let's have some nice hot cha to thaw you out."

There was relief in the lightness of her remark, so I simply responded, "Cha will be good."

It was reassuring that Lily could end this difficult conversation in a comfortable way. She had a number of attitudes to life and a power to her emotions. I admired her caring nature, her brightness and principled attitudes. In fact, I'd never met anyone quite like her. I hoped she could accept my point of view about death and life. In some ways, I felt a fraud, as I'd not told Lily the reasons for my attitude toward remorse and guilt. There was so much she didn't know about how I dealt with the violence of my job or how I felt about her. It was as if we were living in parallel worlds that had to be kept separate.

We entered into her apartment reception area. The plastic bags with food containers and rubbish still littered the floor area. All was dim, quiet and stagnant. We walked across the lobby area to take one of the lifts. The lift took time to arrive, which meant more people congregated around us and waited. Some had foul smelling food in plastic bags. I breathed in shallow breaths as the strange smells were affecting my breathing. The lift door opened and a woman came out pulled by a small dog, which looked desperate to relieve itself. Lily pushed the button for the eighteenth floor. The lift moved at express speed, and after a few stops, the door opened. We crossed to her front door; she opened it and locked it behind us.

"I hope you can put up with my little flat. I know you find it small."

"It's okay. I can relax here."

The fragrance of her familiar perfume filled the room's air. It was a welcome change. I took the gun from my trousers and put it on Lily's shelf between some small green plants and a round jade bracelet. A glow of light came through the window, but the sea was a blacked out blot with a few lights from the ships entering harbour. Lily drew the curtains, but their thinness did little to cut out the light.

She pointed to the shelf area. "You make some green tea and I'll take a shower." I looked over at the kettle. Lily saw me look. "It's all there on the side."

"Are you hungry?"

"Of course. Chinese people take food seriously. I'll phone for a pizza when I finish here."

"I need the toilet. Got to go."

"Okay. I'll organise the food."

I took a pee. The shower room was modern and the toilet was Western in design, which was a relief. Toiletries spilled along the shelves, with some creams and sprays in a small basket on the floor. Given Lily didn't seem to wear make-up, I wondered why many beauty products were littered around the small room. A hairbrush sat on the shelf with long black strands of hair trapped amongst the bristles. Beside the brush was a plastic cup with one toothbrush and Chinese branded toothpaste. There on the shelf was a bottle of Daisy, the Marc Jacobs perfume. This was an intimate space. I washed my hands, enjoying the fragrance of the soap. Finally, I checked my hair in the mirror and came back into the shell of a room.

Lily gathered some things and disappeared into the shower room. "I'll have that tea when I'm finished in here," her voice echoed above the start of the shower.

I made the tea but it got progressively cold. I looked around but couldn't feel neatness was present. The room was like a box full of oddments. I sat, looked out the window and waited an endless amount of time until Lily finished her shower. She emerged in a pretty thigh-length floral gown, attempting to dry her wet hair. Every time she stopped using the towel, her hair fell in black wet strands to her shoulders.

"Your turn," she said.

I went into the shower, and after a couple of minutes, the hot water turned colder. I didn't want to spend time under a cold shower, so turned the water off once it became tepid. I thought it better to remain casual, so wore my trousers and a T-shirt. The shower allowed me to feel refreshed and I looked forward to talking to Lily. I emerged and Lily had made the towel into a turban. She was sitting on the bed holding her phone. Michael Buble songs were playing on Lily's Apple iPad and the atmosphere was relaxed. Lily made a phone call to have pizza and snacks delivered. She gave me a beer from her fridge but took nothing for herself. The tea sat cold on the side.

"Don't worry about me. Cold green tea is more refreshing."

Within twenty minutes from the order for the pizza, a phone call from the courier confirmed it was about to arrive. Lily made sure I took the right amount of money and told me to take the delivery from the building lobby area. Local food in China was quite cheap, so I was surprised at the high cost for the pizza.

The courier was burrowing into a large box looking for the order when I arrived in the lobby. His clothes could have been those of a miner given the ground in dirt from travelling around Dalian. I took the boxed pizza, and its escaping aroma sent my juices running. It's amazing how the smell of such a simple meal can create such a large appetite.

I went back and we enjoyed eating the meal, while sitting on Lily's bed. I was happy to idle away the time. The conversation was about the music and artists we both liked. It was amazing as the playlist Lily chose mirrored my own taste. There was a friendly argument whether Robbie Williams was better than Michael Buble. We finally decided we enjoyed both of them, so didn't bother trying to pick a winner. I argued that Robbie made each song his own, and Lily insisted Michael was cooler than Robbie as he had a stronger charisma. It was a relaxing time after all that had happened. We discussed music and I found Lily also liked jazz, which surprised me. The conversation ended well as we both agreed Adele's second album *21* was one of the best albums ever. We listened to Adele and when the 'we almost had it all' line was sung, we both went quiet and looked at each other.

Lily broke the atmosphere, "I'll clear up tomorrow."

"Not while I'm here." I cleared the packaging and empty drink tins into the bin. Then, took them out of the room and placed them in the big dustbin on the landing, beside the lift. Lily displayed a contented smile, while I cleared everything.

On returning, I said, "No mess, no smell and no need to put off what is required. As you tell me – I'm happier to have things neat and tidy."

"Thanks, my tidy man. Now what side of the bed will please you most, because I've no preference?"

"Good – as I want to be away from the wall."

The conversation was taking the emotion out of sharing the same bed. We were supressing the earlier feelings and being polite to each other. Lily said she wanted to check her social network sites and suggested we would be more comfortable under the bed covers. I got in and placed my back against the headboard.

"I'll leave the music playing beside the bed. Turn it off when you want or it will go off after an hour anyway," said Lily.

She turned out the light, put her gown on a chair and walked toward the bed. The room wasn't dark and I caught a glimpse of Lily's feminine nightdress.

She wore a light green nightdress in a slip style, with shoelace shoulder straps. It barely reached the top of her thighs. Lily's hair was still damp, and the smell of her shampoo drifted around the room. She slipped under the covers, picked up her phone and started tapping away.

Her closeness generated the same emotion I'd experienced on Tiger Beach. I opened my phone and looked at the picture of Lily in her tiger pose. She was beside me and I wanted some contact. The anguish was consuming me. This was not helped by the line of her body form, which was outlined in relief by the bed covers. It was a distraction to my calmness. I slid onto my back and looked toward the ceiling to clear my mind. On seeing this, Lily assumed I was going to sleep. She moved across the bed and softly kissed my cheek. Her perfume was noticeable and the air became filled by her fragrance.

"Goodnight, Harry." I wanted to reach out to her and hold her but managed to control my actions. She went back to her texting and I closed my eyes. On drifting into sleep, my thought was, *If I do everything right, nothing can turn into a problem.* Nothing was straightforward for me though. My last thought before sleep was, *It's wrong to leave behind a complicated emotional situation.* Sleep came without a resolution of what should be said, or done.

I awoke to the bright light creeping into the room through the thin curtains. I squinted, threw an arm over my eyes and waited for them to focus. Lily realised I'd woken. "Morning, it's time to get up," she insisted, while pushing at my body to make me move. I simply grunted. Then she asserted herself by using the leverage of the wall and her legs to push me out of bed.

"No you don't." I grabbed her legs to stop her getting the better of me. "Don't pick fights with me." I pulled her toward me and we ended in a laughing heap on the floor. I felt pleased we both woke in good spirits and this had led to some childish actions. But amongst the giggles and pulling at each other, I became aware of the silky smoothness of Lily's legs. A feeling of passion hit me in the stomach.

This didn't last. She insisted as she jumped up, "It was a draw." Lily brought me back to my senses as she rushed, still giggling, into the shower room to get dressed. I pulled my trousers on, made some tea and waited for her to finish dressing. In the meantime with military precision, I picked up the rumpled bed covers, tucked them in and smoothed them out. Finally plumping up the pillows and placing them four-square in their place.

Lily emerged, took in the neatness of the bed and commented, "Perhaps you'll be welcome here again. I like your room service."

"Don't expect me to look after you on a regular basis. Anyway, I won't agree to be your personal servant."

"Well, I'm getting the measure of you." The morning's atmosphere remained calm as we didn't revisit the events of the previous day. We drank the tea and talked about the breakthrough in knowing more about what had happened. By then, it was time to meet Leo.

"I'm going now." I put my leather jacket on and pushed the gun into my trousers.

"Look after yourself. I feel worried about you." Then, with more emphasis, "REALLY worried."

We embraced tightly and Lily buried her head into my shoulder. "Don't worry. I'll be in contact when I know what's happening."

"Be safe. Those Russians are dangerous." The meaning was in her eyes. I made my way to the door and looked back. She mouthed the words 'be safe' again without any sound. I could only stare back at her.

It's strange how some people can sense the future. Little did I realise that Lily's worry was a premonition. I noted her concern but was not unduly worried. Assessment of risks was second nature when faced with the possibility of potential danger.

Chapter 23
Mother Ship

I waited outside Carrefour watching the speed at which the street vendors put up their stalls. Trestles, coverings and boxes of goods were part of an assembly line of activity. The noises of vendors and heavy traffic from the road merged in the morning rush hour. One loud horn after another sounded in order to get reaction from other drivers. The efforts were wasted as no one bothered to change their driving. I caught sight of Leo coming slowly toward me along the road. He was punctual as normal. At first, the activities of the street seemed ordinary, but then something caught my attention. After looking along the street, there was one aspect that required a second check. Leo drew up to the kerb, while at the same time I noticed a familiar SUV further along the road. It pulled in behind him about another hundred metres up the road, just after Leo stopped. I assumed Leo may have been followed. The SUV in the distance was like the one that I'd seen at Comrade's bar. I moved to the edge of the kerb to place the taxi between me and the SUV. I obtained Leo's attention and signalled him to wait. A small nod from him let me know he understood.

I made my way to the sides of the street vendor's stalls, walking behind different people. I closed in on the SUV. I walked with the crowds past the SUV, then rounded back on it. I went first to the side with the driver. I had taken my gun out and held it under my jacket. The driver was looking forward, but on seeing me from the corner of his eye, he moved his head sideways. A machine pistol was visible on the lap of his passenger. It looked like a Makarov, but I didn't know the model. We'd met before. These were the two slower guys from the fight outside the Institute of Technology. At first, the driver was bemused, but then recognised me and started to move. He grabbed at his gun and I wasn't about to wait for what may happen.

There was no way we could let these guys affect our mission. I smiled at the driver, while bringing my gun into the right position on the outside of his door. He knew the score but was powerless to move quickly enough. The passenger struggled to take his safety off and level the machine pistol at me. I placed the gun against the door. Three cracks from my gun and both men flopped sideways in different poses. I saw the first shot had not hit the driver in a vital area, so shot him again. It was better to make body rather than head shots given the situation in the street. A head shot could break the van's glass and lead to unwanted attention. The result was in my favour as both men were put out of action. In the noise of the day, no one seemed to notice or care. I replaced the gun into my trousers and walked away.

The mistake I'd made in not eliminating the Russians turned the normality of the day upside down. After only walking a short way between the street vendors, there was a burst of machine pistol fire. On hearing the rat-tatting noise, I threw myself to the ground and looked round. One badly wounded Russian had tumbled out, and in a bent over position, let off a second burst. Unfortunately, he'd hit a man with a child. The Russian stumbled forward and aimed another burst. This time, he hit the food stalls and a woman serving. Food flew into the air and the woman spun backwards from the impact.

Before he fired again, a man hit him across the back of the head with a large piece of wood. This was a call to action as other people descended on him, kicking the gun away. It was like a scene from Africa with hyenas attacking their prey. Each angry person was making a small but telling attack. I was convinced these actions would keep the police confused as to what had happened.

I went back to the taxi, only to find a confrontation was going on with Leo. I saw a Chinese person was holding open Leo's door and arguing for a fare to somewhere. Perhaps he was frightened by the actions along the street and wanted to escape the scene. I had a greater need to leave and I was in no mood for debate. I pointed at myself as if the taxi was waiting for me and then pushed the man aside. Leo's voice was angry as he pulled at the passenger front door trying to close it. I got into the back seat and Leo moved off. But he could only shuffle forward on clogged roads as the shooting had caused a major traffic jam. Groups of Chinese people had congregated on both sides of the street trying to see what had happened.

"Let's ensure you're not followed again by more of those Russians." I assumed Leo knew the drill about losing a car tracking him.

"It's good you find those Russians behind me, ah," said Leo.

"I'm always on the lookout for the Russians as they seem to know where I am. I don't know how they can keep tracking us."

I looked out of the window, trying to reassess things. Our taxi skipped in and out of shop glass reflections as I tried to think more clearly. I wasn't clear about why we were being constantly found by the Russians. My thoughts were broken by sirens and police cars passing from the opposite direction.

"Them Russians plenty trouble," he added.

Leo did his job well now. Doubling back a couple of times, then waiting to see if we were being followed. The manoeuvres confused me as I lost all sense of direction.

He turned to me. "We arrive."

We went down an alley and round the back of a small dingy building. A couple of CCTV cameras, which covered our approach, were noticeable as a security measure. The building was nondescript with small bared windows and no business signs, apart from a small trade plate. A roller shutter opened and we drove into a parking bay area. The door shut behind us whirring and rattling. Leo turned off the engine and I looked around. Another Volkswagen Santana taxi van and two other cars were parked in the area. We got out and Leo pointed to where we should go.

He led me to a goods' type lift, with buttons to select any one of the upper three floors. In the lift's corner was a sophisticated infrared CCTV system. It was far more sophisticated than any building in such bad condition would have installed. The lift moved, but the sensation was weird. There was no button to press for a lower-level area, yet the lift went down. The realisation we were going down felt strange. I supposed our descent was generated by someone who was watching us on a CCTV screen. The lift door opened to reveal a basement area. At first glance, the area and layout looked correct given its intended purposes. It was a cavernous underground area, filled with the scent of electrical equipment. Steel shelving supported one piece of electrical equipment after another, creating a massive collection of computers. Coloured wires criss-crossed everywhere through the shelving. The air was surprisingly cold, probably to help the computers work more efficiently. It was like a surreal grotto, as the lighting added a bluish tint to the whole area.

We moved on through a corridor of humming computers until we reached a green demountable looking structure. Inside, there were four Chinese people with headphones, each sitting in front of a screen. They were arched over their computers and never looked up from whatever task was being carried out. At least fifteen other screens blinked with coloured displays. Leo knocked on a door at the end of the room and opened it. Two Western people were sitting in the room, looking relaxed. They were sitting at an oval meeting table. A small Union Jack flag on a wooden stand and a conference microphone was in the centre of the table. Two large screens were mounted on the back wall.

They stood up. "Hello, Harry. Welcome to our mother ship. I am Joseph and this is Isabel."

"Nice to meet at last," said Isabel.

Both had a stance that was upright and military in deportment. We shook hands, but a salute may have been more fitting given their body language. I shook hands with a moderate pressure not wanting to convey a dominant brashness. Joseph looked a 'will do' type, brimming with energy and seemingly excited at the project. His eyes were young in a face aged from the grind and worry of undercover activities. Nothing like the current situation had happened in Dalian. Now it would be all systems go for this secret Dalian unit.

"Do get us a nice coffee, Leo," ordered Isabel in an assertive tone. Although I'm not a military man by background, I admire the British military services approach to getting things done. Isabel conveyed a strong presence and authority. I recognised her voice as the person who had regularly contacted me. She looked at me, "I'm sure a coffee will be good."

"Emm, thanks." I nodded.

"Great work, Harry." Joseph's eyes fixed on me. I was pleased at his enthusiasm in feeling I'd delivered what he wanted. "You brought us some good intel. Now we have it, we know it's big." He nodded at Isabel in confirmation. "Knew we'd get a breakthrough on their secret trial. Those science boffins of ours will have a field day now."

I walked over to the table and we all sat. Listening to Joseph, I got the impression he was a traditional Sandhurst-type character. If it had been an earlier era, he would have had the bowler and umbrella carefully stored for his return home.

Isabel picked up papers from the table. "Another jigsaw we need to complete SAP. Luckily our London people will help."

Joseph's eyes brightened. "Thanks to our efforts, the pieces are falling in place."

"Of course, but this info will lead to a lot of new questions. It's going to be a busy time for all of us," added Isabel, seeming to bring some realism to Joseph's eagerness. "I'll be happier to be involved with more stimulating tasks."

"Your time can now be applied to these secrets. Think you'll love that," said Joseph, looking sideways at Isabel.

Isabel straightened her body. "True. I'm not a fan of simple data handling. I'm looking forward to more interesting work now we have this."

"The big one has landed," he was upbeat. "At last this listening post can go operational. That should excite you."

"And it does. Certainly does! It's good to be operational at last."

I was drawn to Isabel as she seemed a spirited character. She wore a carefully pressed white blouse and black pencil-line skirt, which accentuated her small waist. The blouse had one too many buttons open, indicating she was not a typical, dreary civil servant. Her type of shoes didn't match her other attire, given they appeared sensible with low heels. Her hair was long and parted in the middle, which flattered her slender nose. It was noticeable that her face looked pallid in the artificial light.

Joseph turned to Isabel and patted her knee. "We're certainly going to motor forward on this one."

Isabel looked upward at the ceiling with a disdainful gaze. I wondered if this was a regular reaction and one that had failed to change his behaviour. The way he acted was decidedly old-fashioned.

The copies of the reports and other items I'd collected from the Institute of Technology were laid out on the table. He waved his hand over the different items while looking at Isabel. "This is what our job is about, my dear. Think how happy London will be when they analyse this lot." Joseph was more patronising than anyone I'd met in the service. The more I watched him, the more it was possible to understand him. He was in a time lag and a generation out of date.

Leo came in with a tray full of coffees and a plate of biscuits. "Just what I need," I said. "A real cup of coffee." I picked up my cup in anticipation. "That looks great, thanks."

"Need to have standards. Emm…even here in China," said Joseph. "That's not easy as we're a bit cut off here. We stay here in our special accommodation nearly all the year, which means we don't get out much." He glanced at Isabel. "This place is confined and, well, Isabel gets 'cabin fever'." That was understandable to me, as I would hate a limited life in a basement.

I noticed the green intensity of Isabel's eyes when she responded. "Any sane person holed up here should feel claustrophobic. And especially if the company bores them – and they need more social interaction."

"Look," said Joseph. "Harry here can stay for a drink and chat. It will be a nice break for you. There are some Italian dishes in the freezer, and we should open a nice bottle of wine…or two."

"I'd like a glass of wine." My taste buds went into anticipation mode.

Isabel wasn't going to make small talk for long. She turned to Leo as he raised his cup to his lips. "Leo, get us a couple of the tech boys to run us through the findings they've made so far. Tell them it's got priority and we're waiting for it. And be sure to bring some of our wine back with you."

When Leo stood up, it reminded me to explain to Isabel my earlier comments about him. "Perhaps, Leo has trouble with me as I'm quite fussy, but I'm getting used to him and his driving habits." Leo looked back at me with a strange hooded-eye expression. I looked down, shook my head twice and smiled. Isabel just ignored me.

"I'll chivvy things up," said Joseph, following Leo and letting the door swing shut behind him.

"If things move quickly on the assessment, we'll know what's required," I said, putting down my empty coffee cup. "I'm looking forward to my future orders."

"We'll see what turned up from what you collected. The tech people are excited, as the Chinese are pushing the boundaries of genetic research," she responded.

I took the gun from my belt and placed it on the table. "I collected this from the Russians who tried to attack me."

Isabel frowned. "A Yarygin pistol! It's interesting the Russians don't use lightweight alloys but still go for metal construction. It's because they don't trust using polymers like we do." She picked up the gun and weighed it in her hand. "They nickname this gun, 'the rook'."

"Yes," I said, "but we never moved quickly on design either. Thank goodness we now get a choice of the Austrian Glocks."

"We've different weapons and explosives stored here, but we keep a low profile. We've never needed them. It seems funny because until now, everything was based upon our being invisible."

"What's your role here?"

"I run the monitoring unit. That means I stay in this building most of the time." She pouted seemingly not contented. Perhaps she was bored in being shut away from her social network of friends. "We're like moles, as it's an isolation unit."

I realised why she had a pallid complexion, but there was no time to find out more. The door opened and Isabel turned, probably to check if the wine had arrived. Leo came in and held the door with his foot. Joseph followed, with one of the technical people trailing him. The technical person walked round us in a hurried way. I noticed Leo had two bottles of wine with him. He took them over to a side table with wine glasses and tumblers on it. Without asking, he poured the wine into three glasses and gave one to me. Isabel went to the table, picked up her glass and swigged back half of it.

"Dao here has interesting information for us," said Joseph, without properly introducing Dao. He picked up a glass and slurped the wine. Dao placed a computer on the table and connected an HDMI lead to a port connector. We arranged our seats to view the screen. The lights were dimmed and one TV screen on the end wall became blue. Dao loaded the computer with data from a USB. The rest of us sat expectantly. All was quiet apart from the keys being tapped. The first page was projected. It was in Chinese, so I was reliant on oral translation. Thankfully, Joseph gave a clear synopsis of the content. He was obviously fluent.

"It's the right report. See that." He waved a finger in the direction of the screen and some Chinese characters. "The title is Eagle. Perfect, we have the right files." Joseph fell silent while concentrating on the pages. No reaction came from anyone else. I assumed Isabel could also read the files.

"Next one." A couple of pages were scrolled through. "My god! We need to get expert insight," said Joseph, focussing on the screen.

I was bemused and Isabel said, "Harry, this is extremely important. If my translation is correct, this is about genetic reprogramming."

"It is," confirmed Dao. A few more pages were displayed.

"I still don't understand. What reprograming?" I enquired.

"This is a series of trials to somehow reprogram cells or to generate them in some way. It's about altering DNA," said Dao. "It looks like they use chemicals and oscillating magnet fields to achieve the changes."

"Yes. That's it. They're affecting genes and creating different combinations," added Joseph.

"There's a list with lots of details about the people participating in the trial. And, we have the names of the lead researchers conducting the trials," added Dao.

Dao flicked through a number of graphs and tables of results. There was a diagram, which was probably based upon the equipment used. Next was the picture of what looked like a big cabinet with a heavy metal door and coils of electric cables on round bobbin shapes. They looked like small towers with wired loops. I told the group about Lily knowing a large transformer had exploded.

"Can we trust this Chinese person?" asked Joseph.

I never paused with my answer. "I trust her. She has shown many qualities that make me feel we can work safely with her."

"Let's be ultra-careful. You need to keep a close watch on things," Joseph emphasised everything as if a stern father figure.

"Goes without saying," I said. "What're we doing with all the materials?"

"We've sent the copies to our boffins in London for scientific insight. We also need to wait for London to give us orders for what we need to do," said Joseph.

"I think we've done well from our end," said Isabel, before finishing her glass of wine.

"Certainly have. This warrants a toast. Let's open another bottle," added Joseph, reaching for the bottle. Leo went to the water dispenser, at the side of the room, and returned with a plastic cup of water for himself. Dao went to the side of the room and made a call.

"With pleasure," voiced Isabel. She stood and beckoned me to her. Dao turned off the projector and raised the lights. I went over to Isabel. She put her arm in mine and pulled me close to her body. She exerted sufficient strength to allow me to recognise the contours of her form. My reaction was to feel uncomfortable as I'd already assumed she was lonely and wanted some attention. I felt she wanted to dominate my personal space and take control of the situation.

"We're getting there," said Joseph "Well done, Harry."

"Yes, well done," said Isabel as she pulled at my arm.

"Come and sit down, Harry." Joseph leant back and put his hands behind his head. "Let's all celebrate." I was thankful to Joseph as I could politely pull away from Isabel and relax.

"This Pinot Grigio is good wine," said Joseph, draining his own glass before recharging ours. "Cheers as we've certainly done well." Joseph took on a joyous expression. Perhaps he could see a promotion opportunity from the progress we were making. "Here's to Jinying and our good health."

The taste of the wine wasn't as crisp and fruity as I would have liked. I drank three glasses before I realised it was a Chinese branded wine. I didn't need more, but Joseph kept filling my glass rather than asking if I wanted more. He was a good host, but I noticed he never offered the Chinese staff a drink.

The success of the day and the effect of drinks provided a party atmosphere to the occasion. The talk drifted into areas where we had common experiences. Joseph and Isabel reminisced about the culture of London from museums, art galleries and restaurants to favourite walks. We talked in an approving way about the places we loved or knew of. The conversation was warm and friendly. This acted as a means to strengthen the relationship between us all. It was a mutual reinforcing experience.

"We want you to stay here tonight. That's better than you staying with that new friend in the city centre. We have a spare room for you," said Joseph. "We're not sure about her yet, but it's being checked on. Never know if these types are on the Chinese side."

I nodded but made no other response. It was not worth saying anything positive about Lily as clearance procedures would be the deciding factor. The drink relaxed me and had made me feel tired. I was happy for Leo to take me along a corridor to a small modern bedroom. The room was basic but nicely furnished with what looked like IKEA furniture. There was a small ash wood desk and chair, a double bed with throws on and a colourful striped armchair with modern lines. Table lamps and soft lighting added to the room's relaxing ambience. I texted Lily to let her know what was happening. I also mentioned that if she'd picked up on the noises in the street near Carrefour, not to worry, as everything was perfectly okay. My first choice was to sample the shower, which I found was modern and clean with a rain-shower fitting. Transformed, I stepped out into the room with a towel around my waist.

There were two soft knocks on the door and it opened before I could get to it. There, in a pink satin, kimono-shaped dressing gown was Isabel. Without uttering a word, she stepped into my room, closed the door then locked it. This wasn't good.

My eyes narrowed. I became aware that I would have to deal with this awkward situation. "Did you want something?" The words were a mask, as I already understood what she was intending.

"I enjoyed reminiscing," she said. "I miss many things about England." Her eyes fixed on my bare chest and then skimmed across my body. "One in particular. I've not been close to a man for at least six months."

"I understand that, but you're in the wrong place coming here."

"Don't you know you're tantalising – it will be good for us to share some sex?" I'd already realised that she missed some of the excitement of life, so her willingness to assert herself sexually was clear. I felt no intention to give her what she wanted. I didn't feel I wanted to be the one who was going to spice up her isolated existence. My decision was easy. I considered her a sexual predator, not a potential lover.

"I don't want this," I said softly. "I can see you've misjudged me. You have to go."

"Are you a man?"

"Let's calm things down. You shouldn't have come here."

"Why not? Free love liberates us all."

"Nothing about free love is unconditional. Please go." Isabel didn't turn to go. She smiled, so I explained myself more forcefully. "I don't want physical pleasure with you. I think it's best you leave." I was looking for the harmony and moral balance that I'd become more aware of.

She wasn't upset. "Well, are you sure you want that?"

I paused trying to find the right words. "Look! I think it's best for both of us. Then there's no regret."

"Well, if you don't throw me out, I'm going to stay." She wasn't taking into account my feelings and simply stated, "I'm not leaving."

"In that case, I'm throwing you out."

She sighed then responded, "Don't... I don't want you to."

"This is madness." I was getting irritated. "I don't want you to stay here. So, please leave." Nothing was getting through to her.

"Come on. I'm not mad, Harry." Her eyes widened as she let her dressing gown slide from her body to the floor. She was naked apart from a pair of briefs. The light fell gently on the different curves and provided her skin with a sensual sheen. I looked away to her gown lying on the floor and went to pick it up.

"Get OUT of my room," I insisted, offering her the gown. I held the gown out for her but she didn't react, so I folded it and placed it on the back of the chair. "I'm going back to the bathroom. I want you gone when I come out." I went into the bathroom, took off the towel and put on some clothes. I took my time and cleaned my teeth before going back in the room.

I came back to find Isabel was stretched out on the bed, with one arm behind her head. She moved over to one side of the bed and patted the sheets. "Let's play."

I rolled my eyes. This needed to come to an end. I walked over to the door, unlocked it and threw it open. A glimmer of light came in from the hallway. I went back, took Isabel's gown from the chair, and threw it over her body. Her eyes widened a little, but she never moved.

"You haven't a clue what you're missing," she murmured through pursed lips.

"I'm not interested in anything you may say or offer."

In one movement, I scooped up Isabel from the bed. She smelled of a mixture of wine and perfume. Her arms held on to me round my neck. I carried her outside my room and stood her against the wall, before pulling her gown more tightly around her. Through half-closed eyes, she muttered, "Shame we didn't find a way to enjoy the night." I simply looked at her, thinking she had lost all semblance of her dignity.

I'd nothing to say, so left her there to listen to the door closing and being double locked.

Chapter 24
The Boffins' Assessment

I woke refreshed, then dressed without taking a shower. The phone in the room rang. "Are you ready? You need to be at our conference meeting in fifteen minutes," it was Isabel back to her normal self.

"That's all right. I'll be there."

"Okay. Don't be late." As expected, the conversation ended without politeness.

I came into the main office area and found Joseph, Isabel and Dao huddled round a computer screen, sipping coffee.

"Get yourself a coffee from the pot and some toast," insisted Isabel. She followed me with her eyes as I made my way across the room.

Joseph turned to me, "You'll be interested to know we've got the detail. It's as we thought. Our boffins have told us they are dealing with something related to changing genes or interfering with the science of epigenetics."

"Epigenetics? Sounds important," I said, while in the process of devouring a slice of toast.

"It is. Come with us. We're getting debriefed from London in a few minutes. The scientists understand what's going on." Joseph led the way to a comfortable room with a large screen on one wall. We sat in blue-coloured executive-style seats. It was like being at a private film premier. The screen flicked into life. A couple of inoffensive looking scientists were pictured staring back at us.

"Thanks for staying up late to brief us," said Joseph, without introducing anyone for security reasons. "We understand you have the detail, so can you tell us what you know," he spoke toward a conference-meeting microphone.

"We have studied the materials. It's clearly related to reorganising DNA sequences," said the scientist, taking the lead. "The Chinese are attempting to use aspects of genomics and molecular biology to modify DNA."

"Does this warrant us worrying about the experiments?" Joseph questioned.

"They are developing something that's potentially lethal. They're attempting to modify DNA to use as a form of armour to protect their people. Other groups, not protected by the change, could be affected by whatever viruses or chemicals they release."

"How advanced are they in the game?" asked Joseph.

"When we say epigenetics, this is a whole new branch of biology. We've never seen this before. The Chinese are attempting to change the sequencing of DNA and gene production. This change will remain in the population. Any change they make in DNA can be handed down to future generations. It will remain as part of their gene pool in children. This means children can carry the new DNA protection from birth."

"Give us an idea how important this is?" continued Joseph, staring at the screen.

"Well. We're always going to see biological changes to human evolution and DNA. That's basic Darwinism, where organisms develop over time. But right now, the process is being escalated to develop new forms of warfare. They are far beyond the realm of 'Dolly the Sheep' experiments. The Chinese are trying to use genetic techniques to achieve changes that will give them a military advantage."

"What sort of impact could this cause?" Joseph leant forward.

"Those who develop these new DNA changes will be able to selectively kill people." We exchanged glances, waiting for the right response. The side of Joseph's clenched hand hit the table with a thud.

"Christ. This is an immense national security danger!" Joseph grimaced.

The one talking on the screen looked sideways at his colleague. "My colleague will let you know what they're attempting."

"We can identify they are attempting to unwind some of the DNA strands in their trials and then reprogram certain parts," reported the second scientist. "It's the edge of a new era. Some of the four chemicals that make up DNA are being affected in clever ways." He paused to collect his thoughts. "They're trying to provide new human blueprints by rewriting individual DNA."

"This is worrying, given it's at an advanced stage," said Joseph. "It's definitely worrying."

"Yes," responded the lead scientist. "A virus can be used which produces a mild flu or no effect in a reprogramed DNA person, but the general population will suffer deadly secondary effects. For example, they could select a modified Coronavirus. This would be lethal to anyone not carrying the new DNA."

He went on. "I want to keep this simple, but it's not simple. We've not seen experimental designs like the ones they have utilised. They have used an interesting combination of applications." He picked up copies of the papers and then dropped them back on the table. "They combine chemistry and magnetic fields to change the DNA coding."

"Can you give us an outline of these applications?" asked Joseph.

"Okay. First, they administer repressor proteins to silence active regions of the DNA. Second, they use oscillating magnetics to create an electronic wave targeted at the DNA cells. The energy level from this provides bands of neutrons which affect organic matter. This leads to DNA coding changes." He paused to let the information sink in.

His eyes became focused as if we were in the same room. I realised he wanted to emphasise something. He gave a short reminder of what he'd said. "So, in summary, a minute part of the DNA is first switched off by chemicals. This is possible because DNA is simply a number of chemicals making up a set of rails, or rungs in the double helix, all held together by hydrogen bonds. The targeted chemicals are dosed, and when made unstable, act as receptors for change. After this, a selected DNA area can be affected by the magnetic oscillations." We became focussed, trying to take in his explanation. He added, "We know from research at Caltech University that electrons can act in RNA as a primer for change. The active RNA starts the process, which leads to a new DNA configuration being formed. In normal biology, the DNA would be repaired, but the Chinese experiments overcome this."

"How does the combination of these work together?" asked Dao.

"In simple terms, the membrane of the DNA cell loses its strength by the administration of the repressor chemical. Then, the DNA cell held within the membrane can be modified by a finely targeted electromagnetic wave. The Chinese are using this technique to develop new sequences as far as we can tell."

Joseph changed his body position to look around the room. He paused to give time for others to ask questions. Not getting any reaction he asked, "How near are the Chinese to developing this?" We listened for the possible response of the two boffins, but they sat with expressionless looks.

The lead scientist broke the silence, "Technology in China to achieve this seems to be evolving rapidly and surpassing other nations. We believe they're accelerating their trials, so we must slow them down." He went on, "In fact, the implications of its final use are they could take out selected individuals, world leaders, their older aged people or whole country groups."

"Now we have this knowledge, how do we deal with this?" I asked.

"We can discuss that later. I don't think we need to keep the scientists here any longer unless you have more questions," said Joseph. No one indicated they had anything more to say, so he thanked both men for their inputs and Dao switched off the link.

"There's a need to allocate the planned tasks," said Isabel, once the screen went blank.

"Yes. We need to rack up the operation," retorted Joseph. He pulled his chair round to face the group. "The plan is quite dramatic I'm afraid. London has already cleared the planned actions with the various government agencies."

"So they must have realised the importance of moving swiftly on this," said Isabel.

I wanted more detail. "I never expected the Jinying project to be this extensive. So, can we know the overall objective before we get down to task details?"

Joseph trotted out the obvious. "Our objective is to affect the research findings of the program."

"That's sensible," I confirmed.

Joseph looked in my direction. "We cannot allow this biological warfare research to succeed. I'm sure you realise the necessity of this."

I was more concerned with the short-term actions, so asked, "What does your dramatic plan mean for us?"

"We have assembled a list of those taking part in the research program trials. Using the list, we intend to interfere with the research outcomes," said Joseph.

"Please be clear about this, Joseph." Isabel turned toward him. "The others need to know we're taking out selected people. So, when can everyone know the plans about eliminating a few of the participants in the trials?"

"It's more or less finalised. We'll do it on a planned basis, and with a means of death that will not be easily identified by a pathologist," he replied in a matter-of-fact way. "That will make them think they need to modify their approach, and so slow them down."

"Hadn't we better start?" she asked.

"We're going to get advice on how to administer a substance that provides for a seemingly natural death. London has dispatched a special form of fungal prion already."

"What's a fungal prion?" I asked.

Dao provided the answer, "It's the same sort of thing that causes mad cow disease. We may also use a brain cancer causing agent as well." He looked at me. "The cause of death should mirror the experiment," Dao added. "This is very important now. There's a need to confuse their research approach in order to slow down their efforts. If we get them to think that the experiment went wrong, it should lead to a focus on the pathology of the deaths."

I felt frustrated. "Can't those dumb bastards come up with a better plan than killing young people?"

"This is the plan, Harry," emphasised Joseph.

His emphasis felt unsettling. "Is this final?" I asked. "If it is, then this isn't the best decision or solution. These are innocent people that you will order me to kill. Surely, it's better to destroy the equipment to slow them down." The group turned toward Joseph.

"Christ, no. Think how it will affect international relationships," he responded. It was obvious Joseph would bulldoze ahead with the agreed plan.

I doubted the plan. "We can go for the institute, destroy the equipment and make sure another country takes the blame."

"False news or any news on this is not in the plan, or required. If we eliminate some participants, the Chinese government will continue to cover up these secret experiments," Joseph was adamant. "If by chance they find out what we did, they will suppress the details. Then, no international incident will occur."

Lily's worry about the bad and the good people of the world were whirling in my thoughts. "Eliminate. Let's be clear – you want me to murder innocent people. That's not a good solution." I sensed everyone in the room became tense, but went on. "Get someone else to do this as I can't follow the plan. You need to send me back to the UK."

"Steady on. We know your record. You've eliminated people before," he sounded severe.

"This is different."

"Don't be fucking idealistic. You've a job to do." His jaw stiffened. "Remember you work for the greater good?" He was devoid of compassion for innocent people. It was obvious the final decision was made by London and nothing could change now.

Nothing seemed right, but protest was of no use. I knew the plan had been agreed. "I'm formally requesting a transfer to another assignment."

"That's unfortunate. We'll let London know your reservations and see what they want us to do. I'll let you know," Joseph reverted to a more military style. I sensed he didn't like my attitude to orders. If I'd been in the military, a court-martial would have suited him, rather than having to inform London of my request.

"Where's Leo?" asked Isabel. "He can take you back to a safe house we're going to arrange. We can bring you back in to tie up things when everything is a little clearer. The safe house is more secure than anywhere else."

"He's in the big office," said Dao.

I collected my things and went with Dao into the main office to find Leo. He was busy. Leo took a call, and then went back in the other office to talk to Isabel. I would have left with him, but while waiting, I looked across the room and by chance spotted a small picture of Lily on a screen. I walked over to the screen. Under the picture amongst some Chinese words was the number 18. I looked more closely. I was able to read 'clearance denied – suggest clean', in English amongst other Chinese characters. The one word I reacted most to was, 'Clean'. Until now, I'd followed orders without question, but after seeing the screen, my mind started racing. There was a surge of disbelief, then anger.

Leo came back to pick up the keys to the car. I told him I was going to say goodbye to Isabel. He said he had some things to collect and would wait by the lift. I went back into the inner room and only Isabel was there.

"Are we cleaning Lily?" I asked in as calm a way as possible.

"I'm afraid so. You know the score. The project needs to be free from links to us."

176

"Is it necessary?"

"She didn't get clearance. You need a better place to stay, and we need to have her taken off the security risk list. We'll make it look like a bike accident."

"Taken off! What you mean is die," the words camouflaged the reality for Lily. "So you mean to murder her along with others!"

"Get real. You've been trained not to get close to nationals while on an assignment. So, what's wrong? You should know the reality of these situations."

"It's not right. That's what's wrong. Lily won't be a risk to us." There was a twist of anguish in the pit of my stomach. I decided there was no way I'd let her be taken away from me or this world.

"Too late for a discussion. The decision was made at a higher level."

"Shit. Why do those in power end up being the abusers?"

"Joseph told you we're doing this for the greater good. We'll cut off any lose ends for the sake of security."

"There's no morality in any of this."

She made no comment. It was then I made my decision. Like I'd told Lily, I believed that when it was time to decide on something, there would be no regrets about that decision. I was going to change my life. Whatever the outcome, I knew it would be right and easier to live with.

Chapter 25
Doing Things Differently

What was planned didn't fit my moral compass. There was a struggle between my loyalty to orders and those of conscience. Things until now were straightforward, but I wasn't willing to accept the new ways of working. My discussions with Lily had started to make me think about what was important in life. I'd developed an alternative perspective of who I was and what I did. There was little doubt that the Eagle mission's impact had led me to question myself. I was clear that things had to be done differently, as my allegiance was to my conscience. That clarity gave me the courage to do what was required. Yes – what was going to happen was right, and my life was about to be rearranged in a major way. Amongst these thoughts, I had a flashback to my student days. I remembered Hook had written 'some men are eventful while others were event-making'. I'd always believed that conviction needs to be linked to action. Now I was way beyond being disenchanted; I'd become self-aware. It was now my time to act over future events. A fork in the road had been reached and I was clear on my direction.

My mind was made up so I reacted without a second thought. There was no way things could happen as London planned. I took a deep breath and this caught Isabel's attention. She had no idea of my feelings or how I would rebel against the plans and my country.

"Sorry, Isabel." She lifted her head in a confused way. I took the opportunity to hit Isabel hard on the chin. Her hair flew up and her head jerked backwards. I caught her body with my left arm as it dropped in a limp heap. Then, I dragged her across the room and placed her behind the table out of sight.

There was no time for delay. I broke open the cupboard holding the arsenal of guns and explosives. There were shape charges and C3 explosives, which I placed in a pile on the table. I also took a handgun and its silencer, plus a number of small items to help with my plan. The pile was too obvious to carry. I went into the outer office and asked Dao for a strong bag to hold the things Isabel wanted me to take. Dao asked one of the operatives to give me a holdall. I went back into the inner office, loaded up the holdall and then left, closing the door behind me. For good effect, I made out I was saying goodbye to Isabel.

There was something else I wanted to take. "Give me a copy of the list of the Eagle participants that we need to use for the eliminations, Dao. Isabel wants me to study it." He seemed bemused but did what I asked.

I met Leo and we travelled up in the lift together. As soon as we got out, I tried to phone Lily to warn her. The phone rang and went dead. She'd blocked calls. My phone bleeped with a message: '*teaching now so will talk later.*'

"I need to go to Donghai University first," I told Leo. "There's something important I need to do before going to the safe house." The roller shutters cranked down behind us and we left the building without incidence. I sent a text message to Lily:

'*They are trying to kill you because of me. On my way to you and will phone later. Hide somewhere.*'

Isabel recovered sufficiently to stumble out the room to give the alarm. Nothing was calm in the building after that. Screens showing CCTV images were being scanned, but it was too late for a lock down of the lifts and doors. We had departed just in time.

Joseph knew he had to take full responsibility for the events, and his blood pressure reached the highest point it had been throughout his entire life. He broke out in a sweat when he realised we weren't visible on the CCTV screens. Isabel stood at his side, holding her chin, while rotating it slowly from side to side. "How…did…this…happen?" asked Joseph, in a faltering monologue. He was rightly worried about being relieved of his senior role. Like any retired CEO, he was going to find out how it feels to be powerless and lacking in status. Joseph was a drowning man and there was no one to rescue him.

Isabel felt strong enough to speak. "I should have realised Harry's not to be trusted. He thinks he knows best and enjoys getting on his moral high horse."

"Why? Why?" He became more perplexed. The worry was sucking him down.

"That's your problem. You'd better check his file to understand what he's going to do next."

"Can we track him?" asked Joseph. He looked at Isabel, wondering about the next move. When there was no reaction, he used a more assertive military tone. "Tell me how we'll get that bastard?"

Isabel remained quiet. She crossed her arms tightly together, and her eyes took on an intense look. She was planning to take revenge for her isolation, her rejected advances and the impact on her pride.

"Deal with this, Isabel – now!" Joseph could feel his field agent unit being stripped from him. "Christ, just do it."

Her arms dropped and she spun around. She went to the open cupboard in the inner office and took out two of the remaining Glocks, a machine pistol and some ammunition. Isabel came out with the weapons in her arms, ignoring any further commands from Joseph.

"Fix this... Go fucking fix it!" he ordered to no one in particular. His mouth opened and he took in air to control his emotions.

"Come on, Dao," barked Isabel.

She rushed to the garage area where the Audi S3 was parked. Dao pounded after her. They jumped into the car and Isabel took to the driver's side without discussion. The roller doors creaked open once more. The key was already in the ignition. She started the car, put it in sport's mode, kept the revs to the red line and roared off. Turbocharged air increased torque to maximum levels and tyres squealed. This was a woman on a mission, getting some excitement at last. She opened the voice system in the car. Back in the basement, her people were concentrating on the pursuit. For them, everything was small blobs moving across a map on their monitors. The car tracker system fed back data to pinpoint Leo's road position. This information was relayed to Isabel, indicating Leo was taking a different direction to the university and not the one planned for the safe house.

The S3 was driven with anger and resolve to catch up as quickly as possible. Isabel was hunting her prey. "Get the cleaners on the task to eliminate two targets. Like two minutes ago," she ordered in her military style. "We've got a female target, Lily Wang, and our agent, Harry Long. If I don't kill him first, both will be at the university. So send our people. And make sure you send pictures so they're sure of the targets."

Isabel got updates on where the taxi was in relation to her. The speed at which she drove the S3 meant she quickly reduced her distance to the taxi. She got another update. "You're a block away. They're definitely making their way to the university." It was the message Isabel wanted. Now she could contact Leo.

There was a crackle from the taxi dashboard and then her voice boomed. She was giving a command to Leo in Chinese. Leo's grip tightened on the wheel.

He exchanged looks with me. "FUCK, Harry! What you do, ah?" The taxi pulled over, the brakes were slammed on and it half mounted the kerb. My head banged against the headrest with the impact. The engine stalled and there was a click as Leo locked the doors. I rummaged into the holdall for the gun.

"Move, Move, MOVE!" I shouted. The car remained stationary. "You'll have problems if you ignore me." Leo pushed the button to drop down the gun. I'd already prejudged he would do this. Rather than shoot Leo, I cracked my gun down on his leg. It was hard enough to ensure he had no further thought to try anything.

"Be careful, Leo. I wasn't always happy with you – but I've grown to like you. So, will you leave this to me?" I asked him, while pushing his gun back into the dashboard and out of sight. "Touch that gun again and I'll kill you."

A screeching noise from behind led us to turn round. Leo was starting to panic. "Fuck. Oh… Isabel, she's here!"

I gripped my gun. "Open this door before I shoot you in the leg."

I was hoping Leo wasn't thinking of being a hero. He'd seen me in action on several occasions and had gained full knowledge of my capability. Showing understanding, he used careful hand movements to unlock the doors. The doors clicked and I opened my door. I was ready for action and planning to obtain a tactical edge.

Leo looked over to Isabel and became worried at seeing her tapping her mobile. "She's doing a telephone code. She must be blowing us!" he shouted. Everything was out of control. Leo started to open his door and I'd reacted by diving out with my holdall. A split second later, there was a red and yellow flash beside me, followed by a deafening boom. The taxi lifted by about two metres. From my position on the ground, I saw Leo flying upwards. The explosion rang in my ears as a hot blast surged past me.

Poor Leo hadn't a chance. The explosion was contained to the interior by the reinforcements to the taxi. This directed the force of the explosion to the weakest point, which was Leo's door opening and the floor panel. It was surreal, given the way things turned out. Leo was dead and I'd not known anything about his personal life or even understood him. No need to dwell on his loss as this was self-preservation time. It was time to go into action and enter my zone. I stood up knowing Isabel would have stopped her car at a safe distance. The danger was clear, which triggered my reaction of entering the zone of no worries, no nerves; I became tactical.

Through the smoke and flames, there was the indistinct image of Isabel and Dao, guns in hand, walking toward the taxi. I noticed they were walking toward me over open ground. They should have come closer in their car for more protection. Perhaps Isabel was so incensed, she was losing her sense of judgement.

I scrambled behind the burning taxi, pulling my jacket over my mouth to deal with the smoke. My eyes smarted, and the acrid fumes were making me cough. I peered out over what was left of the back of the taxi. They spotted my outline moving through the smoke. Dao fired a machine pistol, but in a continuous mode rather than bursts. *What a lack of training*, I thought. I ducked and the taxi's protective armour took a number of the bullets. Dao needed to keep using both his arms to pull the barrel down to counteract the upward force of the rounds. He wasted a lot of shots.

I peered over the metalwork to follow Dao's outline. When I was sure of a clear target, I rose, took a breath to steady my aim and took him out with a central chest shot. When raising myself above the cover of the taxi, Isabel had a chance to fire. Before I could get her into my sights, a bullet ripped through my left arm. It turned me round and threw me to the ground. Isabel wouldn't stop now. Her desire to kill me meant she was going to follow up on the sight of my falling.

The pain in my arm was from the exit wound side. I examined it to see how much blood was flowing. If the bullet had severed an artery this would probably take me into unconsciousness in a short time. Thankfully, the flow seemed normal. A combination of adrenaline and survival instinct focused my mind. There was a need to reassess the situation. The taxi was crackling and popping with strange sounds as it burnt. The tyres let off black acrid smoke. Smoke keeps low and can obscure movement. I took a deep breath and crawled around the other side of the taxi. I could use the smoke as a screen to hide me. My lungs were suffering intense pain. I felt a desperate need to come up for air but kept hidden. It was obvious Isabel was making her way toward my previous position. I waited for a moment, then stood pointing my gun in the direction Isabel should be found. She was there on the other side of the taxi. She was keeping low and looking to the ground where she'd seen me spin and drop. My lungs were at bursting point. I aimed to fire but needed to take a breath.

My arm wasn't steady and I missed. Isabel reacted and turned to me. She pulled off a shot, but the bullet missed by a mile. Now I was steady and didn't miss. *Goodbye, Isabel*, I thought, *but what a waste.* She had ended up dead, lying in smouldering debris. I picked up my holdall and walked away, checking my arm for the blood flow. Luckily the damage from the gunshot had missed my bone and large veins. I placed a handkerchief on the wound and pressed hard to staunch the flow. It didn't look too serious.

Chinese people stopped in cars some distance away and were watching, taking pictures on their mobiles and probably contacting the police. Like any onlookers to such a scene, they craned their necks to see, but from a safe distance. I broke into a trot, went through some flats and emerged onto a wide main road. My ears were ringing and ambient noises were muffled. The buildings tracked by like a film in an out of focus blur. There was a need to keep a clear head. The main road was busy and my relief was instant when a taxi, with the red for hire sign, came toward me. I put the holdall over my arm in front of the gunshot wound and hailed it down.

The driver opened his window, leant forward from his seat and asked something. He was obviously enquiring where he should take me. I opened the door and got in but had no idea how to tell the taxi driver where I wanted to go. I knew if I sat in the back of the taxi he wasn't going to refuse to take me. I pointed down the road; he shrugged and turned on the meter. He asked me something again, but only after my stronger gesture to drive did he start off. My thoughts turned to Lily and her safety. I was anxious as I needed to get back.

Chapter 26
Meeting Geoff

"University, the university," I repeated. There was just a blank look and a stream of Chinese from the taxi driver. I tried again, "University," but he couldn't understand where I wanted him to take me. My mouth was parched and I tried to wet my lips. I changed my request. "Donghai," I repeated a couple of times using a different tone. It worked.

"Oh. *Da Xue Donghai*."

"*Shi*," I responded. He now picked up speed, knowing the destination. This driver was a madman compared to Leo. The only thing the driver didn't do was a handbrake turn. His urgency was a relief, as it met my need to get back as quickly as possible.

I took out my phone and tried but failed to get through to Lily. A whoosh of air and a change in noise signalled the taxi entering a dark road tunnel. I caught a glimpse of myself in the taxi door's window. I'd not realised how blackened my face was and how much debris was in my hair. I looked and felt like I'd been through hell. I peered at the reflection and ran my fingers through my hair to remove some of the debris. Seeing my blackened face, I assumed if any spectators had taken pictures of the fight, my appearance would confuse the police. My arm wasn't hurting too much. I checked it and was thankful to see the flow of blood had eased. Luckily my wound was to my muscle.

I hadn't relaxed. The adrenaline continued to course through my veins. I was desperate to contact Lily. I tried to phone twice more before she answered. The beeps of the call were endless… "Come on…come on…"

"Hi, Harry. I've been worried. Where are you?" The relief in hearing Lily was instant.

"I'm coming back. I'll be back with you soon."

"I got the text. Can you tell me what's going on?"

"I'm near the university. You need to go straight to the main office. Meet me there and don't show yourself until you see me."

"Why? Am I in danger from the Russians?"

"No. It's worse than that. It's my people."

"What about you. Are you okay?"

"Things have gone wrong. My arm needs attention as I've injured it."

"I'll take care of you."

"There's something more important. We're both being pursued by professional killers." I took a calming breath. "You're in real danger so take care."

"My God. What's happened?"

"I'll tell the whole story soon. Oh, and don't go near your bike."

After I finished talking to Lily, my phone rang. It was Joseph.

"Look, Harry, it's not too late to come back in. We don't want you doing anything rash."

"I can assure you I've weighed things up. I couldn't go along with your plan to kill some innocent people."

"Harry, I've respect for your work with us. I pulled your file and saw your profile. It indicates your clearance is at the highest level for loyalty. So, what do you think?" There was a brief silence. "We shouldn't have made our decision about Lily without involving you. We failed – so come back in."

"That's bollocks! Things have gone too far," I snapped, disregarding his words.

"Not that far. In China, it's said whether a cat is black or white, it does not matter as long as it catches mice. So, we need you to stay with us."

"What shit are you peddling me? I'll simply be hung out to dry!"

"Let me be clear. You've no prior experience of a country like China. You've found something here that has changed your ideas. We realise that."

Perhaps Joseph had a point as I'd had no concerns over the politics of my actions until now, but why? I wanted to support my country but felt shell-shocked at the events. I needed to be clear about myself. Everything churned around in my mind and my thoughts spilled out. Yes, I had a love of my country. But was that enough if people in charge were making decisions I couldn't agree to. There was a need to reflect on what I believed in. It was possible to return, but if I went back, could I take similar orders? I couldn't. So I was sure the ways of doing things didn't suit me now. One thing was correct because Joseph was right; I'd changed since arriving in China. The change was obvious to him, and any assessment of me would label me a misfit. I was now someone who wouldn't follow future orders without question. There was no way they would let me back. My final decision was clear.

"Sorry, Joseph, I've lost trust in the service. I'm sure you've lost trust in me."

"No. We can square things if you come in," he prompted.

"Nothing makes me believe there's a neat solution."

"You're accountable to Britain, NOT China. Where's your love of country?"

"That accountability doesn't allow for moral questions being asked. I'm not a political pawn of Britain anymore."

"It's your duty to return. There's a need to support your country." I didn't respond. Joseph continued, "Trust us. We'll reprocess you. You'll be sent back to the UK to join another team."

"Bullshit. You'll never trust me again." I heard Joseph sigh. "It's the new politics that worries me. Everything has changed – and you do things differently than in the past. You think you're running a gentleman's club, but that's far from the reality of what goes on."

"No. Nothing has changed in what we do." There was an air of resignation. "We do everything to protect Britain."

"Perhaps you should reflect on the new ways of doing things then. I'm not coming back in and am clear about myself. Goodbye, Joseph," I ended the call with more clarity over the correctness of my decision.

I finally knew where we were. The taxi arrived at the gate to Donghai and I paid the driver. I stepped out and looked around. Close by was a bus stop with a number of Chinese people waiting in their usual disorderly way. One person was squatting on their heels. A couple of people had bags full of shopping in both hands. I joined the group. One bag was open at the top, which made it easy to slip my mobile phone covertly into it. The bus journey would confuse the field base tracking system. I shuffled backwards to let other people push forward and left to make my way into the university. Passing through the grounds, I saw the laundry van with the 'specialist carpet cleaning' sign on it. This was the one that had helped take away the Russian body from my apartment. I gripped my gun but couldn't see anyone in the cab. It was obvious that I needed to take care in case of danger. I walked on smoothing my clothes and brushing hard at my hair with my fingers, trying to release the debris.

At first, I walked briskly but then broke into a jog to get to the English language office as fast as possible. The building was quiet as there were not many students coming or going. I tried to establish the level of risk. A check of the people around the building suggested there were no hidden dangers. I pushed open the main door and ran up the stone staircase to get to the office as quickly as possible. James and Lily turned to look when they heard me enter. Lily reacted by being visibly upset at seeing me in my dishevelled state. Her eyes welled up and a few tears rolled down her cheek before being brushed away. "Harry, you look terrible. What happened?"

James's mouth opened in disbelief. "What on earth is going on?"

"James, this may come as a big shock." I raised my eyebrows. "Someone tried to kill me."

I looked over at Lily. Seeing her generated a strong emotional release. A mixture of concern, relief and fondness swirled in my head. I was aware of my heart beating wildly in my chest. "I was worried about you, really worried." I opened my arms as wide as possible, encouraging Lily to come to me. "I couldn't stop thinking about you." She snuggled into me as my words spilled out, "I realise I really care about you." She gave a sigh. "I need to change my life and want it to include you. Today, my whole situation changed and I can't continue with what I was doing. I don't intend to control my emotion anymore." Lily sniffed in to quench her tears.

James observed us in disbelief. "What does this mean, Harry? I need to know what happened." He felt a need to assess things. "Is this related to the death of Matt by the Russian gangsters?"

Lily pulled away and looked at James sensing his need to assert his authority. I responded to James wanting to move things on by speaking to Geoff. "It's related but also to the deaths of the students. It's urgent that I speak to Geoff. Get him to come here at once – and don't let him have excuses." James adopted a quizzical look, so I explained, "You want to know the answer. Don't worry, you'll get it when Geoff arrives."

"I'll go for a cigarette before I phone him," said James, obviously in desperate need of nicotine comfort. The blood drained from his face as he patted his jacket to locate his cigarettes.

"Phone Geoff first. It's urgent. You can smoke when he's on his way here," I told him in a jarring way. He left pulling out his mobile. I turned to Lily in order to share more details.

"I've given up on my people as they're intent on killing you. I'm here to protect you whatever happens." On saying this, I felt a special feeling and my eyes softened. "Lily, I know, truly know, you're more important than I ever wanted to admit."

"It's okay. You've kept a distance from me. You've held back from my feelings and controlled yours. But now you're showing me what's in your heart."

"So you understand me."

Her response was not unexpected. "Silly you. The real you was always there to see. You just suppressed your feelings." Lily's eyes became misty. "Your shell is tough, but like a tough nut the kernel beneath is much softer." She moved closer to me. "At last, we can be together with this." Her eyes focussed on the blood on my arm. The room was hot and airless yet the windows were open. Distant noises from the street below, of students laughing and talking seemed normal. I became mute as I couldn't find words that were appropriate.

Lily took a deep breath, recovered some composure and brought us back to reality. "Show me that arm. We need to fix it as soon as we can."

I watched her examining my arm and added, "It's not too bad. Just needs patching up."

"I have to find a place where we can be safe." After a pause, she said, "Okay. I know somewhere to go. Come with me after you've seen Geoff."

"We've got to be careful. They're trying to kill you. They'll try to make it look as if an accident happened, so we can't use your bike. It's being set up to crash."

She disregarded my words. "We have to see to that arm." Lily went to the first-aid box on the wall. She pulled out almost the whole of the contents into her bag.

I looked at what she was gathering. "We'll need something sharp, like tweezers and scissors as well."

There were faint noises coming from the hall. I ushered Lily to duck in case there was danger, then levelled my gun at the door. The heavy office door creaked open. Geoff must have been quite near as he came into the office with James. After two steps, he saw me and his mouth dropped open. "Christ. Put that gun down. Why are you pointing that at us, Harry?"

"It'll become clear."

"Why are you acting like this...and look like you do...and you've got a gun?" Geoff frowned. His gaze moved to the blood seeping from my arm.

"I'm the person coming back from where the shit hit the fan," I said, making Geoff aware of my anger. "People are dying here because of what's happening. This isn't ketchup on my arm." My approach must have been a massive jolt to his mind. "I've killed two people defending myself today." I lowered the gun in an effort to calm the situation.

"But why do you want to speak to me? I'm not involved." He took a few more steps into the office.

"Not involved! You're not so fucking smart as you think." I wanted to keep him on edge but didn't want him to clam up. "I know everything about you and Cheng. Why do you think you're here?"

"Ohh. What are you saying?" He looked astonished at my approach.

"Okay. So, tell me about the love you had for Cheng?"

His face tightened, indicating a realisation of his plight. "Well, I really did like Cheng." He steadied himself on a chair, and then dropped onto it. I moved nearer to him so the bulk of my body would create stress. He went on, "Cheng was special...but I never wanted him to die."

"Cut the crap. I asked about your love!" I shrieked. "Did you hear me?" I continued, waiting for the right effect.

"Yes. I did have feelings for Cheng. He was my best friend at one time."

"No! ... No, Geoff. You were lovers, yes lovers. So don't play with words. Say it for Cheng's sake." The tension built in me. The thought of what he had done started to get to me, and I wanted to put my fist through his face. His behaviour in murdering two innocent students had been abominable. "Look! I'm a ticking time-bomb about to go off – tell us!" Geoff looked at me with deep self-pity.

"Cheng wasn't faithful to me...wasn't faithful...he wasn't."

"Focus on when you were lovers. We need the truth."

His mouth opened, but it was a while until the words emerged, "You're torturing me." We waited in silence. He caught his breath and confessed, "Yes. I loved him." Then, he stated more emphatically, "Really loved him." James looked shocked at hearing this.

"I came here to find out the truth." I paused for effect. "So! You need to tell me the truth? Where did you grow the fungi and mould for the mycotoxin that killed Cheng and also Bao?"

Geoff stood to leave. "I don't need to answer. It was an accident." He wanted to run away from the truth.

"Sit the fuck down! And don't give me lame excuses." I was close enough to push him back in the chair. The weight of my arm and grip on his shoulder was enough. I hovered over him, trying to dominate his thoughts. He gazed up at me with a look of resignation.

"Give me the truth," I demanded. He looked vacantly at me, so I tried again, "You need to clear your conscience." I took my silencer out from the holdall and screwed it on. "I've killed several people today and you'll admit what you did – or else it ends here." He probably felt like a spider caught in the vortex of a toilet being flushed.

James looked toward the door. I sensed he could run out given the thought of my using the gun. "James, don't move, please." I moved my gun to him and back to Geoff, which created the desired effect. James nodded solemnly and became a statue.

"Look, Geoff I've the evidence. I know it was the mushrooms you gave them," I said, not telling him it was only circumstantial evidence. "Tell us, then I will let you go. I promise, I give my word." I'd given him a way to get rid of his guilt.

"I suppose you've enough evidence." He became resigned to the knowledge that he'd been responsible. The whirlpool of denial calmed. His voice strengthened and he confessed. "Yes. I made the toxin. I was carried away with the microbiology of creating it."

His dilemma seemed to have been put behind him. He stared at me. "It was only after I gave Cheng the mushrooms that I regretted it and wanted to save him. There was a desire for reconciliation. I rushed back to see him and beg his forgiveness. To tell him it was because of my love."

Lily had heard enough. "What? … Died for love?" questioned Lily, angrily. "Listening to you, I think it was about control."

"Perhaps I was out of my mind." He swallowed and paused. "I don't think I really wanted to kill Cheng. Then I had no idea he would share the meal with Bao." Geoff's emotions were on a roller coaster. "I couldn't bear for him to be with someone else." A few tears ran down his cheek.

James listened to the drama of Geoff with increasing worry. He became unsteady, so eased himself onto the nearest chair. The office had been his domain, his area of control, his place to tell others what he wanted. Now he must have felt like an emasculated bystander.

Geoff drew in air through his nose with a loud sniff. "He should have realised that when he rejected me, all my life was sucked out. Nothing was left." He looked at Lily, James and then me. "So, what else can I say?" He gave an imploring look, put his head down and muttered, "There's no future for me."

Lily couldn't restrain herself. The hurt inside over Cheng erupted, "We don't need to hear anything more. But get real about what happened – I'll tell you about the real you." She composed herself and added, "You were obsessed with your relationship and couldn't bear rejection. There was no real feeling for Cheng. Only pity for yourself so you took revenge because of it." Geoff's head dipped lower. "In fact, you're a weak, self-pitying bastard."

James straightened a little and shifted awkwardly in the chair. He was trying to gain his composure and leadership responsibilities. "Christ. How should I handle this?" He ran the palm of his hand from his forehead to the top of his head. He looked across to us, then fumbled inside his jacket. His hand was shaking as he took out a cigarette to smoke in the office. Something he'd seldom done before.

I held up the list I'd brought with me. "When you tell the dean and others about what you've been told by Geoff, I also want you to tell them about the names on this list."

"What's the list for?"

"This list is from an experiment called Eagle. It will be used to randomly kill a few of the people on it. These are names from the medical trial that's taking place. It's the same one Cheng and, Bao were in. The Russians are going to kill them like they killed Matt." I was still careful to protect my country and so lied to James.

James seemed like he was coping better with what was happening. "I'll do my best." His hands gripped the paper with the list of names. There was a lot for James to take in given what had happened under his management with Geoff, Matt and now me.

"Give it priority as lives could be at risk."

"Leave it to me." James stood and went over to sit behind his own desk. He felt he had a task to complete. Having responsibility for the list helped revert him to the comfort of his management role. I nodded in affirmation to James. The old worn leather chair at his desk creaked as he slipped into it. He settled back in his chair, looking over the list. I looked over at Lily, raised my eyes a little and nodded to her as a signal to leave. We left the room with Geoff sitting passively, staring emptily into the middle distance. James remained seated, his head dropped while he scratched it, contemplating his next decision. He was focussed on the list of names placed flat on the desk in front of him. Both men, for different reasons, were shell-shocked at events.

Lily led me down the back staircase for safety. Our eyes readjusted to the daylight, and I scanned the road for anything suspicious. We went over garden areas and past the back of different building blocks. She insisted on carrying my holdall in case I developed problems with my injured arm.

"You did well in getting the confession." The holdall swung heavily in Lily's hand.

"Well, I reduced his options in what he could say." I grinned to emphasise my meaning.

"What do you think will happen now?"

"Geoff will run, but in China, he will not escape the authorities. James will do his duty by informing the dean."

"He will be executed you know?" she said. "He'll be shot or given a lethal injection."

"Yes. The evidence against him is overwhelming. Killing him will create an international outcry about Chinese law and sentencing. That will not be a problem. The authorities will be relieved, as it will divert attention from the medical experiments."

Lily stopped and looked sideways at me. "What are your plans now?"

"Quite dramatic. I want to blow up a building."

"What? More danger?" she stressed her vowels.

"It's necessary."

"You have the option to pull out."

"No. It's become a matter of principle."

I clambered over a low fence. Lily waited, looked across the fence and a pained look crossed her face. "I want us to be together. Don't risk our future."

It was obvious Lily wanted it to end, but I was determined to complete my plan. What I was planning meant it was a dangerous mission. I needed to risk our future as acting alone meant I had no support network. I made things clear for her. "I'm going to go to the Institute of Technology to destroy their equipment. It will look like an accident, but until I go there, I'm not sure what I can achieve."

"But are you sure you need to?"

"Look. When you take a stand, there's no middle ground. I'll stand up for clear principles and do what I believe in."

"You could leave it to others."

"No. Do you remember when we talked about your father? You said we sometimes have to take a stand. This is mine. It's the only way to stop those in the medical trial being killed. They're the innocents in this. I don't want them to die."

"You have strong morals."

"Yes. I hate those who say they have conviction but never show action."

"Okay. I know why you're doing this. I can help do whatever it takes. But first, let's do something about that arm. I'll show you a safe place so we can have some privacy."

Lily led the way around lightly wooded areas and paths. I followed, wondering where we would end up.

Chapter 27
Hiding Away

We'd not gone far when Lily stopped. "This is where Matt stayed. His place will be empty until they recruit a new member of staff." We were standing in front of a non-descript university apartment building. I was hoping Lily had decided on some safe shelter for us by selecting Matt's old accommodation.

I scanned the area around the building and everything seemed normal. "This looks good. Hotels are easily monitored and leave trails that can be identified. It's far better here."

We went up the stairs and arrived at a door that was locked. I leant against it and it was solid. Luckily the door lock wasn't a deadlock. There was a cheap Yale pin-type latch with about five or six pins in the tumbler. This was the easiest type to pick.

"Do you have a hairpin, Lily?"

She had a pin that was thin enough to pick locks. I made it into two thin lengths that could pick the lock more easily. Lily looked on as I guided the pin in and moved it around listening for the pins in the lock to move. It clicked five times and I tried the door. The tumblers had been turned, but the door still held. The jamb was tight on the door.

Lily sat on her heels and became impatient. "Open sesame, please!"

I pushed on the door with my good shoulder and it gave way. Dust particles shimmered as the light broke through. The relief at the door opening was tangible. Lily reacted with, "Thank goodness. We can relax now."

We both stepped through the door, smiling at each other as a pleased reaction. Lily double locked the door from the inside by means of a catch. She also found a bolt on the door and slid it across for added safety. I surveyed the room. There was nothing to personalise it. A book was splayed on a faded bedspread and a jacket hung on the back of a chair. There was a stained leather satchel on its seat. The walls and shelves were bare of anything creative. Books, pens, dust and papers were the only adornments. The surroundings portrayed a lack of artistic temperament. It was austere and functional. Perhaps Matt spent his time in the bars and restaurants to escape the room's monotony.

Lily put down my holdall and looked at me. It was a special look that only those who are close can share. This drew me to her eyes and exotic look. The feelings moving between us became intense. They had the quality of tingling expectancy. Catching her gaze, I could see her emotion had morphed with mine. We closed the space between us knowing, just knowing. The tension broke. She kissed my lips in a full, soft expression of emotion. Her lips were full, moist and warm.

I held her and she looked at me with mutual affection. "I remember when I first saw you. You looked so handsome and strong. I liked you from the start, Mr Harry Long." Her eyes focussed. "But it's the way you act that made me fall in love."

I told her my first memory. "From our time together in Labour Park, I was captivated by you." The worries which had previously plagued me evaporated, and I felt reassured about my feelings. I looked at Lily. "I feel I've thrown off so many worries over us."

She looked up at me. There was an intimate feeling of a bond having developed between us. It was intoxicating as it had developed beyond mere attraction and allure. The strength of the emotion was overpowering. Lily was in an 'act and do' mode though. She was rightly worried that I needed to wash off the dirt from my encounter with Isabel.

"I feel our emotion, but let's fix that arm first," said Lily. "I think you need a shower to get you clean." She looked at my arm. "I can then dress your wound. Afterwards, we can relax with each other." I gazed into her eyes but found them unreadable. I was searching for an understanding of her Chinese behaviour.

I followed her request, undressed and stepped into the shower. To my complete surprise, Lily entered the bathroom. She undressed, the shower door opened and a naked Lily joined me. Her skin looked smooth and translucent from the warm water cascading over it. I felt unrestrained passion. There was a burst of emotion where the world whirled and throbbed. She acted a little nervously and didn't say anything. We kissed. It was a soft rather than passionate kiss. It had been a telling kiss though, and I realised more was to come. The passion of the moment increased and sent my world spinning. Our feelings swirled, our lips swelled from expectation, our giddiness increased – and we shared, celebrated and consumed each other. Our relationship was taken to a different level. I was tumbled into a world of inconceivable feelings.

"I'm in ecstasy, but I'm getting out of this shower now," she took control. "You'll need that arm looked at," said Lily, washing off the soap and stepping out the shower. I savoured the memory of the past few minutes. Lily went to dress while I continued to let the shower wash over me to recover my senses. The soap whirled, and bubbles popped as the water flowed over my body. I felt renewed so stepped out. A curious stillness and calmness descended on me. The steam that had eddied around us had condensed into a fogged mist covering the bathroom walls and mirror. I took a towel and dried myself before leaving the bathroom. Lily was dressed and sorting out the first-aid items from her bag.

I searched through Matt's clothes as I needed to change. I opened a drawer and saw a few socks and underwear. His wardrobe had only one suit, a jacket and a couple of pairs of trousers. Hangers held a few shirts. They were not up to the quality of my choice. I selected some clothes, dressed and lay on the bed awaiting Lily. On the side was a picture of Matt and the girl from Comrade's bar. Only a few books were in the room. There were several paperback thriller stories and a couple of travel books of China. I flicked through a travel book of China, noting the superb scenery, especially in the Yunnan area. From the back of the book, some pictures fell out. They were of Matt and Amanda standing on the side of a mountain or beside a lake. '*Fond Memories xx,*' was written on the back of one picture.

"This picture is interesting," I mused.

"No idea about it. Now let's clean out the wound so that it doesn't turn sceptic. I'll boil the kettle." Lily went over to the small kitchen area and sorted out the medical equipment she'd brought with her. After sterilising the implements in a bowl, she examined the wound. "I'll need to clean the entrance wound. It may have some foreign material in it." She examined, scraped, disinfected and dressed both wounds in no time. I was reassured everything had gone well when she told me she'd finished.

I checked the neatness of the dressing. "Thanks. You're a good nurse."

"Perhaps we can relax now that arm's fixed." Lily gave me an intense look.

We sat on the couch and embraced a second time. I hugged her slender form. The world paused as I enjoyed the purity of the feeling. It went from the physical and ascended to the spiritual. Our souls met in unison once more before calmness finally descended on us. We were both spent and drifted into a light sleep still locked in each other's arms.

Lily was the first to wake. I watched her walk over to the TV. She caught my gaze and smiled. "We need to get some food. Also, we need to find out what the news is showing given what has happened in Dalian." She switched the on the TV and used the remote to flick through a couple of channels. The news was in Chinese delivered at rapid speed. A change in the topic of a political meeting report revealed a picture of the outside of Comrade's bar, with a dark area of bloodstain. A serious-sounding newscaster delivered the story. Familiar pictures flashed across the screen. The news piece went on to show a passport picture of Matt Groom, the burnt-out taxi, turned over stalls and dead stall holders. The marketplace was shown as a cordoned off area. Lily listened intently. Finally, a doctor was interviewed in front of a hospital, followed by a statement by a senior policeman.

"They're saying Dalian is suffering from a wave of Russian crime, drugs and prostitution. The report is giving the public an answer to what is happening. The presenter says the enemies of the country will be hunted down."

"All governments want their people to have easy answers," I responded. "I'm glad there are no links to us on the news." Lily went into the bathroom. "We need to organise the rest of our day," I called out.

"I think it's best if I go out alone to get some food to bring back, while you stay here. It's less likely I'll be noticed," was her direct response.

She emerged ready to go out. "I understand, but you need to be careful as you're a link to me and the British think you're a threat." She appeared calm at my warning, so I continued, "Keep looking around for danger."

After Lily left, I went through some of the rest of Matt's drawers. Most of his belongings appeared normal, but at the back of one drawer, I found a picture of Geoff and Cheng in an intimate embrace. Given its poor quality, the picture had obviously been enlarged from a smaller picture. I assumed Matt had shown this picture to Geoff as a means to stop his relationship with Cheng.

There was a knock on the door. It appeared too quick for the return of Lily. I picked up the gun and shouted, *"Zao!"*

"It's Lily." Lily brought back a hot takeaway with some drinks. We both must have had good appetites as we sat on the bed and devoured it all. We were left relaxed facing each other across the debris of plastic cups and boxes.

My mind turned to what lay ahead. "I need transport to go to the institute. Any ideas?"

"I've an old bike stored at the back of the campus," Lily suggested. "I only use it when my Shadow is being serviced. I'll take you."

"No. You're going to stay here until I return. I don't want you involved." My eyes bored into Lily's. When it came to her, I couldn't be dispassionate. Knowing the institute, I was well aware of the amount of danger it involved. It was normal for me to act independently and to handle explosives, guns and fights. Lily lacked my experience, so I didn't want to involve her.

"But I'm already involved, so can help you out. Sometimes you need to consider me, rather than doing everything your way." There was a stubborn look across her face.

"Oh God. I've no sway with you." My hands clenched. "Look. I'm going to blow up a building. It's a job for a professional."

Lily looked straight at me. "We're both involved in this. So stop trying to act alone." She was not going to listen to reason. "I'm going with you," she insisted. "Sooner or later you'll realise what help I can offer."

I thrust my finger at her. "You need a restraining order."

She wasn't impressed. "I wouldn't be restrained because those medical trials will lead to people dying So, I won't agree, won't be restrained and won't stay here. I'll be at your side."

"You're as tough as they come."

"Ohh, Harry, you've always acted to protect me. Stop shielding me. You need to accept equality and that in some ways, I'm stronger than you."

"I'm serious." I put my hands on my hips. "I know about the danger out there. There's a need to protect you."

"Why are you English people so serious about being serious? I'm not a child."

"I have my professional belief of knowing what's best for you."

"I'm happy to deal with that. Stop playing by your rules of being my guardian, my protector. Women go to war these days and I'm coming."

My job taught me the need to be careful about a dangerous situation, but Lily's words jarred on me. I was silent for a moment, while taking in their importance. I shrugged as if to say I don't care if you disagree, yet knew what she said was true. Seeing Lily's reaction to my shrug, I spoke before she did.

"Okay, okay, I know I can't stop you." There was no sense in arguing any longer. Knowing her strength of character, I relented. "Your bike will get us there."

"So let's leave."

"First, it's the Institute of Technology building to finalise my plan. Afterwards, you'll need to tell me where in China we can hide away."

"It's difficult as there are many places to choose."

"Perhaps we'll be best outside China," I said, wondering if Lily would want that.

I gathered my old clothes into a bundle and we cleared up our mess. "We should go. Let's find that old bike."

"Not so fast. Let me look at your arm before we leave?" She checked the dressing. "It'll be okay." She looked around the room, then at me. "Things have become complicated, but we can finish this soon and be together."

"We have one last task to carry out before we can relax. Then all this will be behind us. We're going to destroy the institute and what it stands for," I said. "But I won't have you die on me. I won't."

Lily looked relaxed. "Can't wait for us to put this behind us."

"Well, after a building is blown up. Are you okay with that?"

"Yes," she nodded. "I'm fine." I could sense there was no tension in her. Her strong spirit was evident. I'd accepted she was my equal.

We closed the door and walked toward the stairs. I looked back from the stairs to the room that had provided profound significance in our relationship. It was not a room I would have chosen but one where we achieved perfect fulfilment. It was where our lives had changed forever. I tried to seize the moment, to keep it with me forever.

I felt the strength of our emotion and asked, "Do you think in the end love conquers all, Lily?"

Lily skipped down the last steps. "Courage plus emotion does. In your case love took its time."

"Yes. It took time for me to realise what was important in life."

"Lysander had the famous line, 'the course of true love never did run smooth,' AND that's us."

Just before exiting, I took Lily's hand. "Yes, I do love you and have to agree it's been a bumpy ride. But now I feel fully committed to our future."

She looked back at me. "It's good that we can share so much now."

We exited and I squinted at the brightness of the outside light. Lily asked me to wait out of sight while she went to get her motorbike. We parted, and Lily walked across the road while I waited at the side of the building. Little did I realise how soon events were going to get even bumpier.

Chapter 28
Institute Visit

What I didn't know was Isabel had sent the two Chinese field agents to Matt's apartment. Perhaps they had tracked Lily's phone.

"Harry, run!" Lily screamed.

She'd been seen by the two 'cleaners' sent to track us. They'd probably been told to forget the motorbike and concentrate on rubbing us out. I looked across the road to assess what was happening. There, in full flight, was Lily, chased from behind by two Chinese men. I saw the distinctive overalls of the men chasing her. They looked like the two who had come to my room to take away the Russian body and clean up. They both had handguns.

"I'll cover you!" I shouted, while grabbing the gun from the holdall.

A car was approaching along the road in front of me. It would arrive at the same time Lily needed to get across the road. They were about to coincide in space and time, but Lily was in full flight and not about to stop. The seconds went into slow motion for me. Real time slowed into frames of elapsed events. The situation felt grim. I held my breath and my heart rate increased, as I realised they were on a collision course. The car kept coming on the same line and finally veered to miss her. As it passed, I raised the gun to take aim. One of the Chinese men dropped on one knee and used both hands to steady his aim at Lily.

"Don't run straight – weave!" I yelled, hoping Lily would understand. She did, but three shots sounded. Birds wheeled into the air at the noise. The sound was from a large calibre handgun, possibly a forty-five calibre. One bullet hit a tree sending off shards of bark, while the other two passed by.

"Get behind the tree!" Lily crouched low, desperately trying to take cover. Fear was etched across her brow. Everything went quiet and the rasping of crickets became more audible than anything else.

The kneeling Chinese man focused on me. I was another three metres beyond Lily and a bigger target. I had no cover so turned sideways. We both fired at the same time, with two rounds in quick succession. He missed me. The size of the Chinese man's gun would make it difficult to steady it. One of my rounds seemed to go through his shoulder. Wherever it hit, he was in enough pain not to continue the fight. He rolled left, rolled right and then crawled backwards.

The second Chinese man had taken a position on the other side of the road, behind a tree. He peered round the tree and raised his gun using both hands. He was so near I could see the black mouth of the gun barrel and his levelling of the gun to take aim. A second car was coming along the road with a driver oblivious to what was happening. The Chinese guy steadied his aim as the car approached. It was no use staying where I was as I was too exposed. My thoughts were racing as to my next move.

I decided to do something he would not expect. I used the bulk of the passing car to run alongside it, keeping as low as possible. This gave me a new position along the road. I had wheeled round to attack him from the side. As the car passed on, I ensured my gun was pointing to his last position. He thought his position was safe, but now I was sideways to him. Now he was exposed. Taking advantage of my new position, I shot at the upper bulk of his body. The bullet went through his chest and he flew sideways. He was prone with his gun beside him.

"Okay. Run!" I yelled. She reacted immediately.

Lily ran toward me, and as she reached me, I pulled her behind me to use my body as a shield. I looked to see what had happened to the man with the shoulder wound. I could see a couple of Chinese people huddled around him. I reloaded my gun and asked Lily to take us on a safer detour across the gardens to the bike. We jogged off at a fast pace, ducking past shrubs and across patches of grass. The pace was tiring but we pushed on never stopping. After a while, I felt we were safe and so slipped the gun back in my trousers.

"That was close. I think we're okay now," I panted.

Lily stopped and bent forward taking in air. "What a mess. It never ends."

"I'm about to end it," I said with conviction.

We walked on until we came to a car park behind a low-rise building.

"This is it." Lily pointed to a shrouded object behind some cars. "Here's my other bike."

I saw what Lily was pointing at. We had arrived at a bike-shaped object. It was a mysterious bulky shape covered in an old tarpaulin. The tarpaulin was covered in bird droppings and moss. We pulled the cover away. I was hoping a pristine bike would appear from below the tarpaulin. What she exposed was old, dusty and in need of attention. I stood back and watched Lily shake the bike to see if there was petrol in the tank. A swishing sound of petrol relaxed me.

"Wish we had a magic wand to turn this into a Shadow," I joked.

"I love this bike, so be grateful. It's an old Chang Jiang motorbike that belonged to my father. It'll do the job."

The first attempt to start it ended in a quiet plop. Thankfully, Lily kicked started the bike on the third attempt. To my relief, it had started. It spluttered and needed to be revved to keep it going but was in working order. We set off with the engine thumping out a range of notes. It didn't sound right, and I hoped it was simply a broken exhaust pipe. I would have been surprised if there were any spare parts available to mend this dated, leftover from the past.

"When I was a child, this bike had a sidecar attached to it," shouted Lily over the engine's agitating sounds. "Get on."

I climbed on a separate rear seat with a hoop grab handle at its front. This was definitely a different riding experience. We set off and in no time, arrived at the Institute of Technology building.

I directed Lily to go to the side of the building where I'd previously climbed over the wall. On our arrival, I noticed the land next to the institute was being developed. I looked across at the large building plot. "Park there," I suggested.

She rode the bike onto the land of a new building development site beside the institute. We bumped up and down on the dirt of a new roadway before the discordant sounds of the bike's engine ceased. I got off; dust was swirling around my feet. I stared back at the institute trying to figure out the best way to enter. The problem was how to get into the building without creating attention. I could get over the wall by standing on the bike first but still needed to enter without setting off a door alarm.

"Any ideas how to get in?" I asked, thinking aloud.

We looked around. "That's it," she pointed.

"What. Are you sure?" It was a crane. "Can you drive it?"

"Only way to find out is to follow me."

There was a tracked mini crane sitting beside a fence at the edge of the building site. It was like an army tank with a large derrick on top.

Lily led the way to the crane. "We're in luck. It's what we need."

One look in the cab of the crane and I was lost as everything was written in Chinese. However, there were levers with direction arrows that seemed intuitive. We discussed the controls and arrows. Lily seemed to have grasped the fundamentals of the information. She sat in the operator's seat, and reaching up, she located the key in the universal hiding place behind the visor. Without any delay, she managed to get the crane's engine working. The engine throbbed into life and sent out plumes of acrid blue smoke. Her elation was evident. "Great. The operating length of this crane will reach the upper windows."

She managed a short practice swivel of the arm and the bucket attached to it. It swung in a precarious way. "I can get this round to the height of the institute's windows. It's noisy, but the office workers must have heard it working on this site."

"Okay let's do it." I grabbed my holdall and under it was a screwdriver on the cab floor. I added it to my holdall as it seemed a handy tool. "I'll climb onto the gantry."

"No even better. I can lift you in the bucket of the crane."

Lily lifted and swung the arm and bucket in different directions. She was a natural. I gave her the thumbs-up sign and clambered into the bucket. She lifted the bucket to the right height and length and swung it across the road over the grounds of the institute. With a slight rocking and shudder, she managed to align me with the window I'd previously exited from. I stepped from the bucket to the windowsill.

This entrance would be more difficult than the previous visit. I realised the possible dangers were much greater now. I crouched on the sill, cupped my hands to my eyes and looked through the window. I didn't like what I saw. I needed to think quickly to deal with the problem which faced me.

Chapter 29
Destruction Time

There were two people walking along the corridor. My immediate thought was to act like a workman mending the window. I took out my newly acquired screwdriver as it would help me. The holdall was placed on the window ledge and I positioned my head to hide my face as much as possible. I made a movement as if scraping my screwdriver along the edge of the window. The action was carried out without sound to minimise unwanted attention. I caught a glimpse of the two people walking by. They passed without stopping. I waited a few minutes and looked again. I could see the corridor was now clear. I applied the screwdriver to the bottom of the window. There was instant relief when the large window prised open. I entered the building, dropped down and quietly closed it. Lily must have been watching as the distant clanking of the crane could be heard, as she moved the arm back over to the building site.

I made my way along the corridor to get to the emergency staircase. A photocopying machine was humming and whirring with its printing. The noise was coming from a small room off the corridor. It signalled danger as someone would be there to collect the copies. The printing stopped and there was an undesirable silence. I had nowhere to hide so continued on. A young-looking secretary, in a smart black suit, emerged from the photocopying room into the corridor. My anguish set off a trickle of adrenaline. She walked toward me with a sense of purpose. As I expected, she looked at me with surprise. I used the word, *"Ni hao,"* as a greeting. The surprised look turned to a smile, and the young girl walked on past me.

My strides quickened. I made my way along the corridor to get to the emergency staircase. The room with the transformer that powered the magnetic equipment was my target. As it was a service room, it shouldn't be occupied. That would allow me to place the explosives while being undisturbed. I pictured the building plans. The layout of the building was known, but although I knew the floor level, I wasn't sure of the transformer's exact location. I fixed on where the area of the transformer room would be.

I knew what I was going to do. The plan for the explosion was to create confusion about what had happened. I wanted the Chinese investigation to think that the experiment equipment had failed again, as with the students' experience. I wanted them to concentrate on the cause of another but bigger explosion. This was to complicate any investigation by linking the detonation to the earlier problems of the transformer malfunction. The hope was that if the transformer was identified as being at the site of the explosion, it could confuse the investigation and halt the trials.

I knew the room was up a level on the next floor. I went into the building's middle emergency staircase and up the stairs. Coming out from the stair void into the corridor, there was another unexpected challenge. The room I wanted access to was guarded. As I opened the door, the guard turned round. He saw me immediately as I entered the corridor. He was sitting at a small desk; a short fat man in a baggy blue uniform, with a peaked cap that was too large for him. He was opposite the lift exit, guarding the entrance to the transformer and medical treatment room. Looking at him, perhaps the term guard was too exaggerated a way to describe him. He looked sleepy and not up to protecting anything. This was no professional person. He seemed ill equipped to do anything but check the security passes of those entering. It was important to react after his drowsy-eye gaze fixed on me. The contents of my holdall flashed through my mind.

I walked toward him with a confident gait, making out I was looking for a pass in my holdall. Half way toward him, I stopped and put my hand in my pocket as if my pass were there. I shrugged, then walked on and pointed to my holdall. Pointing to the holdall confused him as to what was meant. He soon found out my purpose. I placed my hand in the holdall and brought my gun out, holding it by the barrel. I struck him with the butt to the side of his temple. It was such a fast movement that he never flinched. One second he was looking at me and then he was slumped across his desk. I placed him with his head on the desk in his hands as if he were sleeping. Once I felt things looked normal, I opened the door he controlled for access. There was a short corridor and from this area, one door led off to the left and one to the right. Things weren't clear. I wasn't sure what door to use so listened at both doors. I could hear a humming from inside one of them. It sounded like the transformer, so I turned the handle. I opened the door just far enough to peer inside. This wasn't the room.

One look and I knew it was the wrong room. This was the room where the medical trials were carried out. A few people were at the far end of the room and some looked in my direction. Most were more intent on their work and showed little interest in me. I used the tactic of pointing to my holdall again and shut the door. It was my best, if only, idea. In the short time the door opened, I noticed a number of large silo-like enclosures were lined up against one wall. They were sending out the droning noises. On an opposite wall, there were racks of drugs and medical equipment.

I went to the door opposite, but the door was locked. The screwdriver was the quick answer. The lock wasn't solid and the screwdriver, acting as a lever, forced the door open. I looked in. Two large grey cabinets covered in sheet metal stood in the room. Pipes, like massive old-fashioned radiators, came out from the sides of the cabinets. These aided the cooling. Large cables, the thickness of an arm, emerged in groups of about five from the middle of the cabinets and disappeared into the floor. It was clear these would run to where the medical trials were carried out in the room I'd looked into. Three dials were on each cabinet and were at a steady state. The room hummed with a low-level sound and was slightly warmer than the outside corridor. At the top of the cabinets were air ducts which vanished into the ceiling.

I sorted out the holdall. I got out my shape charges and placed them near the steel supports at the sides of the room. I examined the structure to decide where to place the charges for the maximum effect. The shape charges, being directional, had to be placed carefully in position. The main charges were going to cut though the steel girders that supported the building. The logic was once the girders were cut through, it would destroy the support for the building. Then the building's weight above the transformer room would cause a chain reaction and lead to the building's collapse. I took out the C3 plastic explosive and pushed it into place. I choose the base of the transformers and the tops of each of the cabinets. I noticed a label was attached to the cabinet with the symbol of a lightning bolt and under it Chinese characters – probably stating danger in Chinese. I smiled at the thought.

The shock wave from the full explosion was planned to create secondary damage to all parts of the building. There was going to be a delayed two-stage explosion to confuse the initial analysis. I wanted the early solution to look as if the transformers had blown, causing more serious secondary damage. However, once investigators assessed the cut pattern damage to the steel girders, they would work out that shape charges caused it.

I just needed to set the time for the detonation of the charges. The time was set for fifteen minutes for the C3, followed by a short delay for the shape charges to blow. The fifteen minutes would allow as many people as possible to get out of the building without being hurt. I turned to leave but noticed the guard slumped over his desk where I'd left him. I slapped his face and he made a couple of groaning sounds. He had started to recover, so I pulled him into a more upright position.

Next, I went straight to the fire alarm, hit the glass with the screwdriver and prodded the button to set it off. I walked along the corridor and sent a second alarm off. The two alarm indicators would show on the main security control board and prompt the security people to treat the situation as serious. Being a modern building, the alarm sounded with loud claxons and intermittent honking.

"Honk, Honk...Hong...Hong...Hong!" rung out, and reverberated off the walls.

It wasn't the orderly evacuation that I expected. A stream of people emerged from different rooms and places around me. Joining them, I made my way along the corridor. The flow and ebb of people continued with most making for the emergency staircase. We passed some who were not aware of evacuation procedures as they were waiting for the lift. I reached the emergency staircase at the end of the building and joined in the wave of bodies descending. Intermittent alarm sounds, some shouts and a clattering of shoes on concrete signalled the exodus. The staircase led down to the corridor to the exit or further down to the emergency doors. I remembered the emergency doors were padlocked on the outside. I assumed the security staff would unlock all the doors. If not, the weight of people could probably break the lock to open the doors if they needed to. Although the building was new, it was clear from what I saw that no proper evacuation drills had been carried out. I followed a wave of people who were streaming out the door, which led to the reception area and main entrance.

The blasts of the fire alarm spurred people along. People were carried along with the momentum of the group until they spilled out through the main doors and down the entrance steps. I rushed along with a heightened sense of exhilaration that I'd managed to carry out my plan. How wrong; relief turned to shock. The people I saw outside the institute were definitely not anticipated.

Chapter 30
Old Contacts

People were rushing from the institute via the reception area and steps. I joined the general flow moving toward the outside area. Once outside the building, I looked at my watch. Twelve minutes to go before the building was trashed. I descended the steps and my heart jumped a beat. The black S-class Mercedes was sitting directly beside the entrance to the building and about twenty-five metres away from the exit staircase. Whoever was in it, would see me amongst the exiting Chinese staff. There was no way they would miss spotting me.

The front passenger car window opened and a loud voice bellowed out. It was obvious they had been waiting for me. "Nice to see you, Harry. Come here and say hello to Lily," it was the crushed-gonad Russian back again. His heavily accented voice carried over the background noise of people leaving the building. I went from disbelief to desperation and back again.

The rear car door opened and I saw Lily had her hands tied behind her back. My throat became dry and my breathing wasn't regular. A red mark showed on her face. My heart began beating violently against my ribs. But the shocks were not finished, as sitting next to Lily was Matt Groom. There was a menacing look in his eyes. I couldn't grasp things. It was him, and I could see he held a gun to the side of Lily's body. The misjudgement I'd made angered me. I felt incompetent as all the early signs had been there for me to realise Matt had something to hide. I should have paid more attention after seeing him exiting the institute on my first visit.

The big Russian looked at my holdall. "You give that bag to me. Carefully do it. Remember we have Lily here. Okay?"

I looked into the rear of the car, "Are you okay?"

"I'm alright." She nodded to reassure me. Matt prodded her with his gun.

"Leave out the chat," ordered Matt.

Time expanded and slowed. I had no idea what to do but faced up to things by regaining my composure. I squared my shoulders and became more resolute. In a couple of paces, I was by the side of the car. Grudgingly, I handed the holdall through the window to the Russian. Looking through the open car window, I saw he was holding a machine pistol, aimed, through the door, at my body.

People were making their way to the other side of the road from the institute. They formed into different groups of those dressed in white coats, business suits or causal wear. The groups looked back to assess the situation. There wasn't any smoke or a fire, so they chatted calmly amongst themselves or were using their mobiles. There was no evidence of worry or panic. It had become an enjoyable break from the routine of daily work.

The Russian put the machine pistol across his legs still pointing it at me. With one hand, he rummaged inside my holdall and only found the handgun, its silencer and the screwdriver. I stood by the car door trying to come up with an idea of how to deal with this new dilemma.

"Go search him, Matt, and I'll cover Lily." Matt gave his gun to the driver and got out of the car to search me.

He got out of the back of the car and patted me down. "Nothing on him," said Matt.

"Nothing? So what is it you do or see in the building? What you British know?" the Russian snapped. He went on. "We realise you were involved in this alarm going off. What you found?" The driver and Matt remained silent.

I looked at Matt. "So you're a Russian puppet?" I felt a strong loathing. He glared back.

"I did what I had to. I'm a field agent like you." He was acting far stronger in his new role.

"I want you to let Lily go. She cannot tell you anything as she's innocent," I told the big Russian. They all remained quiet and said nothing. Their tactic of silence worked as I needed to negotiate. "If you let her go, I'll tell you everything."

The Russian shook his head in a slow, defiant way. "Just tell."

I had to continue with some explanation, so needed to say more. "I took pictures on my mobile phone, but it was knocked from my hand in the rush to get out of the building. It's an incredible medical trial in there. If Matt goes to the top floor now, there's no one there. He can take pictures," I said, trying to gauge the timing of the explosion. "It's a military experiment you'll be able to photograph."

"We'll decide when and what we do," said the Russian, taking control.

I eyed the Russian. "So you killed Gary, then planted Matt's identity onto him," I said. "But killing Gary doesn't make sense to me."

Matt looked me full in the face. "Ha, ha. You're not as clever as you think, Harry. You didn't get it at the time. I fooled you in Comrade's and you didn't see through my story." He had all the answers. "The girl set up Gary's death for us."

"Sure, I was fooled." The regret in saying this hurt. "Once you convinced me that Geoff was behind the student deaths, I made the mistake of believing in you."

Matt smiled. "Yes. You dumb fuck. You bought every word of it."

"So why did you kill Gary?"

"The Chinese MSS were on to me. I had to disappear before they picked me up."

The seconds were ticking away. Each moment was agonising as if time was frozen. There was a need to do something. I tried to worry them by saying directly to Matt, "You're not as clever as you think; it's such bad timing. You've lost an opportunity to get into the building as everyone will return soon."

The big Russian intervened, "Matt couldn't do all we wanted. He tried to bribe the institute's officials to let him know something about the experiments and how the students died – but they didn't do what we expected. They talked to the Chinese MSS about him." He turned, looked over at the institute building and saw only a few people were exiting. "Matt, go and show Harry what we can do. Go! Find out as much as possible."

The agonising wait was over and my mind became lighter. Matt ran across the road and disappeared up the steps of the institute. The Russian spoke to his driver. "Tie his hands behind back."

The driver got me to face forwards while he tied my hands behind my back. He secured them tightly with a plastic tie clip. I could tell my hands were too secure for me to free them. He pushed me forward and I took a stumbling step toward the car. I was focussed on only one thing. My mind was counting down the minutes in anticipation of the explosion.

The Russian pointed. "Get in the back."

I got in and sat next to Lily. "I'll get you out of this. We—"

The big Russian struck me across the side of my face with his fist. It came out of the blue. My head jolted sideways and I suffered a spinning sensation. "Concentrate, Harry. Your lives depend on it." He never worried me as I was calm and focussed in knowing what I would do when the explosives detonated.

The big Russian smirked and lifted his finger as if to say something. Before he said anything else, there was a small explosion, followed by an almighty one. Both Russians looked across the road in stunned bewilderment. A shock wave went out into the street and rocked the car. The explosives had done their job. Both Russians had lost all concentration due to the scene of the Institute of Technology's top two floors collapsing onto the first floor.

Their surprise and bafflement gave us an advantage. I shouted to Lily, "NOW! Kick their necks!" The anger was boiling inside me. We needed to position ourselves and sight our targets. At my shout, both Lily and I lifted our hips sideways and struck. It was an instantaneous reaction fuelled by rage. They never saw our strikes coming. We used the sides of our feet and kicked with bitterness and supercharged energy into their necks. The ability to get leverage from the seat helped in delivering several devastating kicks. Both thigh and buttock muscles delivered enormous amounts of power. The accumulated effect of the kicks was to render both Russians senseless.

I looked at the Russians slumped forward in their seats and back at Lily. "Fuck. What a relief." We both sat up taking in deep breaths, but the air was polluted. Beyond the car, the air was filled with a smoky haze. It was even possible to taste the clouds of fumes coming off the destroyed building.

"Huh, listen." There was a distant wail of sirens. "We need to get away from here. Let's go before we attract an audience." The institute was reduced to a single storey with a concrete staircase, seemingly hanging in mid-air as the only part remaining of the upper floors. It was a stairway in mid-air to nowhere. Flames lapped around different parts of the building, while billowing smoke blackened the steel girders, which now stood up like a broken set of railings. The smoke twisted and curled above groups of stunned onlookers, who were in shock and timidly moving further back from the building.

We scrambled from the car as best we could and stood with our hands securely tied behind our backs. Lily looked around trying to decide what to do. She dropped down and managed to free her hands by bringing her tied hands from her back, over her buttocks, past her legs and round to the front of her body. She'd slipped her tied hands from the back to her front. I tried, but couldn't achieve what she had. She watched my failed attempt to pull my hands past my bottom before taking control.

"Come on. This way," said Lily, walking to where the shards of glass had hit the pavement. She carefully picked up a suitable piece. I turned around and Lily sawed away at my plastic tie. It severed and then it was possible for me to do the same for her.

The distant noise of the fire service trucks got louder and in minutes, a number of different vehicles arrived with ladders, pumps or rescue equipment. Everything had been transformed into a major incident scene. Pulsing lights of the emergency services lit up the carcass of the building. Scania and Volvo fire engines drew up in a long red line outside the remains of the institute. Firemen rushed to set up their equipment. More sirens announced the arrival of police cars and a couple of ambulances. Emergency services spread out amongst the devastation of rubble and twisted metal. Almost every onlooker from the institute was staring at the devastated scene, taking pictures or talking on their mobile.

We needed to move fast. "Help me pull the Russians out. We'll leave them beside the road to be found." We dragged them out and I went back for the gun that could be traced to the people I'd shot. I wiped it clean of my prints and placed it in the hand of the big Russian. It would now be covered in his prints.

"That should help the police investigation. I'm hoping they'll blame the Russians for this, as well as for the other shootings," I said. I was going to walk away but before leaving, for some inexplicable reason, I picked up the screwdriver and put it in my pocket. It was a good job I didn't make the move more theatrical, as Lily had already raised her eyebrows at my action.

"It's a good idea to use the Russians. There's been a lot of coverage about Russians being mixed up with crime in Dalian. The police will arrest them," she commented.

I pointed to the building site. "Let's get back to your bike."

"Where are we going?" asked Lily.

"I've no idea as long as we travel a long distance away from here. I just hope your worn-out bike will make it."

Lily dipped her head, "Good. That means it's all over. This is what you wanted, so tell me it's ended."

"Nothing left to do here," I said. "Nothing."

"It's going to give you closure. You did what you believed was right." She caught my eye. "How are you feeling now?"

"I realise being in China helped me reflect and know myself better. What has happened in the last few days wasn't simple for me."

"I think you have a spiritual side that was never properly developed or showed itself."

"I realise you've taken time to understand me." She smiled softly, and I went on, "I never came to China looking for any spiritual change, but you, and your culture, opened up my mind to an alternative way of thinking."

She straddled the bike. It was time to leave. I stood looking at her. We both pulled out our sunglasses at the same time as if we had rehearsed it. "Com'on, take me to the South West. We can tour Yunnan and pass over the mountains into Laos, then how about living in Thailand?" Lily crunched the bike into gear and held it on the clutch. The engine idled and spluttered as Lily waited for me to get on.

I knew we felt a shared moment of harmony. I knew it; I'd got it. I'd accomplished what I felt was right. There was a sense of fulfilment of doing something that suited my destiny. The karma I'd found was with me. I wasn't left wanting anymore. After a life of following orders, I was my own self at last.

I got on the bike and Lily let out the clutch. We set off in a cloud of dust. The institute was giving off acrid smoke and what had been beautiful glass shapes, from the first floor up, had collapsed into a mass of rubble. Firemen were training hoses on the burning building or going in through the partly collapsed entrance area. One fireman was calling over a policeman to one of the injured Russians. The fireman was holding up the machine pistol and looking quite tense.

We rode off in silence, looking forward at the road in front, not back at the institute. I realised the short time in China had become my portal to enter a new world. I had a realisation of who I really was. I'd morphed and been transfigured into a global citizen. I knew what I cared about and what my values were. I realised this was symbolic of how I would live the rest of my life. How could any other adventure be better than the one I was about to embark on?

* * *